THE WAR-TORN

For over a hundred years, war ravaged the lands of Khorvaire. Dynasties rose and fell, fortunes were made and lost, and new wonders and unspeakable horrors entered the world.

With the War now over, an uneasy peace struggles to settle over the battle-ravaged lands.

But what of the soldiers, nobels, spies, healers, and wizards whose lives were forever changed by decades of war? What of those who have no home to which they can return? What does a world without war hold for those who have known nothing but bloodshed and death? What fate lies for these, the War-Torn?

THE
WAR~TORN

THE CRIMSON TALISMAN
ADRIAN COLE

THE ORB OF XORIAT
EDWARD BOLME

IN THE CLAWS OF THE TIGER
JAMES WYATT

BLOOD AND HONOR
GRAEME DAVIS

EBERRON

BLOOD AND HONOR

THE WAR-TORN • BOOK 4

GRAEME DAVIS

Wizards of the Coast

BLOOD AND HONOR
The War-Torn • Book 4

Cover art by Wayne Reynolds
Map by Rob Lazzaretti
First Printing: September 2006
Library of Congress Catalog Card Number: 2005935541

9 8 7 6 5 4 3 2 1

ISBN-10: 0-7869-4069-7
ISBN-13: 978-0-7869-4069-1
620-95589740 -001-EN

U.S., CANADA,
ASIA, PACIFIC, & LATIN AMERICA
Wizards of the Coast, Inc.
P.O. Box 707
Renton, WA 98057-0707
+1-800-324-6496

EUROPEAN HEADQUARTERS
Hasbro UK Ltd
Caswell Way
Newport, Gwent NP9 0YH
GREAT BRITAIN
Save this address for your records.

Visit our web site at www.wizards.com

To the two most important people in my life:

My father, David Davis, who has always supported me despite not being entirely sure what it is I do; and my wife, Gina Laurin, who knows, but supports me anyway.

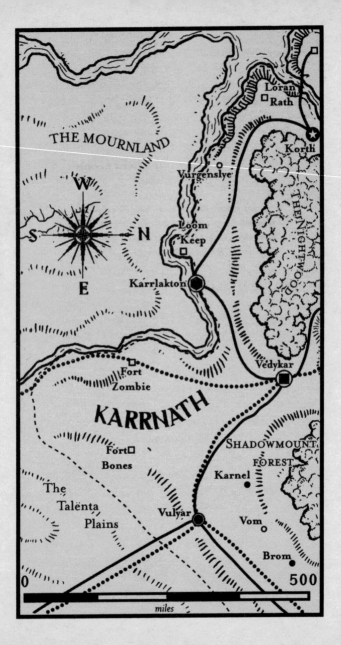

TABLE OF CONTENTS

THE COMPANY OF THE SKULL
CHAPTER 1

Late Barrakas, 998 YK

"Lieutenant Mordan?"

The officer paused in saddling his horse and shot a glance over one shoulder. Lank blond hair framed a tanned face, its fine features concealed by a growth of stubble. His eyes seemed to make the newcomer uncomfortable. Narrowed almost to slits by years of scanning the Talenta Plains for enemies, they were a pale blue-gray like chips of ice.

Their gaze took in a short, slightly overweight young man standing in the stable doorway. His face was red and sheened with sweat. Mordan suppressed a groan as he looked the newcomer up and down—wide eyes, fresh uniform, no scars. *Dol Arrah*, he prayed, *please don't let this be Tarmun's replacement.*

"What?" said Mordan.

"Uh, the adjutant said I should report to you, Lieutenant," said the newcomer. "I've been assigned to your squad. Brager, Trooper Edvan Brager." He tried to force a smile.

"Well, hooray for you, Brager," said Mordan. "Ever ride an undead horse before?"

1

The new recruit brightened. "Not in combat, but I used to work at the Ministry for the Dead. In supply. I tested undead horses before they were shipped here and to Fort Zombie."

Mordan grunted. At least he was used to the beasts. That had to count for something.

"So who did you cross at the Ministry?"

"Lieutenant?"

"I assume you're here because you got kicked out and had nowhere else to go?"

"Oh, no, Lieutenant. I got tired of counting their legs and riding 'em across the warehouse, and—"

"And you decided to see if life in the Company of the Skull's as glamorous as it is in the stories?"

Brager's smile faded a little. "Uh, yes."

Mordan finished cinching his saddle and turned to face him for the first time. "Well, it's not. But you'll have plenty of time to find that out for yourself. Take your gear over to barracks block C and report to Sergeant Grasht. He'll show you your bunk—and if he talks about eating you, he's just being friendly. Be ready to ride out in fifteen minutes. Dismissed."

Brager saluted, turned crisply, and left. Mordan started to speculate on how long he would last. A bet on the life expectancy of a new recruit was a cherished tradition in the Company of the Skull.

* * * * * * *

Fifteen minutes later, a half-dozen riders stood in a rough line in the courtyard of Fort Bones. The summer sun beat down on them, turning the famous bone walls blinding white and glinting off the masterwork breastplates of the skeleton troopers who stood on the parapet.

Mordan glanced along the line. Brager was at the far left-hand end, with a crossbow on his back and a longsword at his side. He was still red-faced and sweating, but at least he didn't look so nervous. Next to him was Garn, a female dwarf, astride her skeletal pony. He'd had to call in a few favors to get it, but she was just too short for a full-sized horse.

At the middle of the line was Grasht, the massive half-orc, with his greatsword on his back. His stirrups almost reached the ground. Beside him, Cardel the half-elf wore his usual smirk. Sharp-faced Kalla sat ignoring him, and Mordan decided he didn't want to know what Cardel had just said to her. At the end of the line, and a little way off from the skeletal horses, a wiry halfling in the dyed and painted skins of a plains hunter stood beside a reddish-brown glide-wing. A leather-bound saddle adorned with silver studs was strapped to its back, and its long face was painted with markings that echoed the wooden hunting-mask that hung round the halfling's neck. Though he was not an official member of the Company of the Skull, Dern's knowledge of the plains and his skill with Redwind, his glidewing, made him invaluable.

"Attention!" snapped Mordan. "It seems one of the advance posts on the Plains has lost a patrol. Our orders are to get it back or find out what happened to it."

A cynical murmur ran down the line. The improved Karrnathi skeletons were useful enough in battle, but their sense of direction was notoriously bad. If something had happened to their living officer, they could have wandered all over the place. Mordan tossed a leather scroll-case to Garn and another to Dern.

"Here's their route," he said. "We'll start at the outpost. Let's go."

"Hey, lieutenant?" Grasht was already looking unhappy.

Mordan anticipated his question. "Yes, Grasht, we will be riding through the night." A loud groan issued from the troops. "There have been reports of Valenar activity in the area, and if they're behind this the Captain needs to know right away." He paused, struck by a sudden thought.

"Brager," he said, "did you ever sleep in the saddle back at the Ministry?"

Brager shook his head. "No, Lieutenant," he replied. "Endurance testing was done with sandbags."

Cardel muttered something, and Grasht stifled a chuckle.

"Well, now's your chance to learn," Mordan said. "Get sleep whenever you can. You'll need it. Just take care you don't roll over."

As the rest of the troop laughed, Mordan signaled them to move out.

＊ ＊ ＊ ◎ ＊ ＊ ＊

The Talenta Plains stretched away to a curtain of heat haze. Mordan signaled the squad to halt, took off his broad-brimmed hat, and wiped the sweat from his eyes. Squinting in the harsh light, he scanned the horizon.

"Kalla!" he called, pulling out his flask. "Are you sure we're on the right trail?"

The trooper slid from her horse, trotted a little way in front of the line, and dropped to a crouch. She stared at the ground for a few seconds, then looked up.

"They've been this way," she said. "Here's one hoofprint split almost in half, and this other one looks like a bone-end where the hoof must have come off. If they were living horses, they wouldn't still be moving."

Mordan wiped his mouth and stowed his flask again.

"Garn, where's their next stop?"

The dwarf fished the map out of a saddlebag. "They were supposed to head east another fifty miles or so, to a rise with a small rock spire on the top. Then back north till they hit the lightning rail, and west back to the fort."

Mordan nodded and turned back to Kalla. "Were they headed the right way?"

The shifter nodded, raising one arm to indicate where the tracks led.

"Why don't we just say the Valenar got them and go home?" grumbled the half-orc.

"You know why," said Mordan. "There's valuable military property to be recovered." The skeleton troopers of Fort Bones were equipped with masterwork armor.

Grasht snorted. "The Valenar got their armor. We all know it."

Behind him, Cardel snickered. "Maybe they did, maybe they didn't," he said. "You may be too rich to care, but I could use the bounty. Or could it be you're afraid of running into the Valenar yourself?"

Grasht spat something in his own language and half-drew his massive sword. Mordan rode between the two as fast as his lurching undead mount would move.

"That's enough!" His voice was more tired than angry. "Grasht, move up to the head of the column. Cardel, you're at the back. Move out!"

❂ ❂ ❂ ❂ ❂ ❂ ❂

The sun was low in the sky when a batlike silhouette appeared above the horizon, drawing closer through the diminishing heat-haze. Within a few minutes, the reddish-brown glidewing was circling above the patrol. His face hidden behind a snarling beast-mask of painted wood, the rider gestured back the way he had come and made a chopping gesture across his own throat, indicating death—or the dead. Mordan waved an acknowledgment, and the column of riders changed their course to follow the flying scout.

The splintered bones of the lost patrol stood out white in the gathering dusk. Grasht kicked at half a skull and spat on the ground.

"Told you!" he said. "The Valenar aren't going to leave masterwork armor lying around. This is pointless!"

Mordan scanned the wreckage. "Not entirely," he said. "Now we know what happened to them."

Kalla looked up from the edge of the debris. "Valenar horses, for sure," she said. "See how long the strides are? They came in from that way, surrounded the patrol. Seven of them. Five elves for sure. The other two didn't dismount so I can't tell. Looks like a couple were wounded, but not badly. They headed back over there." She pointed to a low ridge on the horizon. "Their hoofprints are a little deeper going away, like they were carrying something."

"There goes the armor," muttered Cardel. Grasht shot him an I-told-you-so look. Mordan nodded his thanks to Kalla and walked over to where Dern was tossing scraps of dried meat to his glidewing.

The troopers began gathering up the bones without waiting for an order. They were all familiar with the task. Cardel hummed as he worked—a patriotic Karrnathi song about the glory of the dead who rose again to serve their country. The others ignored him.

Grasht, as usual, was complaining. If Fort Bones needed more material for its walls, he muttered to himself, he'd be happy to kill a bunch of recruits and use their bones instead.

Then they wouldn't have to come all the way out here, and he'd have something to eat into the bargain. No one had ever actually seen him eat a human, but he liked to play the savage half-orc.

His grumbling was cut short by a yelp of pain as an arrow caught him in the shoulder. Mordan whirled to see seven Valenar raiders bearing down on them. He cursed Dern for not having spotted them and drew his longsword.

The glidewing leaped into the air as the troopers scrambled to their steeds. Facing a charge of Valenar cavalry was bad enough while mounted. No one wanted to be caught on foot.

Vaulting into the saddle, Mordan edged his mount into line with the others. He drew his longsword and waited, trying to judge which of the Valenar would be closest to him when the charge hit. Beside him, Grasht had pulled the arrow from his shoulder and was hefting his greatsword. The others closed ranks. Kalla had begun to shift, extending her claws and crouching on her saddle, ready to leap at the first elf that came near. Brager was fumbling with his crossbow. Cardel was already aiming.

The elves loosed a volley of arrows at full gallop. A couple rattled off the bones of the undead horses, but none struck the riders. Cardel replied with a shot from his heavy crossbow. It struck deep into the thigh of one of the elves, who winced but kept riding.

Dern's glidewing swooped low above the charging Valenar, but the horses ignored it; trained for war, they would not spook so easily. As the winged reptile pulled up into a sharp turn, Dern reached behind him into a saddlebag.

Brager had finally loaded his crossbow and loosed a bolt at the Valenar leader, but it glanced off his mailed shoulder.

The elves stowed their bows in back-holsters and drew the distinctive Valenar double scimitars. Their leader held a slim and deadly-looking rapier straight forward from his shoulder as he gave his warcry.

A few yards before impact, Dern's glidewing swooped low over the elves once more. The halfling had one hand on the reins, and a bola spun in the other. The glidewing banked sharply as Dern flung the bola, entangling the legs of one of the Valenar horses. It crashed to the ground, pitching its rider from the saddle.

Mordan twisted his mount to the side, parrying a slashing blade and chopping at his attacker's arm. From the corner of his eye, he saw Grasht countercharge the Valenar, knocking one of the elves from his horse with a sweep of his greatsword. Kalla threw herself at another of the elves, dodging his blade and dragging him to the ground.

With the impact of the charge spent, Mordan felt safe to dismount. Garn and Grasht did the same, but Cardel and Brager remained mounted, circling the melee and loosing their crossbows from a distance. An elf slashed down at him. Mordan dodged, responding with an upward thrust that caught the rider just beneath the ribs. Dropping his double scimitar, the elf clutched his side. A second slash bit into the elf's thigh, jarring against bone. He fell from the saddle.

Looking round for a fresh enemy, Mordan saw Garn standing with her back to her skeletal pony, her paired maces smeared with blood. A fallen elf lay at her feet, and another was approaching her cautiously, his double scimitar weaving a complex series of arcs in the air. Focused on this opponent, she was unaware of the Valenar leader behind her. His gray cloak was flung over one shoulder to clear his sword arm, and his rapier was drawn.

Mordan shouted a warning and started to run, but the dwarf was too far away. Before he could reach her, the rapier struck at her pony. It collapsed into a pile of bones, exposing her back; a split second later her eyes widened in pain, fading as she looked down at the bloody tip of the rapier protruding from her chest.

With a cry, Mordan cut down the elf trooper, swatting one blade of the double scimitar aside and plunging his longsword into the elf's chest. Wrenching the blade free, he stepped over the elf's body and faced the Valenar leader.

The battle raging around them seemed to recede as the two regarded each other. The elf leader was tall and well-built, with silver eyes and an expression of arrogant amusement. A gem gleamed in the hilt of his rapier—perhaps a dragonshard, Mordan thought. The weapon must be enchanted to drop an undead pony with a single blow. The cloak was probably magical as well—elven cloaks were famed for their ability to conceal their wearer in any terrain. Along with his fine mail and the elaborate gold brooch that secured his cloak, it was clear that the Valenar leader was an individual of wealth and position.

Mordan was unarmored, and the elf no doubt took this for foolishness, or perhaps a concession to the summer heat of the plains. But Mordan had been fighting the Valenar long enough to know that the key to victory was speed rather than protection.

He struck an overhand blow at the elf's head, stepping back out of the range of the rapier when his opponent parried the blow. The arrogance faded from the elf's face. He had not expected a human to strike the first blow or to attack so swiftly. With a nod, the elf raised his rapier to the ready position, and the two circled each other.

The elf tried to distract Mordan with a sweep of his cloak, but Mordan twisted aside from the probing rapier that followed it. He feinted to the left before bringing his sword back in a fast slash to the right that forced the elf to jump backward.

After a few probing attacks, the Valenar swept with his cloak again. Mordan ignored it, preparing to dodge the thrust he knew would follow. But he was wrong. Under the cover of his cloak, the elf had drawn a broad-bladed dagger with his left hand. Seeing the flash of the blade, Mordan sidestepped a blow that would have struck his sword hand, but the Valenar was one move ahead of him. A backhanded slash of the dagger struck his left wrist hard, sending a jarring pain the length of his arm.

Gritting his teeth against he shock of the wound, Mordan glanced down. His left hand lay on the ground twitching. Blood pumped out of the stump of his wrist. His vision was starting to blur. He had only a few seconds to act.

A feint with his longsword forced his opponent further to his left. The elf watched his blade, ignoring the maimed left arm. That was his mistake. Twisting aside from a rapier thrust, Mordan slammed the bleeding arm against the Valenar's own wrist. There was a small flare of black energy, accompanied by a brief sizzling sound, and the elf yelped in surprise, momentarily off-balance. In that instant, Mordan stepped inside the elf's reach and spun round, reversing his sword and stabbing backward at the exposed torso. His longsword pierced the elf's mail coat, and he heard a grunt of surprise that turned into a soft, bubbling wheeze as the elf collapsed.

Mordan's left arm was ablaze with pain. Beside the loss of his hand, the dragonmark on his shoulder burned, as it always did when he used its power. He stood for a moment, fighting the darkness that pressed down on his eyes, and then fell on top of the dead elf.

CHAPTER 2

Late Barrakas, 998 YK

Mordan awoke in a low tent, with an elderly halfling woman leaning over him. He tried to sit up, but she shushed him and pressed him back. He was too weak to resist. His left hand ached abominably.

The next time he opened his eyes, he found Dern sitting beside his bed. The halfling scout looked at him solemnly as he struggled to sit up.

"Drink this," Dern said, handing him a mug of steaming broth. "You've lost a lot of blood, but you're going to be fine." He paused, then said, "Perra couldn't save your hand. I'm sorry."

It wasn't till Dern spoke that Mordan looked down and saw the tightly bound stump of his left wrist. Odd, he thought, still light-headed from the effort of sitting up, I could swear I can still feel my hand. He took the mug in his right hand and sipped at the hot, bitter broth.

"I thought your Jorasco healers could fix anything," he said after he had drunk.

Dern grimaced. "Some of them can," he said, "but not all."

Mordan drained the mug, feeling his head clear and his pain subside as he did so. Whatever Perra's limitations, her healing potions were effective. He pushed his lank blond hair out of his eyes and swung his legs off the cot—actually two halfling-sized beds lashed together—stooping in the low space. He was still a little light-headed, but felt strong enough to walk. He looked for his sword, and as his eye lit on the elegant elven rapier beside his cot, he remembered the battle.

"I saw Garn fall," he said. "Is she . . . ?

Dern nodded. "We wrapped her body and put it on her pony," he said. "We figured she'd want to be sent back to the Mror Holds. Perra cast a preserving spell on her."

"Anyone else?"

Much to Mordan's relief, Dern shook his head. "Nothing serious."

Mordan swung his legs off the cot and got to his feet. Dern held back the flap of the tent.

Outside, the troopers sat on brightly colored rugs, in the open middle of the camp. Grasht hoisted a drink as four giggling halfling women brought him a huge rack of hammertail ribs, tottering under their weight. His shoulder was bandaged where the arrow had struck him; it was just a flesh wound, and as he told anyone who would listen, he'd had worse. Around him, the others relaxed and enjoyed the hospitality of Dern's tribe. There was a moment of silence as Mordan appeared, followed by a loud cheer. The troopers shuffled to make space for their leader, and he motioned Dern to sit beside him.

"How did you miss them?" he asked as more food arrived.

Dern was too good a scout to overlook a troop of Valenar cavalry in open terrain.

"I don't know." The halfling grimaced, more in puzzlement than apology. "Maybe they were invisible. Their leader's cloak would have hidden him, but it couldn't have covered all of them and their horses."

"At least none of them had any spells," said Mordan. "Maybe they used a scroll or something."

"They must have seen me, though," Dern said. "They didn't charge till Redwind had landed."

"They saw all of us," said Mordan. "No question of that."

"You don't like hammertail?" Dern asked, half-rising from his cushion and gesturing at the meat before Mordan. "Could be there's some hardhead or flatmouth." Halflings were particular about their hospitality, even those outside House Ghallanda. Mordan reached for the food.

"No, it's good," he said. "I was thinking, that's all." He fell to eating with deliberate relish.

Screams of laughter erupted behind Mordan, and he looked round to see Grasht squaring off against a skin-clad halfling warrior in a clear area beside the main firepit. Grasht was wielding a tent-pole—a center-post as thick as his opponent's waist—like an oversized quarterstaff, and the halfling was circling him with a thin stick in one hand.

A crowd had gathered around them, laughing and shouting encouragement as the halfling ducked under Grasht's sweeping blow and darted in to tap him on the chest with the stick. Mordan shook his head and smiled. The halflings had always liked Grasht. With his size, his bluster, and his swagger, they seemed to regard him as a curiosity. He certainly enjoyed their hospitality.

When the feast was over, Mordan went to pay his respects to the group's elders, who sat on brightly colored rugs in the middle of the camp. Mordan had met Lath Yoldrum and old Hazlon several times in the past—their tribe had been providing the Company of the Skull with scouts and outriders for years—but they always made an impression on him. Neither would have stood much taller than his belt-buckle, but somehow their presence was bigger than they were. Hazlon, the tribe's shaman, was an arresting sight with his brightly colored headdress, necklace of lizard teeth, and feathered staff carved from the leg bone of a clawfoot lizard. Yoldrum, on the other hand, was dressed in dyed cloth and tanned hides like any member of his tribe, with his graying hair drawn back in a hunter's ponytail. Only the quiet strength in his dark eyes and the scars of man hunts set him apart from his people.

"You are better," the lath observed. "That is good."

"I'm alive, thanks to your healer," said Mordran, using the dialect of the Plains out of courtesy, "but I think my fighting days may be over." He held up his stump.

"That might be a good thing." The lath shrugged. "You can go back to your people and live in peace."

"I don't have any people," he said.

Hazlon chuckled softly. "Your quarrel will be mended," he said, without further explanation.

Mordan made a non-committal face. He had never talked to anyone about his family. The old halfling was probably guessing. Everyone who signed on with the Company of the Skull had something in their past. The shaman's eyes rested briefly on the rapier that Mordan wore.

"You should keep that sword," he said. Etiquette had

prevented Mordan from asking if it was magical, and he was glad that Hazlon had raised the matter.

"It belonged to the leader of the elves we fought," he said.

"I can feel it humming," said Hazlon. "It's strong against the dead who walk. The Valenar knew they'd be fighting your dead soldiers. You'll find it useful."

Mordan bowed his head to the old halfling. It would have been impolite to point out that the undead of Karrnath were on his side, or that the Company of the Skull had nothing to do with them.

"Thank you for your help and hospitality," said Mordan.

As he began to stand, Hazlon put a hand on his arm.

"You have a brother," he said, "with the name of a king. There is trouble around him—and great danger. Your people need you." His expression—and the fact that he spoke in the common tongue of humans—convinced Mordan that he was deadly serious.

"I didn't know you spoke our language," he said.

Hazlon's habitual smirk came back. "There are many things you don't know," he said, as if talking to a small child. He pressed something into Mordan's hand: a small leather bag on a thong. "This will protect you," he said.

INTERLUDE

Thirteen-year-old Kasmir ir'Dramon gritted his teeth and fought with all his strength. Laughing with savage glee as he pinned Kasmir down, kneeling on his chest and holding his wrists against the ground, his older brother's face blotted out most of the sky. Kasmir felt the bump of the anthill pressing into his back, and the ants were starting to crawl inside his clothes. He struggled as they stung and clenched his jaw tighter to stop himself from crying. Gali held him firmly, grinning all the time. Over Gali's shoulder Kasmir saw the laughing face of his brother's friend and classmate, Berend Hintram, who was staying for the summer. They had both just completed their first year at Karrnath's prestigious Rekkenmark military academy and were still wearing their cadet's uniforms.

The stinging became unbearable. He twisted his left hand free from his brother's grasp and punched Gali's side. Rage grew within him, but he was unable to get free.

Suddenly, his shoulder burned as if it were on fire. There

was a strange fizzing sound, and Gali screamed. Kasmir scrambled to his feet as his brother fell backward and rolled off him. Kasmir tore off his shirt and frantically brushed the ants off his skin, where red welts were already showing. He slapped at the burning spot on his shoulder, staring at the strange, twisting design that had appeared on his skin. Then he noticed that Gali wasn't moving.

His brother lay still in the grass, his face white and his breathing shallow. The outline of Kasmir's hand stood out gray and dead against the pale skin where he had hit him.

Servants came running, followed by his mother and father. Their visitor stood and stared in shock. They gathered round his fallen brother and took him into the house. Kasmir stayed where he was, rubbing his arm and trying to understand what had just happened. Then his father came and dragged him into the house, and he found himself surrounded by angry, shouting faces.

Kaz Mordan jerked awake, and sat up rubbing his eyes. Outside the window, the blue-gray light of dawn was creeping over the land. They would be in Vedykar soon.

Even with the money he had saved from his pay and bounties, the lightning rail was an indulgence, but it was the quickest way home to Vedykar. He stared out of the window of the steerage cart, ignoring his fellow passengers as they ignored him. He no longer wore the insignia of the Company of the Skull, but his clothing and his demeanor marked him as different from the other good people who rode the rail.

At the back of the cart, a group of dwarves played a game with stone tiles, drinking, betting, and arguing with equal enthusiasm. The other passengers were a cross-section: merchants from Irontown and Vulyar, travelers of indeterminate profession and status, and a single bone knight from Fort Zombie, dressed in his macabre-looking bonecraft armor. He and Mordan had exchanged a nod of professional courtesy when they boarded, but clearly the bone knight wanted to be left alone as much as Mordan did. Some people were overawed by these necromantic warriors, but to Mordan they were no more than herders, controlling Karrnathi undead in battle just as a houndmaster would control a pack of dogs.

Watching the landscape slide past, lit by occasional flares of blue light from the elemental-powered craft, Mordan thought about what the old halfling had told him. He thought about Kasmir ir'Dramon, turning the name over in his mind and trying to get used to the feel of it again. He had been Kaz Mordan of the Company of the Skull for so long that his real name felt strange, like a set of clothes he hadn't worn for years. His mind went back to the last time he had heard it—after his disgrace at Rekkenmark, when his father had disowned him and banished him from the house.

In particular, he remembered Gali—the golden boy, the son and heir, named for King Galifar, first in his class at the Rekkenmark Academy, the Vedykar Lancer with a shining breastplate. He remembered the smirk of pure satisfaction his brother had worn as he watched their father rage and threaten. Now, Mordan thought, he was going home, where he wasn't welcome, to check on his brother, who hated him. He wondered if the high and mighty Galifar ir'Dramon would do the same, but deep down he knew the answer.

As the lightning rail got closer to the town, he began to recognize places and landmarks, but they seemed like memories from another life. Disembarking at Vedykar, he found his way to the edge of his family's estate easily enough, but things had changed in his absence. The well-ordered fields and orchards of his youth were brown and strewn with weeds. The cattle were thinner, and the tenant cottages dirty and in need of rethatching. Like his neighbors, Adalbert ir'Dramon had prided himself on the condition of his estates. Something had changed.

At last, he reached the main gate. It had been designed to impress; the driveway swept between the griffon-topped gateposts, which framed the house perfectly on its low hill. But the gates needed paint, and the griffons were encrusted with lichen and bird droppings. Even the house seemed somehow darker and sadder, hunkering down upon its hill rather than standing proudly atop it. He paused for a moment in the gateway to take in the scene.

"What do you want?"

Mordan started as a harsh voice broke his reverie. He couldn't remember the last time anyone had been able to sneak up on him. He turned to see a stocky man, just past middle age, brandishing a crossbow. As their eyes met, the man's jaw dropped a little.

"Master Kasmir?" he breathed, lowering the crossbow.

Mordan nodded. A smile somehow didn't seem appropriate. "Hello, Adrik."

"You're back?" The gamekeeper looked uncomfortable at the idea.

"Not for long," Mordan replied. "I need to see my father." Adrik scratched his head and stared at his boots.

"You'll find him changed, Master Kasmir," he said. "Ever since . . ."

"Ever since he threw me out?" Kaz suggested.

Adrik shook his head sadly. "No, Master Kasmir, though it has to be said he never was the same after that. No, this is"—he checked himself—"well, it's not for me to say. Best you

hear it from the family. Good day to you, Master Kasmir."
With that, he turned and trudged away along the inside of the
wall without looking back.

The other servants reacted in much the same way when
Kaz arrived at the house. Many of them looked at him as if
he were somehow familiar but they couldn't put a name to
the face. He was leaner and harder than the disgraced cadet
they remembered, and his eyes had acquired the permanent squint of one accustomed to scanning the sun-baked
grasslands for enemies. In some eyes he saw disapproval; in
others, he thought, a trace of pity. His presence seemed to
make everyone uncomfortable. It was understandable, he
told himself. He didn't expect to be welcomed like a returning hero.

Steeling himself, he knocked on the huge door of iron-
bound oak. He knew that his father might refuse to see him,
and order him off the estate as he had done before. But
when Sattel the butler admitted him to the house, his father
chanced to be looking down on the hall from the upstairs
landing. Kaz noticed how tired he looked, and how old. For
an instant the two regarded each other without emotion.

Then, a spark of recognition flashed across the eyes of
the elder ir'Dramon, and his face twisted into a mask of rage.
Hurling himself down the stairs with an incoherent cry, he
flew at his son's throat.

"Vulture!" he howled, as Sattel tried to drag him off.
"Have you no respect for our grief?"

Kaz remained still, frightened that he might hurt the old
man if he resisted. He tensed the muscles of his neck against
his father's grip but kept his arms passively by his sides.

The disturbance brought several other servants running,
and they helped Sattel restrain their master, finally helping

him to a tall-backed chair that stood against the staircase. He trembled with a mixture of rage and exhaustion, spewing curses at his son.

"Adalbert?' Kaz recognized his mother's voice before she came out of the drawing-room. "Whatever . . . ?" Her voice trailed off as she saw Kaz. For a moment he thought she was going to cry—she had been crying the last time he saw her—but she took control of herself with a visible effort.

"Sattel, take the master to his bedroom and give him some brandy," she ordered. "Milla, bring tea to the drawing-room. Levro, take our visitor's cloak. The rest of you, back to your duties. Quickly, now!" The knot of servants stopped staring and went about their business. As Kaz relinquished his cloak, his mother stared in shock for a moment at the stump of his left wrist. Then she motioned her son to follow her.

"I knew you'd be back when you heard," she said coldly, once the tea had been brought.

Kaz looked at her. "Heard about what?"

"Oh, yes," she said with a derisive snort, "You're very good at protesting your innocence. You always were."

"Did something happen to Gali?"

At the mention of her elder son's name, the brittleness went out of Grethilde ir'Dramon. Her hand shook slightly as she set down her teacup, and tears stole into her angry eyes.

"On the Day of Mourning," she said, her voice husky with emotion, "the Lancers were deep inside Cyre. They were all killed." Her words tailed off into soft sobbing.

Kaz closed his eyes, trying to absorb what his mother had said. Gali was dead? The halfling shaman's warning made it sound as though he was in danger now—but the Day of Mourning was more than two years ago.

"So," his mother's cold voice brought him back to the present, "now you're the heir, you've come back to claim your birthright. Well, you may not have long to wait—the sight of you nearly killed your poor father. As if he hasn't endured enough already."

Kaz felt very tired. He set down his cup and rose from his chair.

"You needn't worry about that, mother. I'm going."

For the first time since had arrived, his mother looked startled. "What . . . ?"

"I came to find out about Gali, that's all." He turned to leave the room.

"Oh, that's right!" Her voice was like a slap. "You just go off back to—to Dollurh, or wherever you've been hiding! Walk away from your family, from your responsibilities, from me and your father!"

Kaz shook his head wearily. He had learned early that there was no way to win.

"I'm sorry about Gali," he said softly, "but we both know things would be worse if I stayed. And I'm not the heir to anything here—father made that quite clear when he threw me out. Besides, I'm still wanted." He paused, but for the first time he could remember, his mother was at a loss for words. "You're right about father," he continued. "He needs help. Cousin Thandred's next in line, I think. Maybe you should talk to him."

He left the drawing room without a backward glance.

A Meeting

CHAPTER 3

Olarune 17, 999 YK

K az Mordan, you are under arrest!"

The man looked up from his drink and cast a jaded glance over the huge, battle-scarred half-orc officer. His narrowed blue-gray eyes took in the uniform and lingered for a moment on the badge of the Royal Swords, the national guard that maintained and enforced martial law in Karrnath. His gaze passed over the heavily muscled arms, the unsheathed greatsword, and the neck as thick as a man's waist.

"Knock it off, Solly," he said, "I'm not in the mood."

The half-orc's features seemed to melt, then the figure shrank, turning into a perfect replica of the seated man: the same lank, jaw-length blond hair, the same slitted blue-gray eyes, the same fine features masked by a three-day growth of stubble, the same missing left hand. The only difference was the grin. The changeling slid into the shadowy booth, facing his original across the table.

"So have you got anything for me, or not?" Mordan asked.

Solly half-shrugged. "Well, yes and no," he said.

Mordan took a deep swallow from his mug of Nightwood ale. "I'll take that as a no," he said.

Solly raised the stump of his left wrist, sprouting a hand from it and wagging a finger slowly in front of his face.

"Not so fast," he said. "Maybe I didn't find what you're looking for"—he leaned forward a little—"but I've got something that's almost as interesting."

"What?" Mordan asked wearily. "Another map to the Cyran bullion vaults in Metrol?"

Solly widened his eyes and clapped his hand to his chest in mock offense. "Would I do that to you?" he asked. "No, I sold that to the bunch of new faces in the corner. This is for real." He shifted again, to what Mordan took to be his natural form: a slim humanoid with white hair that flopped over a half-formed face like pale clay. His eyes were like dark holes in the snow. Mordan held his gaze.

"Very well," Mordan said. "What is it?"

"Looks like you've got competition," the changeling replied.

Mordan raised an eyebrow. "Meaning?"

"Someone else has been asking about the Vedykar Lancers."

"Asking what?"

"The same as you—where were they posted, last known position, and so on. Except she didn't know their name. She's working from a sketch of a badge."

"She?"

The lower half of Solly's face opened in a crude leer.

"I thought that would interest you." Chuckling, he shifted his face to portray a human woman in her mid-twenties. Her features were fine but strong, with a determined chin and long auburn hair.

"And that's not all," Solly continued. His voice was husky and feminine, with a strong Thrane accent.

"What else?" There was a pause, and the woman cocked her head expectantly. Mordan pulled a small leather purse from inside his cloak and tossed it across the table. It was caught in mid-air, with a soft clink of coins.

"She had another badge," said Solly. "She wanted information on both of them."

Mordan frowned. "Whose badge?"

"You tell me." Solly shrugged, shifting back to his usual form. He reached inside his jerkin, pulled out a scrap of paper, and pushed it across the table.

Mordan leaned forward, his habitual squint narrowing as he looked at the design—a white skull over the number sixty-one, in red on a black background. After a few moments, he straightened up, shaking his head.

"Never saw it before. How long has she been asking around?"

"A couple of days. That's all I know."

"You sure?"

Solly spread his hands. "If you want to pay me more money, I'll make something up."

Mordan thought for a moment. "Keep an eye on her, and let me know what she finds out."

"And if she asks me?" Solly asked. "After all, everyone comes to me eventually."

"Tell her what you've found out for me, which is nothing. There's no record the Vedykar Lancers were ever here, nobody knows where they were, and you don't know the other badge. But keep me out of it."

He finished his ale and rose to leave. He glanced over at the corner table, where a group of adventurers pored over a map and talked in low, urgent tones, then shook his head with a sad smile and stepped out into the damp evening of Karrlakton, beneath the sign of the Black Dragon.

● ● ● ◉ ● ● ●

The fog was trying to turn to rain, as it usually did at this time of night and this time of year. The moisture was too heavy to hang in the still air but too light to fall, and it clung to whatever touched it. The cobbles were slick underfoot, reflecting the pale light of the few remaining everbright lanterns; most had been broken or stolen and sold. The fog muffled sounds and robbed the scene of all color.

Wrapping his cloak about him, Mordan walked along the waterfront at an easy pace. Across the river, invisible through the dank fog, was the dead-gray mist that marked the edge of the Mournland. Newcomers to Karrlakton were often nervous when the evening fog rolled in, fearful that the Mournland might have crossed the river; but it hadn't moved since the inexplicable destruction of Cyre more than four years ago. It had stopped at the borders on the Day of Mourning, and there it had stayed ever since; nobody knew why. And, as Mordan knew from his own experience, the dead-gray mist of the Mournland was neither cold nor damp.

The docks and warehouses he passed spoke of better times. Beneath the grime and peeling paint they were large and solidly built, a relic of the pre-war days when goods flowed through Karrlakton from Cyre, the Talenta Plains and all points south and east. Many of the buildings still showed damage from the War—some were reduced to rubble, while others had only a few scorch-marks on their walls.

When the Last War broke out, the strategic location that had served Karrlakton so well through centuries of peaceful trade became its greatest weakness. It had been pummeled by wave after wave of attacks from across the river. Despite this—or perhaps because of it—the city had served as a major military depot. Almost every unit posted to the Cyran front or the Talenta Plains had passed through Karrlakton, which made it a logical place to look for traces of the lost.

Peace had done little to restore the city's fortunes. Cyre was no more, and the Valenar elves pressed hard on the Talenta Plains. Things—strange, twisted, unnatural things—sometimes came out of the Mournland and tried to cross the river. Not as often as rumor maintained, but often enough to be a danger. River trade collapsed as merchants began to move their goods by safer overland routes. Adventurers, fortune-seekers, and bandits flocked to the waterfront district as an easy stepping-off point for expeditions across the river and into the Mournland; in their wake came everyone who could sell them equipment or services—legal and otherwise—and many others who thought they could turn a profit.

The Black Dragon was one of several waterfront taverns frequented by these freebooters. It had a reputation for being dangerous, but in truth only the obnoxious, the inexperienced, and the foolish came to any harm there. The authorities regarded it as a nest of vipers, but the Royal Swords seldom ventured into the waterfront district.

"Repent!"

The howl of the street-corner prophet was barely recognizable as a human word. He stood glassy-eyed on a crumbling jetty, facing across the river toward the unseen Mournland, bellowing into the fog. Blood and pus oozed from the fragments of colored stone that were hammered into his forehead, and from the mystical patterns carved into the flesh of his arms and torso. The symbols were repeated on his tattered clothing, in paints of various colors and in other, less readily identifiable substances. An open book hung around his neck on a heavy chain, its pages blank. He wore a spiked helmet of vaguely hobgoblin design, with a battered and jaw-less skull impaled on the top. Cones of incense glowed dimly within its eye-sockets, their smoke mingling with the fog.

"Beware the Dragon Below!"

Perhaps, in his mind, he saw a congregation, hanging fearfully on every word as they cringed at his feet; in reality, there were few people abroad on the waterfront, and they paid him no heed.

"Lo, Great Khyber did loose his breath upon the wicked world, and there opened in the heart of sinful Cyre a vast chasm, glowing with the power of His vengeance! And disso-lute Cyre was no more! And so the rest of this immoral world shall fall before His wrath! Repent and believe, for only the faithful shall be spared!"

Despite his ragged clothes, the man raved and gestured with the authority of a high priest—which, perhaps, he thought he was. No one knew why the Mournland had stopped at the bor-ders of Cyre, and no one knew whether it might spread across the river as suddenly and unexpectedly as it had appeared. The morbid, the fanatical, and the unhinged came from far and wide to be close to this looming, unknowable threat.

Mordan turned down an alley between two warehouses, heading away from the dark and turbid river. He stepped over the huddled bodies of sleeping beggars who sheltered between the warehouse walls, and over the occasional body whose blood mixed with the greasy water in the cracks between the stones, indicating a more permanent sleep. Although his gait was still brisk and confident, he kept his hand on the hilt of the bejeweled rapier that hung at his side beneath his cloak.

His slitted eyes swept the shadows as small, half-seen shapes skittered out of his way.

His pace slowed as he approached a shabby-looking warehouse that stood a couple of streets back from the waterfront. There was no sign over the weathered door, and nothing could be seen through the grimy window set into it. As he reached for the handle, the door opened suddenly, and a cloaked figure pushed past him, hurrying off down the street. Catching a glimpse of the man's face in the gloom, Mordan stopped in his tracks, staring at his retreating back. After a moment's deliberation, he set out after him, treading softly and taking care not to be seen.

"Stop right there, friend."

Mordan cursed and spun round, drawing his rapier. He found himself facing a figure dressed in the Brelish style and standing just beyond the reach of his sword. In one hand, he held a short, stubby wand of black metal, tipped with an orange crystal. There was a pause as the two took the measure of each other: the stranger's narrow features and pointed ears hinted at elven blood, although his figure was more human in its proportions. A half-elf.

"Nice wand," said Mordan. "What does it do?"

"You want to find out?"

"Not especially."

"Then put your sword away."

With a shrug, Mordan complied. The half-elf relaxed a little but still kept the wand pointed at him.

"I saw you and your changeling friend," the Brelander continued. "What's your interest in the lady?"

"What's yours?"

The half-elf smiled. "Since I'm the one holding the wand, why don't you answer first?"

Mordan shrugged again. "It seems she and I have a common interest."

"And what might that be?"

"A certain cavalry unit, lost in Cyre on the Day of Mourning."

The half-elf considered this for a moment.

"Karrnathi?" he asked.

Mordan nodded.

"This cavalry unit have a name?"

"The Vedykar Lancers. But she doesn't know that."

There was a blur of motion, and the Brelander recoiled with a yelp, clutching his wrist. His wand clattered across the cobbles. Before either of them could react, two bulky figures moved to block the alley in front of them. One was a half-orc, and the other appeared to be human. Mordan glanced over his shoulder at a soft sound behind them. Another group of thugs had moved into place, cutting off any hope of retreat.

"Hello, Mordan," slurred the half-orc, hefting a massive club.

The half-elf raised an eyebrow. "Friends of yours?" he asked.

"Not exactly."

"Ikar wants to see you," said the half-orc. "He's very unhappy about that last Metrol run."

Mordan shrugged. "You win some, you lose some," he said.

The half-orc snorted. "Ikar doesn't like to lose," he said, taking a step closer.

Mordan stayed as still as a statue. His eyes narrowed, hardening like chips of ice. "Then he shouldn't have sent you, Slarn." His voice was quiet, but had an edge like steel. "You and your clowns couldn't—"

He never got to finish the sentence. Twisting to one side as the half-orc's club narrowly missed his head, Mordan drew his rapier and put his back to the wall of the alley. The half-elf did the same, drawing a shortsword as the thugs fell into a loose semicircle around them. The one that Mordan had taken to be human opened his mouth in a feral snarl, his teeth elongating and his features warping into a bestial mask.

There were two others beside the half-orc and the shifter. One was a wiry halfling with quick eyes and a deadly-looking curved tangat. A Talenta boomerang in his sash explained what had happened to the Brelander's wand. The other was an elf, armed with a pair of shortswords.

The shifter lunged toward Mordan's companion, slashing with fingernails that had grown into iron-hard claws. The half-orc swung his club at Mordan's head again. The others tensed, ready to exploit any openings created by comrades' attacks.

The Brelander brought his sword up to a guard position, blocking the shifter's attack, and followed through with a slash that cut deep into the creature's shoulder. Mordan sidestepped the half-orc's club, touching his opponent's shoulder with the bound stump of his left wrist. There was a flare of black light, a smell of scorching, and the half-orc howled in pain, dropping his club and clutching his shoulder. Although the blow had not been hard, it had left a grayish mark on the half-orc's hide.

As the half-orc dropped back, the elf leaped forward, his two shortswords weaving a complex pattern in the air. Such a display might have intimidated an untrained opponent, but Mordan flicked one blade aside with his rapier, stepped inside the slashing arc of the other, and slammed his pommel backhanded into the elf's chin, dropping him to the ground like a sack of coal.

The Brelander, meanwhile, was in a stalemate with the wild halfling, blocking one attack after another but unable to land a blow against his agile foe. The half-orc, recovered from the shock of negative energy from Mordan's spell, charged with his club, only to stop short. He looked down in surprise at the small puncture in his chest, and then at the dark blood on the end of Mordan's rapier. He wavered and then fell down dead.

Mordan turned to face the shifter, but he was already limping down the alley as fast as he could go. Finding himself alone against two opponents, the halfling backed slowly after his fleeing comrade, his dark eyes flicking from Mordan to the Brelander and back again. Mordan spoke a phrase in the Talenta dialect and the halfling's eyes widened in shock; stowing his tangat, he turned and ran. They let him go. When he turned out of sight down a side-alley, the two slumped against the wall, catching their breath. It was a few moments before either one spoke.

"So what was that about?" asked the Brelander, stooping to pick up his wand. He stopped abruptly as the tip of Mordan's rapier came to rest lightly on his wrist, and took a step backward, straightening slowly.

Mordan stepped forward, planting his feet on each side of the wand. "Oh, you know," he said, "business. Well, they told you my name—how about yours?"

The half-elf spread his empty palms in a gesture of acquiescence. "Tarrel d'Medani, at your service," he said, with a half-bow.

"Medani, hmm? Inquisitive?" asked Mordan.

Tarrel nodded. "Yes, but I don't have the mark. Speaking of which, what did you do to that big one? Are you a 'Mark?"

Mordan shook his head. "I'm an aberrant. And I think it's my turn to ask questions. You can start with why you were pointing that wand at me."

"Do we have to do this here? Your . . . business associates may be back with reinforcements." As if to emphasize his point, the fallen elf started to stir, groaning softly. Mordan silenced him with a savage kick.

"Honor to the fallen foe," said Tarrel, quoting a Karrnathi saying.

Mordan spat. "Honor is as honor does. Besides, I don't like elves. I spent too long fighting the Valenar."

Tarrel nodded. "That explains the rapier," he said. "I thought it looked like elven work."

"It was a fair trade," said Mordan. "He got my hand; I got his sword and his head." Picking up the wand, he tucked it into his belt. He glanced in the direction where he had last seen the cloaked man, and shook his head ruefully. "Let's go," he said.

THE BADGE

CHAPTER 4

Olarune 17, 999 YK

The two walked in silence, wary of another attack. They came to the entertainment district, where the streets were well-lit and lined with restaurants, small theaters, and taverns. Mordan stopped at a restaurant whose colorful façade mimicked the styles of the Talenta Plains. Its door pillars were carved and painted to resemble the legbones of a huge plains lizard, and the frontage was covered with brightly dyed fabrics, arranged to look like the side of a tent. A sign hung over the door, reading LATHON'S WELCOME in the common tongue, its letters styled in imitation of halfling script.

Inside, the lights were low, and the smell of spices and roasting meat filled the air. Somewhere out of sight, a weaving pattern of rhythms was being pounded out on a drum. The walls were hung with brightly painted skins in an attempt to recreate the atmosphere of a lath's tent—or at least, to satisfy the expectations of city-dwellers who had never seen one.

Instead of the traditional cushions, patrons sat on chairs arranged around tables, built to accommodate human-sized customers. The wooden pillars supporting the ceiling were carved into forms suggestive of animal bones, and the walls were painted with deliberately crude images of huge lizards.

Dressed in a colorful parody of Plains costume, a halfling waitress bustled up to them. Mordan spoke a few words in the Talenta dialect. Her eyes flicked to the charm-bag that hung around his neck, and she smiled broadly.

The waitress led the two past the tables, showed them to a cushioned booth furnished with a low table. It was scarcely four feet from floor to ceiling. Mordan slid into the booth with practiced ease, sitting cross-legged on the floor. Tarrel hit his head on an animal-fat lamp that hung over the table, but eventually made himself comfortable. Tarrel looked around, but the waitress had disappeared.

"So is there a menu?" he asked at last.

Mordan smiled. "Menus are for the cogarak," he said.

Tarrel looked at him blankly.

"It's a halfling word," Mordan explained. "It means someone who doesn't know their way around."

"Of course," said Tarrel. "You fought the Valenar, so you were on the Talenta Plains. So you got a taste for halfling cooking?"

"This place isn't authentic," Mordan replied, "but it's about the best you'll find in Karrlakton. And don't worry about a menu—she'll know what to bring us."

"Oh, so you're a regular here? What's your usual order?"

"It's not like that. When a guest arrives, the cook brings out the best he has. It's the custom."

The food, when it arrived, was surprisingly good. The meat might have been real threehorn, rather than the heavily seasoned beef enjoyed by the other patrons; the spices were well-blended, and the vegetables were a valiant effort to recreate the flavors of the Plains with local ingredients. The meal was accompanied by two steaming mugs of tal—Mordan couldn't quite place the variety, but he thought it was redbush.

"So," said Mordan as they ate, "who's the redhead, and why is she asking about the Vedykar Lancers?"

Tarrel shrugged. "I was hoping you could tell me."

"Why are you interested in her?"

"I'm working for her family. She and her unit were presumed dead in the Mournland, but a spell placed her here in Karrlakton a few days ago."

Mordan raised an eyebrow as he put down his mug. "A spell like that costs a lot of money."

"They can afford it," Tarrel said. "They're an old military family, and they wanted the body back for burial. Now, they want their daughter back—whatever it takes."

"But she seems to have other ideas." Mordan said. "And it looks like her ideas include tracking down the Vedykar Lancers. There's another badge, as well." Mordan pulled Solly's sketch out of his jerkin and put it on the table. "This one," he said. "I've never seen it before. I don't even know if it's Karrnathi."

"Well, it's not Brelish," said Tarrel, "nor Thrane, Cyran, nor any other nationality I've looked into." He paused for a moment, then turned his hands palms up. "And that's all I know."

The two regarded each other in silence. Mordan reached into his belt, put Tarrel's wand on the table, and pushed it across to him. He took it with a silent nod of thanks.

"She's looking for the Vedykar Lancers," said Mordan,

"and so am I. You haven't been able to track her down in Karrlakton?"

Tarrel shook his head. "Don't believe everything you read about Sharn inquisitives," he said. "We can only follow the evidence, and she's not leaving any. My guess is that she has some scores to settle with these two units."

"Well, she's in the right place," Mordan said. "Karrlakton was the main depot for our forces going into Cyre. If that's where she encountered the Lancers, they should have come through here, and there should be a record of their deployment."

"Should be?"

"Yes, but there isn't."

Tarrel clicked his tongue in mock disapproval. "That's not very Karrnathi," he said. "I thought you people were serious about records and regulations."

"I thought so too," said Mordan, "until I started looking. The official story is that the Vedykar Lancers were deep inside Cyre on the Day of Mourning and were lost along with all the thousands of others. But there are no records of their movements for the previous six months."

Tarrel's ironic smile faded. "None?"

"Not in Korth, and not at the Lancer's headquarters in Vedykar. They came back from a tour in Cyre, they were brought back up to strength and re-equipped—and then they vanished."

"Interesting," said Tarrel. "I know what that usually means in the Army of Breland."

"Right," said Mordan. "Some kind of secret mission."

"What kind of cavalry were they?"

"The kind with shiny breastplates and bright plumes on their helmets, who ride behind the King's coach in parades.

Sons of the great and good, graduates of Rekkenmark, filled with honor and tradition."

"The kind that might not want the War to end, like that General . . . Ervus?"

"Eschus. General Rolund Eschus, upholder of the Tradition of Victory," said Mordan. "No, I don't think they went renegade," he continued. "They might not want to stop fighting, but they wouldn't defy an order from the King. They'd obey it to the letter, all the while complaining loudly about the loss of honor to themselves and Karrnath. What was the last trace of your girl?"

Tarrel reached into his coat and pulled out a battered notebook. He leafed through it for a few moments, then stabbed at a page with his finger.

"She was with a ranger unit operating behind the lines in northern Cyre. They last reported back on seventh of Vult, 993."

"Almost two months after the last official record of the Lancers' movements."

"Right."

Mordan leaned back in his seat and thought. "Has your client gone to the gnomes?" he asked.

Tarrel shook his head. "They can't. Money's no object, but because of their rank several members of the family have access to Thrane's military secrets. You know what the gnomes are like."

Mordan nodded. The gnomes—particularly, though not exclusively, those of House Sivis—loved other people's secrets, and the price they asked for their knowledge, though always high, was not always in cash. He had made inquiries himself with the few gnomes he trusted, and been unable to meet their price.

"So," said Tarrel, "you're the local expert. Where do you go in this town to find out about secret missions and missing units?"

"The same place I was going when you stopped me," said Mordan. "Bald Falko's."

"Why?"

"Because if anyone can identify this badge, he can. And because when you stopped me, I was watching one of the Vedykar Lancers come out of his shop."

* * * ⊚ * * *

Inside, the warehouse looked bigger than it really was. The clutter stretched away in all directions until it was swallowed by the darkness: spears and swords standing in barrels, piles of armor in every kind of condition, saddles, odd pieces of uniforms, belts, equipment pouches, and almost every other kind of item that an army could conceivably use. A single oil lamp cast a tiny pool of light over the center of the room, and there, like a spider in a web, sat Bald Falko, perched on a camp stool at a folding map table, scribbling in one of the many ledgers he used to keep track of his stock.

He looked up as Mordan and Tarrel entered—or at least, his eyes did. His head didn't move. Squinting over the top of his battered spectacles, he made the sour face that he used as a greeting.

"Friend of yours, Mordan?" he asked, casting an unwelcoming glance over Tarrel.

"This is Tarrel," Mordan replied. "He's looking for some of the same things I am."

Falko raised his eyes briefly to the ceiling.

"Then he's as much out of luck as you are," he said. "I

told you I'd let you know if I found anything on the Vedykar Lancers."

"Actually, we've got something for you," said Mordan.

"I'm not buying today," Falko replied, turning back to his ledger. "Now if you don't mind . . ."

"We're not selling," said Mordan. "We need a unit badge identified."

Falko closed his ledger and pushed it to one side. "Let's see it," he said, pushing his spectacles back up his nose.

Mordan handed over the sketch Solly had given him. Falko's lip curled in disgust as he looked at it.

"Who drew this?"

"Solly," Mordan replied.

Falko made a noise deep in his throat. "I should have known," he said. "You might as well dip a spider in an inkwell and drop it on the paper. Where did he get the design?"

"From someone else who's looking for the Vedykar Lancers," said Mordan. "They have sketches of this and the badge. . . ."

"And you want to know if the two are connected," Falko finished the sentence for him. Mordan nodded.

"Well, I'll do what I can," said Falko, without much enthusiasm, "but working from a sketch of a sketch—I don't know." He peered at the sketch in silence. "It's Karrnathi," Falko said at last.

"You're sure?" asked Mordan.

Falko fixed him with a glare. "Of course I'm sure! It's a Karrnathi shoulder patch—look at the shape, and look at the style of the numbers! I can tell that, even with Solly's penmanship. The skull looks like the D pattern, which would mean the unit was raised between Aryth 991 and Eyre 993.

That's when they went to the E pattern, which has a wreath around the skull—even Solly couldn't have missed that."

Falko pulled a book from a stack by his elbow, and started leafing through color illustrations of military badges. After a while he stopped, spun the book around to face his visitors, and pushed it across the table.

"See this one?" he asked, stabbing one design with a cracked and grimy fingernail. "That's the closest there is in here."

Kaz and Tarrel bent over the open book. "The number's different," Tarrel observed. "So's the color."

Falko snorted. "So it's true what they say about Brelish inquisitives," he said sarcastically. "I didn't say this was the same badge—just the closest one." He spun the book back around to face him, and flipped to the back pages.

"Six-twenty-nine," he muttered to himself as he ran a finger down column after column of numbers.

"Ah, here it is," he said after a moment. "Yes—this badge belonged to the Third Risen Patriots, before the undead troops were merged into the overall army command structure. They were initially commanded by the Ministry for the Dead, as you may know, but that arrangement created so many operational difficulties that it was abandoned after less than three months. Olarune 992, I think it was."

"Help me out here, Falko," said Mordan. "What does that badge tell us about the one in the sketch?"

"Tell us?" he echoed. "Nothing, on the face of it. No, you have to read between the lines. I'm thinking that your badge belonged to a unit raised by the Ministry—therefore, probably an undead unit—sometime in the winter of 991-992. The fact that it's not on record makes it likely that the unit never saw action—or more likely, it was merged into the army command structure before it was deployed. The army would have changed the badge to conform to their own standards at that time . . ."

"Sorry to interrupt," said Tarrel, "but the original sketch came from a military source in Thrane. That implies . . ."

"It could imply all sorts of things," said Falko. "Faulty observation and reporting of a different badge, obsolete information obtained by espionage—or even deliberate mis-information put out by our military counter-intelligence bureau."

"Or an encounter in the field," said Mordan.

Falko shot him a despairing look. "No," he said firmly, "not with this badge. Quite impossible. No undead forces engaged Thrane troops until Nymm of 992 at the Battle of Asken Ford, and by that time they were all under army command—with army-style badges."

"All of them?" asked Mordan.

"All of the units on record."

"And if this unit isn't on record and was still under Ministry command?"

Falko took off his spectacles and rubbed the bridge of his nose.

"Then it would have to have been some kind of short-lived experimental unit like the Ghoul Corps . . ."

"Or a secret unit," said Mordan. "That would fit with the Vedykar Lancers dropping out of sight, if our Thrane source met both of them at the same time."

Falko shot a nervous glance at Tarrel. "In that case, we're talking about official secrets," Falko said. "And as Karrnath is still under martial law, it would be dangerous to go poking into them. Especially in front of a Brelander. No offense."

"None taken," said Tarrel.

Mordan broke the awkward silence. "Someone was here a couple of hours ago. Human, male, dark hair with a slight curl, scar on the left side of his chin. I'm guessing he wore a Rekkenmark ring."

Falko looked up at him sharply. "None of your business."

"Don't be so sure," said Mordan. "He used to be in the Vedykar Lancers."

Falko's eyes widened a little. "Are you sure?" he asked.

"Fairly sure," said Mordan.

"Probably a chance resemblance," said Falko. "Everyone's been looking for someone since the War ended. It's easy to make mistakes."

"Maybe," said Mordan, "maybe not. What did he want?"

"Why don't you ask him yourself?" said Falko. "I'm not in the habit of discussing my business dealings."

"I don't think he'd be very talkative," said Mordan. "Since the government says the Lancers were wiped out in the Mournland, one of the heroic dead wouldn't want to be identified walking about here in Karrlakton. And since I'm paying you for information about the Lancers . . ." he let his voice trail off significantly.

Falko sighed. "He's looking to sell some surplus equipment. I told him I wasn't buying, and he said he was expecting a shipment of masterwork longswords, plus some armor and shields. I said I'd look at the swords, but I wasn't interested in the other stuff. Happy now?"

Mordan thought for a moment. "Longswords," he said, half to himself. "Did he say what kind of armor and shields?"

"Half-plate and light shields." Falko replied. "I know what you're thinking, but that mix of equipment is far too common to be conclusive. And he didn't mention any lances, saddles, barding—nothing to suggest a cavalry regiment. I'd guess medium infantry, but I'll be able to tell you when he brings the swords in tomorrow. Assuming you're right about him, I'd say he either transferred to the infantry before the Lancers' last posting, or the whole regiment was dismounted for some reason."

"I doubt that," said Mordan. "Not with their long and glorious history on horseback. They'd mutiny first."

"I thought you said they'd never disobey an order," said Tarrel.

"Stopping the war without a clear victory is one thing," Mordan replied, "but dismounting the Vedykar Lancers is another."

Tarrel shook his head. "I'll never understand you Karrns," he said.

Mordan turned back to Falko. "I'll be back tomorrow," he said. "Save me one of those swords and tell him you might have a buyer for the rest. I'd like to see the shields, as well."

Falko raised an eyebrow. "Are you going to pay for them this time?" he asked.

Mordan flashed him a grin. "Of course," he said. "I'm thinking of putting together an expedition."

Falko raised his eyes to the ceiling.

"Well, thanks, Falko," Mordan said. "If we find out any more, I'll let you know."

"Mordan?" said Falko as they turned to leave.

"What?"

"If you find an original of that badge . . . ?"

Mordan smiled. "I'll get you one if I can."

"And anything else with that insignia. It must be very rare."

"Good night, Falko."

"He's quite a character," said Tarrel, once the two were out of the warehouse. Dusk had given way to night, and it was as dark outside as inside.

Mordan nodded. "He knows a lot about the military, though."

"I can tell," said Tarrel with a chuckle. "It looks like he has most of their gear."

"He's a collector," said Mordan. "Swords or facts, he doesn't care. I'm not sure he even wants to sell most of what he's got."

"So who's your mysterious Lancer?"

"Name's Berend Hintram," Mordan said. "He was at Rekkenmark with the one I'm looking for, class of 991."

"Your boy have a name?" asked Tarrel.

"Does your client?" Mordan shot back.

Tarrel held up his hands in mock surrender. "I was just thinking, if I come across anything while I'm looking for my client's daughter . . ."

"Galifar ir'Dramon," said Mordan. "Last known rank was first lieutenant."

Tarrel raised an eyebrow. "Ir'Dramon," he repeated. "That sounds like a good family."

Mordan shrugged. "They used to be," he said, "but times have been tough lately. They don't pay as much as your client, I'm sure of that."

"So why are you working for them? Karrnathi loyalty?"

"You could say."

A distant bell boomed through the fog, striking the hour.

"It's late," said Mordan. "I'm going to get some sleep. I'll meet you outside Falko's at noon. With luck, Hintram will have made his delivery by then."

Inside the warehouse, Falko rummaged through another stack of books, pausing occasionally to glance back at Solly's sketch of the mysterious badge. There was a soft sound behind him, and he turned round with a start. A pair of eyes bored into his, and a gentle voice told him to be still.

CHAPTER 5

Olarune 18, 999 YK

Karrlakton's waterfront looked little better by day than it did by night. The fog was gone, but everything was still gray. Looking across the river, it was impossible to tell where the grayness of the overcast skies ended and the grayness of the Mournland mist began. The walls and roofs of the warehouses were a darker shade of gray, relieved only by the occasional splash of green where moss or some other plant had found a foothold between the stones.

Tarrel turned up his collar and wondered what Mordan was learning from Falko. They had seen Hintram arrive by wagon, unload several bundles into Falko's warehouse, and drive away a few minutes later. Mordan had gone inside while Tarrel followed the wagon. He had changed out of his Brelish clothes, which would have made him too conspicuous on the waterfront, and into some rough laborer's clothing provided by one of Mordan's contacts. He kept a safe distance from his quarry, but the driver seemed to have no idea he was being followed.

The wagon headed east along the waterfront, following wheel-ruts left in the cobbles by centuries of traders. Tarrel tried to imagine what the place had looked like in its prime, with vessels from across Khorvaire crowding its docks, loading and unloading cargo from all over the world. All he could see were the results of war and neglect. The docks stood mostly empty. Instead of bustling merchants and stevedores, there were beggars huddled against the warehouse walls, taking what shelter they could beneath the overhanging roofs.

The farther east the wagon went, the worse everything looked. The cobbles became patchy and then ran out altogether; the warehouses became more ruinous, and the thoroughfare more choked with trash and debris. Finally, even the beggars disappeared, replaced by fat, greasy rats that skittered from cover to cover.

At last, the wagon reached a warehouse close to the gap-toothed city wall. A wooden jetty reached a little way into the water, with moss and mildew speckling the boards that were still there. Off the end of the jetty, a couple of pilings stuck a foot or so out of the gray, oily water, showing that the jetty had once been longer. Opposite the jetty stood a warehouse whose front had been almost demolished—whether by a wartime attack or by something that had crossed from the Mournland, it was impossible to tell—and patched up with canvas, broken timbers, and whatever else came to hand. A half-orc lounged on the nearest corner, obviously a lookout. The wagon was almost fifty yards ahead of him by now, and he slipped into an alley out of sight.

Reaching into his coat, he pulled out a small mirror. It was mounted at an angle on a slim iron handle, and allowed him to look around the corner without being seen. As he watched, the half-orc pulled a sheet of canvas aside, and the cart went into the crumbling warehouse. The lookout returned to his post on the corner.

Tarrel watched for a few moments, then put the mirror away and pulled out a wand. It was different from the one Mordan had returned to him: a smooth, featureless rod of something that looked like glass. Touching it to his chest, he muttered a few words, and vanished.

⊛ ⊛ ⊛ ⊛ ⊛ ⊛ ⊛

"I told you," said Falko.

Mordan examined the sword. It was masterwork, but not cavalry pattern. With its asymmetric, spiked quillons and jagged blade, it was ugly but brutally effective, designed to be wielded with strength rather than skill. He looked at the crown and skull emblem stamped on the hilt.

"Undead?" he asked.

Falko nodded. "The armor and shields, too," he said. "Standard issue for zombie units. It makes sense, I suppose. With the undead forces being demobilized, I expect I'll be seeing a lot more of their surplus equipment. In fact, I'm surprised no one's brought any in before."

There were plenty of adventurers in Karrlakton who would be eager to get their hands on masterwork weapons. But Mordan was no closer to the Lancers.

"Did he tell you anything?" he asked.

Falko shook his head. "Cash only, no names, all business," he replied. "I don't suppose he came by these honestly."

Despite the Treaty of Thronehold, Karrnath was still on a war footing—partly to counter the Valenar threat to the south and partly in case the fragile peace should break. The country's notorious undead troops were being demobilized but not disbanded. The Ministry for the Dead had set up great mausolea to hold them in case of future need—and to act as a deterrent against outside aggression. Their equipment was supposed to go with them. The military would not be disposing of masterwork weapons at a time like this.

Mordan laid the sword back on the table. "Anything more on the badge?" he asked.

Falko looked blank. "Badge?" he asked.

Mordan frowned. It wasn't like Falko to forget anything. "From yesterday," Mordan said. "You said it was a Ministry pattern, but you couldn't pin it down."

Falko knit his brow in concentration, as if trying to remember something from a long time ago. "A badge," he said, absently. "I think . . ." He mopped his brow with a large kerchief. He seemed unsteady on his feet.

"Are you ill, Falko?"

Falko sat down heavily on his camp stool.

"No," he mumbled. "I—I'm fine. Just a headache. I should probably get some sleep. I'll remember tomorrow . . ." his voice tailed off, and his head sagged toward the tabletop.

He didn't even react to the splintering sound of the door being kicked down.

❦ ❦ ❦ ❦ ❦ ❦ ❦

Tarrel approached the warehouse, mentally counting down the duration of the invisibility spell. He worked his way along the back alleys, taking care not to step in any puddles or give any other sign of his presence. He'd been an inquisitive too long to assume that being invisible was a guarantee of being unseen.

The back of the warehouse was more intact than the front, but no cleaner. Mold and moss grew in the cracks between the stones, and dark stains showed where more than a century of rain had washed down from the eaves. Another tough leaned against the wall beside the single back door, dressed in scuffed and filthy leather armor. Tarrel approached as near as he dared and examined the door. The lock was old and the hinges rusted, and his eye caught a stray glint from the door-jamb; looking closer, he saw that the doorway had been outlined in gold dust, magically securing it. It would be almost impossible to open quietly, even if he could overpower the guard.

He stopped and sniffed. Mixed in with the damp, rotting timber, and garbage that made up the smell of the waterfront, there was something else. It was a heavy smell, sweet and sharp in equal measure. It was a smell of decay, but stood out from the overall decay that marked the area. He couldn't quite place it, but he knew it didn't belong there.

Stepping softly past the lazing guard, he went down the side of the warehouse, trying to identify the smell. The smell got stronger as he came to the front of the building, and he guessed it came from inside. A few window-slits were set high up in the walls, allowing light inside but too high for him to see through, even with his mirror. The walls were just as damp and slippery here as at the back of the building, making climbing risky. He could hear something going on inside—a low conversation, a shuffling, and the occasional creak—but nothing that told him what was happening.

He had about a minute of invisibility left and decided to risk looking at the front. Maybe he would be able to see something through a gap in the makeshift repairs. Keeping an eye on the half-orc lookout, he moved as quietly as he could. Cautiously, he reached out a hand toward a loose flap of canvas—but it was flung back before he touched it.

Spinning round to face the door, Mordan caught a glimpse of two bulky figures rushing toward him. Behind them, another one was raising a wand, barking a command word. Instinctively, he threw himself aside, rolling behind a rack of pikes. Something pale and shapeless shot past the spot where he had been standing.

A second glance told him more about the intruders. There were four of them, all wearing the uniform of the Royal Swords. The wand-bearer had drawn a sword like his comrades, and they advanced cautiously into the warehouse. Mordan looked round at a muffled whine from Falko's stool; he was struggling uselessly against a mass of sticky strands that enveloped him and anchored him to the table and floor. Mordan pulled his cloak over his head; it had come from the same place as his rapier, and blended with the shadows.

"Royal Swords!" announced the leader of the group. "Come out and keep your hands where we can see them!" He and one of the others edged toward Mordan's hiding-place, while the other two set about cutting Falko loose from the web.

Peering between the pikestaffs, Mordan could see their heads move as they looked around. They hadn't spotted him yet. He waited until they came closer, and then kicked the rack over, springing to his feet.

One of the Swords was quick enough to get out of the way, but the other was taken by surprise. He raised an arm to protect himself as the pikes clattered off his head and shoulders. Mordan ducked behind a stack of boxes and began to edge toward the door. He had no intention of fighting the Royal Swords if he could get away. King Kaius had kept Karrnath under martial law despite the peace, and royal justice was both harsh and summary—especially for those who killed the King's officers.

Peering out from underneath a set of barding on a horse-shaped stand, Mordan saw three pairs of feet heading toward the door. The middle pair moved clumsily and still bore traces of the magical web; the other two were heavily booted. Falko was protesting feebly, but his captors ignored him. A sideways glance told Mordan that the other two Swords were still looking for him.

Carefully pulling a light mace from a barrel of weapons beside him, he threw it in a high arc across the warehouse. It came down with a crash on a stack of helmets, spilling them noisily across the floor. Falko's captors continued half-dragging him toward the door, but the other two turned round and looked toward the source of the noise. He found a pouch of sling bullets under a table, and threw it after the mace as he moved into the cover of a group of barrels. It landed close by the helmets with a soft rattle. One of the officers took a step toward the sound.

Falko and his captors were outside now, leaving Mordan and the two others in the crowded warehouse. Chancing a glance over the barrels, he saw that one was moving toward the upset helmets, but he had lost sight of the other. He listened for footsteps but heard nothing.

He had a clear path to the door, and decided to run for it—but the other Royal Sword had anticipated his move. Stepping out from behind a rack of armor, he blocked Mordan's way.

"Oh, no, you don't," he said, raising his sword with a vicious smile.

As Mordan twisted away from the slashing blade, he heard the footsteps of the second officer approaching at a run. He backed away from the first, tipping over a barrel to slow him down, and snatched up a leather harness from a pile of horse-trappings beside him. Spinning round, he threw it at the second officer's legs, tripping him. He only had a second to act before the officer regained his feet.

Mordan leaped over the prone body of the fallen officer and ran toward the back of the warehouse. Glancing up, he saw the pale square of a grimy skylight; he vaulted onto Falko's table, and from there to the rafters. Holding his cloak over his head, he punched through the filthy glass with the stump of his left arm, then launched himself upward, through the skylight and onto the roof.

Without waiting to see if the Royal Swords followed, he ran along the roof and jumped across the narrow alley to an adjoining building. Crouching on the roof, he listened for sounds of pursuit, but heard nothing. The Royal Swords must have come for Falko; he just happened to be there at the wrong time, and they weren't going to waste their effort chasing him—especially since he didn't draw steel on them.

Dropping softly to the cobbles, Mordan headed back to the Black Dragon. He didn't follow the Royal Swords, because he knew where they would be taking Falko—to the Palace of Justice in the city center. What he didn't know, yet, was what he was going to do next.

● ● ● ◉ ● ● ●

Stifling a gasp, Tarrel stepped aside. Hintram had almost collided with him as he came out. He froze, certain that he must have been spotted, but the human simply exchanged a few words with his half-orc lookout and strode back into the city. Tarrel ducked between two warehouses and found a secluded spot where there was a large puddle. Crouching over it, he waited until he could see his own reflection in the scummy water. Then he set off after Hintram. He threaded his way through the back-alleys, roughly paralleling the man's course and catching an occasional glimpse of him between buildings. As the street became busier at the western end of the waterfront, Tarrel felt safe to drop back and mingle with the crowd, keeping his quarry in sight.

The waterfront was not the only part of Karrlakton to have suffered destruction. As an industrial center and Karrnath's second city, it had endured constant attacks from Cyran forces across the river. Karrnathi architecture was solid and imposing, but nearly every building in the city was either damaged, recently repaired, or in the process of being repaired. In some places, entire groups of buildings had been destroyed, leaving fragments of walls and chimneys standing out above piles of rubble. As he followed the wagon, Tarrel passed several sites that were being cleared of debris, and a number of new structures under construction. The laborers were a mixed bunch, and as well as native Karrns he saw Cyran exiles, warforged, and even an occasional hobgoblin from Darguun in the south.

Hintram led him to a large hostelry south of the city's main square. Its gilded pillars and gaudy paintwork were meant to convey opulence, but they reminded Tarrel of some of the places in Firelight, Sharn's infamous pleasure district. An ornately carved sign hung over the door, bearing the name GOOD AS GOLD picked out in gilt on a bright red background. The words stood on a bed of carved and painted gold coins.

Tarrel hung back as Hintram went inside, judging the lay of the land. The people entering and leaving the establishment were better dressed than he was in his laborer's disguise, and he didn't want to go in looking out of place and risk attracting attention. At the side of the building, down a dark and narrow passage, he saw an outside privy, obviously provided for the use of the establishment's patrons. It appeared to be empty, so he ducked inside and closed the door.

He had hidden his Brelish clothes close to his lodgings, and by the time he had retrieved them, cleaned up and changed, his quarry might have moved on. If Mordan was right, Hintram was the only link he had to one of the badges his client's daughter was hunting down. He couldn't risk losing his only solid lead.

Rummaging inside his tunic, he pulled out the glassy wand again, then changed his mind. Invisibility had its uses, but the Good As Gold was a busy place, and he would be discovered right away if anyone bumped into him. Pulling on a leather strap under one arm, he unbuckled a scroll-case and thought for a moment. He murmured a single syllable, and the scroll-case opened. Taking out a scroll, he read aloud, still in a low voice. The air around him shimmered, and he became a slightly stout human dressed in the style of a Karrnathi merchant, rather than a grimy half-elf laborer. Stowing the scroll-case again, he stepped out of the privy, wrinkling his nose fastidiously and making a great show of dusting down his clothes. Then he went inside the hostelry.

The interior of the Good As Gold was as ostentatious as its street frontage. The tables and chairs were carved with vines and foliage, but were too solid in their construction to be entirely tasteful. The red and gold theme of the sign was carried on in the upholstery, with velvet and tassels everywhere. The serving staff, dressed in a uniform that suggested a noble livery, bustled between the kitchens and the tables. In addition to the large common room, several smaller private rooms ranged along the outside. Some had their doors closed.

Tarrel scanned the room but saw no sign of his quarry. He picked an unoccupied table with a clear view of the doorways to most of the private rooms, and ordered food and drink. It had been a long morning, and he was glad to take a break.

He suspected that Hintram was behind one of the closed doors, and took his time over his meal as he watched and waited. After ten minutes or so, a waiter knocked on one of the doors and took in a pitcher of wine. As the door opened, Tarrel caught a glimpse of his quarry, who was laughing and drinking with an older human man. This individual was well-dressed, in conservative but stylish Karrnathi clothes, and so fat that he occupied almost all of the small room by himself. He was making a point—or perhaps delivering the punchline of a joke—by waving a half-eaten joint of meat at his companion.

The waiter served the two and left, closing the door behind him. Although Tarrel had caught a glimpse of a window behind the fat man, it seems that the door into the main part of the hostelry was Hintram's only practical way out, so he decided to wait. His meal—a cold plate of cured meats and cheeses with dark, heavy bread fresh from the oven, accompanied by a mug of the Nightwood Ale he had heard so much about—was not as fancy as some cooking he'd had, but the serving was generous and the ingredients were good quality.

As he ate, he made a mental image of the fat man, meaning to ask Mordan if he knew him. Judging by his clothes and Hintram's deferential attitude, he was a person of some consequence in Karrlakton, and he wondered what business he might have with a smuggler of stolen weapons.

He was finishing the last of his cheese when someone else knocked on the door of the side-room. Like Tarrel, he was a half-elf, but he was younger and more muscular. His clothes—black breeches, calf-length boots, and a black leather jerkin over a plain white shirt—were less showy than those of the inn's other patrons, and so was the shortsword that hung by his side. He went inside.

A few moments later, he came out again, accompanied by Hintram and the fat man. Their demeanor had changed; clearly the messenger had brought bad news. As they left, Tarrel tossed a handful of coins on his table and got up to follow them.

A RESCUE

CHAPTER 6

Olarune 18, 999 YK

So you're just going to leave him there?" asked Solly. They were sitting at a booth in the Black Dragon, waiting for Tarrel to make their rendezvous.

Mordan shrugged. "Have you got a better idea?"

Solly grinned. "I do," he said, leaning closer across the table.

Mordan winced slightly, and listened without enthusiasm.

"Look," Solly continued, "I just do my half-orc officer act, and we pretend you're my prisoner. You said they were chasing you all over Falko's shop, so there's probably a reward out for you. Then after we're inside, we find Falko and break him out. It's simple."

"Simple enough to get us killed," Mordan replied. "Do you know how many Royal Swords are in the Palace of Justice at any time?"

Solly waved a hand dismissively.

"Oh, you can take care of them," he said. "I've seen you with that rapier of yours. They won't stand a chance."

"And if I kill any of them, the Royal Swords will hunt me all across Karrnath and not stop until they've hanged me. No, thanks."

Solly looked puzzled at that possibility. "But . . ." he said.

Mordan cut him off. "No," he said. "I don't know what kind of trouble Falko's in, and I don't want to know. He's a big boy."

Solly gave him a sour look. "Some friend you are," he said.

Mordan took a drink. "I don't stick my neck out for anyone," he said. "And if you want to mix business with friendship, you can start by charging me less for all the information you haven't been giving me."

Their conversation was interrupted by Tarrel's arrival.

"So what's new?" he asked.

Mordan sighed. "Falko's in jail, and Solly wants me to get myself killed trying to break him out," he said.

Tarrel raised an eyebrow. "In jail?" he repeated. "What for?"

Mordan shrugged. "Could be a lot of things," he said. "Most likely trading in stolen goods. Those masterwork swords belonged to Fort Zombie. They came and got him soon after you left. Nearly got me, too."

"So," said Tarrel, "they're not from your lancers. Are you're still sure the supplier was one of them?"

Mordan nodded. "I'd never forget that face," he said.

Tarrel looked at him questioningly, but he didn't elaborate. "Well," said Tarrel, "I've got better news. I followed him to an old warehouse, way out at the far end of the docks. He's got some muscle keeping an eye on it. I didn't get a look inside, but after he dropped off the wagon he went back into town. Ever hear of a place called the Good As Gold?"

"Yes," said Mordan. "It's a place for second-rate merchants who want to pay first-rate prices for third-rate food."

"He went there for lunch," Tarrel continued, "and met with someone in a private room."

"What kind of someone?"

"A very large kind of someone. Human, male, older, white hair, seemed important. Know him?"

Mordan cursed under his breath. "Leonus Dabo," he said, "one of our friendly local crime lords."

"Well," Tarrel continued, "they looked pretty friendly. Then a messenger came—he must have brought bad news, because they dropped their smiles and left in a hurry."

"Where did they go?"

Tarrel shrugged. "Hintram went back to his little hideout. I don't know about Mr. Big."

Mordan ran his hand through his hair. "So what have we got?" he thought aloud. "Hintram is selling stolen equipment from Fort Zombie to Falko, and he's doing some kind of business with Dabo. What is it—protection for his smuggling operation?"

Tarrel shook his head. "No," he said. "I've seen people pay protection money. They look scared or they look angry, but they don't smile and laugh. This is some kind of deal that makes them both happy. Is the fat man looking to equip a private army?"

"If he were," said Mordan, "Hintram would have gone to him with those masterwork swords, not Falko." He looked around for a moment. "Did you see where Solly went?"

● ● ● ◉ ● ● ●

The desk sergeant ran a finger down the columns of the day book.

"No Falko here," he said, looking across the desk at the primly dressed lawyer's clerk.

"But that's quite impossible," the young man protested, in cultured tones. "Several witnesses saw him taken into custody only a couple of hours ago."

The sergeant sighed and picked up a quill.

"Do you know the names of the arresting officers?" he asked.

"No," replied the clerk, "but there were four of them, all human. Does that help?"

"You just described eighty percent of our patrols," said the sergeant, putting the quill down again.

"Well," said the clerk, "they obviously had orders to arrest him. Can I at least see the warrant?"

The sergeant sighed, a little harder. He hated persistent clerks. "Can't find the warrant without the name of the accused," he said.

"I already told you," answered the clerk, "it's Falko."

The sergeant smiled, the self-satisfied smile of a player who was about to make the winning move in a game of Conqueror.

"And I already told you," he said, "that there's no Falko in the books." He closed the day book with a slap.

"Listen," the clerk lowered his voice and leaned across the desk a little, "my firm has authorized certain—shall we say, out of pocket expenses for this case."

The sergeant looked hard into the young man's eyes, then slowly opened the book again.

"I suppose it's possible he gave a false name," he said. "What's he look like?"

Behind the clerk's earnest face, Solly stifled a laugh at the thought that a name could be false and a face could not. He covered his chuckle with a cough and concentrated on maintaining his disguise as he gave the sergeant a description of Bald Falko.

* * * ⊛ ⊛ * * *

"I've heard no one can lie to a master inquisitive," said Mordan. "Is that true?"

Tarrel half smiled. "I can usually tell when someone's lying," he said.

"But can you force someone to tell the truth?"

"Sometimes," Tarrel replied. "It's not infallible. A lot depends on how the questions are asked. What's on your mind?"

"Now we know where to find Hintram," said Mordan, "we could just grab him."

Tarrel thought for a moment. "We'd need a plan," he said. "He's got at least a couple of goons guarding that warehouse."

"Simple," said Mordan. "We just watch the place and wait till he leaves. I know of a few quiet little spots where we can talk without being disturbed."

"I don't know," said Tarrel. "It's risky."

"Have you got a better idea?" asked Mordan.

"Well, answer me this," said Tarrel. "Suppose we do manage to capture him without attracting attention, and suppose I can get him to tell us what he knows. What happens next? Your fat crime boss isn't going to be too pleased about us messing with one of his business associates."

Mordan shrugged. "Once I've got what I want, I won't be staying around," he said. "I didn't come to Karrlakton for my health."

"That's fine for you," said Tarrel, "but what's in it for me? I still haven't picked up the trail I'm looking for."

"Well," said Mordan, "your redhead is looking for the Vedykar Lancers just like I am. If we find them, you might find her."

"Except she doesn't know about your friend Hintram," he said. "I wouldn't either, if you hadn't spotted him and I hadn't stopped you."

Before Mordan could answer, Solly appeared at their table, looking very pleased with himself.

"Who's buying?" he asked brightly.

Mordan scowled. "Buying what?" he asked.

Solly's grin widened. "I found Falko," he said. "They didn't take him to the Palace of Justice after all. Guess where he's being held?" He signaled a barmaid. "Harika, how about some service over here?"

"Where?"

"Go on, guess," he said. Then, turning to the newly-arrived barmaid, he said, "A large Cyran brandy and another of whatever these two are drinking." He jerked a thumb in Mordan's direction. "He's paying."

The barmaid looked at Mordan, who nodded. "This had better be good, Solly," he said as she went back to the bar.

"I'll give you a clue," said the changeling, shifting his face into the shape of a fleshless skull.

Tarrel shrugged, and Mordan just glared. With a sigh, Solly's face went back to normal.

"The Ministry of the Dead," he said, unable to resist adding a deep, sinister timbre to his voice. The waitress, who had just returned with the drinks, gave him a sideways look but said nothing.

"The Ministry?" echoed Mordan. "Why would they want him?"

"How about those swords?" ventured Tarrel. "Weren't they from undead troops? They probably want to know where he's getting them."

Mordan cursed under his breath. "He'll tell them about Hintram," he said. "We don't have much time."

"Who's Hintram?" asked Solly. The other two ignored him.

"Not so fast," said Tarrel. "Falko doesn't know where to find Hintram, and we do. Besides, we don't know that he's told them anything."

"I don't want to take the risk," said Mordan. "We're going after Hintram now." He drained his mug and got up to leave.

"We?" asked Tarrel. "You speak for yourself. I'm not doing anything till I know what he's told them. And, if possible, what they've been asking him."

Solly finished his brandy and smacked his lips with a grin. "I can help you there," he said.

Mordan raised his eyes to the ceiling.

"You two do what you want," he said, and left.

❦ ❦ ❦ ❦ ❦ ❦ ❦

"Don't ask me, mate," said the huge, scarred half-orc in the Royal Swords uniform. "I'm just following orders—and orders were to bring him here."

The Ministry guard looked at the officer and his prisoner suspiciously. The prisoner was a half-elf, dressed in the rough clothing of a laborer.

"Whose orders?" he asked.

The half-orc shrugged. "My sergeant didn't say," he replied. "All I know is, he's something to do with that one who was brought in from the waterfront this morning. He's the one that got away."

"Oh, right," said the guard. "I did hear something about that. In you go."

"Where d'you want him?" asked the half-orc. "I wasn't told who to take him to."

"Typical," said the guard, grimacing in sympathetic acknowledgment at the incompetence of superiors. "Hold on—I'll find out."

He pushed the door partway open, beckoned someone from inside, and a muttered exchange took place. After a few moments, he turned back to the visitors.

"You go with Detlev here," he said. "He'll see you right."

The half-orc gave a curt nod of thanks as he half-dragged his prisoner inside the building. They followed the Ministry clerk up several flights of stairs and along a long, narrow passage, finally reaching a stout-looking door of iron-bound oak. Taking a ring of keys from his belt, he unlocked it. As he did so, the half-orc officer released his prisoner, who pulled a scroll from inside his shirt, muttered a few words, and made a swift gesture. The clerk turned at the sound.

"I need you to do me a favor," said Tarrel in a friendly voice.

The clerk blinked a couple of times, looking from the half-elf to the half-orc, who stood by silently. "What?" he asked uncertainly.

"Nothing much," answered Tarrel. "I just want you to show me where you're keeping Falko. You know, the man who was brought in this morning."

The clerk blinked again, as if trying to clear his head. Then his mouth opened, and he started to run. He didn't get far; the half-orc tripped him and his head hit the stone floor hard. The two wrestled him through the door, and closed it behind them.

"I thought you said this would work?" said the half-orc, in Solly's voice. He had one hand over the clerk's mouth.

"Magic isn't infallible," Tarrel replied, quickly tying the clerk's hands and feet. "Sometimes people can resist it." He pulled a rag out of his breeches and stuffed it in the man's mouth.

"See if there's somewhere we can hide him," he added. Solly nodded, and trotted ahead, listening at doors and looking through keyholes. After a few moments, he opened one of the doors and beckoned.

"Broom closet," he said. Tarrel half-carried the groaning clerk into the small room and leaned him against one wall. Closing the door behind them, the two carried on.

"What now?" asked Solly.

"Same plan," said Tarrel. "I'm your prisoner, and you have orders to put me in with Falko." He offered his wrists to Solly, who tied them loosely with a short length of cord, and they walked on.

❦ ❦ ❦ ❦ ❦ ❦ ❦

Mordan hurried along the waterfront, hoping he would reach Hintram before the authorities did. If they caught him, if they realized that he was one of the officially dead Vedykar Lancers, if there was a cover-up—Mordan would lose the only lead he had to show for six months of searching. That all depended on how quickly they made the connection from Falko to Hintram.

He wondered how much Falko had told his captors—how much he really knew. With luck, it was no more than he had already told Mordan: an anonymous seller and no questions asked. But he knew the Ministry of the Dead had magical resources. Maybe they would be able to track Hintram through the swords, or by some other means. There was no shortage of rumors about the necromantic power wielded by the Ministry, and only the Ministry itself knew for sure how much was true.

He wondered, too, why Hintram was trading stolen undead weapons in Karrlakton. It was a far cry from the proud tradition of the Lancers, and further still from any kind of secret mission. What if the official line was true, and the Lancers had really been wiped out on the Day of Mourning? Perhaps Hintram had left the regiment before their final posting—deserted, or even been thrown out? Mordan decided he would worry about that when he heard it from Hintram himself. At least Hintram should be able to shed some light on the Lancers' fate.

As Mordan walked, he became aware of a commotion coming from a few streets away. Looking up, he saw a column of dense black smoke rising into the air. People were running toward it—some were carrying buckets. Falko's warehouse was in that direction, and his heart sank. Quickening his pace, he headed towards the smoke, and his fears were realized. Falko's warehouse was on fire.

A crowd had gathered round the building. Some were trying to put the fire out, using everything from magic to buckets of river water, while others were risking the smoke and flames to save what they could. The front door had either been broken down or burned off its hinges, and people were throwing weapons and armor into the street, or running off with arms full of whatever they could salvage. Knowing the waterfront district, it was unlikely that anyone was acting out of neighborly concern, but—as Mordan observed with a wry smile—most of it had already been stolen at least once before Falko acquired it.

He headed east again. The fire probably wasn't a coincidence, and he suspected that Hintram had something to do with it. If he knew that Falko had been questioned by the Ministry of the Dead, he was probably as nervous about them finding him as Mordan was. The fire could have been set to destroy anything linking the two of them. Mordan remembered what Tarrel had seen in the Good As Gold; perhaps the messenger had been one of Dabo's men bringing the news that Falko had been picked up.

The evening fog was rolling in off the river, and Mordan began to worry about finding the half-ruined warehouse that Tarrel had described. A bank of especially thick fog was moving steadily toward him along the waterfront, so thick it obscured all vision. Everything was quiet.

As he walked, Mordan tried to put himself in Hintram's shoes, to anticipate what he would do next. If the authorities in Karrlakton were onto his weapon-smuggling scheme, he might leave town and try his luck somewhere else. But there was still the question of his business with Dabo. Whatever it was, it might be enough to keep him here, at least until it was concluded.

A rat skittered out of the fog, almost running into his feet. Mordan knew the waterfront rats, and they were usually quite fearless. What had panicked this one? He stopped and listened, scanning the fog for any sign of danger, but there was nothing—except a smell.

It was vaguely familiar, but Mordan couldn't place it. Blindly, he took a few steps into the fog, and the smell became stronger. Then he saw a vague shape, half-hidden in the mist:

a horse, harnessed to a wagon that was still invisible in the fog. It was coming toward him, but it made no sound. The horse's hooves, the wheels of the cart he supposed it was pulling, even the sound of the river—all were gone. There was complete silence.

Mordan backed out of the mist, and as he did so the sound of the river returned. He had experienced silence spells before, fighting the Valenar elves with the Company of the Skull. Casting the spell on an arrow and shooting it into the midst of the enemy—or even better, into the body of the enemy commander—was a favorite ambush technique. It prevented orders from being heard, and the hapless victims of the ambush couldn't hear their attackers coming. He had seen inexperienced troops massacred in the ensuing confusion.

As he stood back, the patch of dense fog rolled slowly by him, and he guessed that it, too, was magical rather than natural. Someone wanted to make sure they were neither seen nor heard. Mordan watched the fog recede, and then walked toward its center.

Again, all sound ceased, and the fog became so dense he couldn't even see his own feet. Moving cautiously forward, he began to make out a shape—the back of a covered wagon. As he got closer, he realized it was the same one he and Tarrel had watched Hintram drive up to Falko's warehouse that morning, carrying the stolen swords. This delivery, Mordan guessed, was probably for Dabo.

He undid the back flap of the canvas wagon cover and pulled himself inside, moving carefully. He might not have to worry about noise, but the driver would still notice a sudden jolt. Securing the flap behind him, he peered through the dimness to see what the wagon was carrying. The fog was as

71

thick inside the cart as outside, and the canvas blocked whatever little light came in from outside. As his eyes adjusted to the gloom, he suddenly remembered why the smell was familiar.

All around him, standing close together and rocking slightly with the motion of the cart, were a dozen zombies.

INTERLUDE

Olarune 18, 999 YK

Master, I have news."

The old, white-haired elf on the carved throne leaned forward a little.

"We intercepted a communication to the Ministry of the Dead from their office in Karrlakton," the messenger continued. "Two enquiries have been made about Unit 61 in that city. One was by an arms dealer, now deceased under unclear circumstances, and the other by a female vampire, who apparently questioned a Ministry clerk under magical domination. Both had a copy of the unit badge and suspected a link with the Ministry, but apparently they knew little else. The message from the Ministry branch office notes that Unit 61 is officially posted as missing, and asks for instructions. That is all."

The messenger winked out of existence, and the elf sat back, absently stroking the skull at the end of the left arm-rest. His silver-blue, almost colorless eyes half-closed in thought.

After a moment, he turned to the pallid, robed lackey who stood by his side.

"Tell Rolund I wish to see him," he said.

A few minutes later, the lackey returned with another. This individual was tall and wiry, with fierce eyes and features that had once been human. On the shoulder of his worn and besmirched uniform was a patch bearing the image of a skull and the number 61. He made a brief obeisance before the throne.

"Rolund," said the elf, "I have work for you. There is a vampire loose in Karrlakton—one of ours, if I'm not mistaken. Female for certain; I suspect she may possibly be a Thrane with red hair. Her activities are becoming inconvenient. I want you to find her, observe until you have identified all her associates—and then destroy them all. Take Aeren, and leave immediately."

"With pleasure, master," the creature's voice was like the grating of a mausoleum door.

"Oh—and Rolund?"

The figure stopped and looked questioningly back at the elf.

"After that, visit our agent in the Ministry. Explain to him the necessity for more complete information in his future reports."

The assassin grinned and left the chamber.

Complications

CHAPTER 7

Olarune 18, 999 YK

Mordan froze and held his breath, but the zombies didn't move. Their eyes glittered in the dim light, and they shifted occasionally to keep their balance, but they gave no indication that they even knew he was there. The canvas was closed at the front as well as the back, so he couldn't see the driver. He guessed it would be Hintram, on his way to sell the undead owners of the weapons he had offered Falko.

As the cart went on its way, he sat and stared at them. Each one had been someone's son or daughter, brother or sister—had laughed with family and friends and played with children—but now they were just nameless corpses. Propaganda called them the Risen Patriots; having given their lives once in the War, they were re-animated by the Ministry of the Dead to fight again.

Now the war was over, they were supposed to be going to their well-deserved rest. Mordan had fought with undead troops on the Talenta Plains. Despite its name, the Company of the Skull was composed of living mercenaries, but they were headquartered in Fort Bones alongside regiments of skeletons. He had seen them on the battlefield, striding relentlessly forward until they were destroyed or the enemy broke, and he knew the fear they inspired. He knew, too, that Karrnath's decision to use undead troops in battle had been controversial and placed Karrnath beyond the pale of civilized nations in many eyes. Although it didn't appear in the Treaty of Thronehold, the demobilization of the undead forces was vital to the new peace.

Mordan guessed that someone at Fort Zombie was diverting undead troops from demobilization and Hintram was selling them on the black market, along with their equipment. The question Mordan couldn't answer was how Hintram, the wealthy son and fashionable Lancer, had become mixed up in this business. Were any of the other Lancers involved? Was Gali?

He had become so used to the magical silence that when the spell wore off, the sudden return of everyday sounds made him jump. Opening the canvas a little, he peered out the back of the wagon and saw that the fog had dissipated as well. They were away from the waterfront now, heading toward the center of Karrlakton, and dusk was falling.

At last, the wagon came to a construction site that was surrounded by high wooden fences. Hiding everything but the tip of a lone chimney-stack, they concealed everything that was going on inside. Hintram slid down from the driver's seat and knocked on a makeshift gate set into the fence. After a few moments it opened, and there was a brief conversation with someone inside.

Mordan took the opportunity to slip out of the wagon and into the gathering shadows. He would capture Hintram later, when he wasn't surrounded by zombies. Even unarmed, they could be dangerous, and Hintram could easily escape in the time it would take Mordan to dispose of them.

The gate opened, and the cart went inside. While he waited, Mordan examined the outside of the site with a tactician's eye. The fence was not unusual; postwar reconstruction efforts fed a lively trade in cheap building materials of indeterminate origin. But a glance confirmed that it was unusually well-built, without any gaps or holes that might allow a glimpse of the inside. It was more than would be needed to keep thieves out, or guard animals in.

Several minutes later, the gate opened again and the wagon came out, noticeably lighter on its axles. Mordan followed it on its return journey to the waterfront. At last it turned down Chandler's Alley, a narrow thoroughfare on the western end of the docks. It was perfect for what he had in mind; he glanced around, and there was no one in sight.

A short sprint brought him to the back of the wagon, which could neither turn nor back up in the narrow lane. Drawing his rapier, he vaulted through the open canvas, landing with a thump inside the cart. Before Hintram had time to react, Mordan cut through the canvas and placed the tip of his rapier lightly on the back of the man's neck.

"Keep driving," he said, "and do as I tell you."

● ● ● ◉ ● ● ●

"Damn," muttered Tarrel. He and Solly—still in his half-orc guise—stared through the bars of the cell. Falko lay on the floor like a rag doll, staring at the ceiling with sightless eyes.

"Is he dead?" asked Solly.

Tarrel didn't answer. Instead, he fished a small leather pouch out of his clothing, and unrolled it to reveal a set of lockpicks. "Keep a lookout," he said.

Solly went to the corner, where he could see both Tarrel and the entrance to the holding area. Tarrel bent over the lock in the cell door for a few moments, and it opened with a click. He gestured to Solly to stay where he was, and went inside.

Tarrel had seen plenty of dead bodies in his career as an inquisitive, and he could tell at a glance that Falko was dead; he had to establish how he died, and if possible, when. With the practiced ease of a master inquisitive, he set about examining the body. The limbs were stiff, indicating that he had been dead for at least a few hours, but there was no obvious sign of any wounds, or even bruises. At last Tarrel found what he was looking for—a small puncture mark behind Falko's right ear. There was no sign of what had caused it, but he noticed a trace of a resinous substance sticking to Falko's hair close to the wound. Tarrel cut the hair off with a small knife and wrapped it in a handkerchief. There would be time to identify it later.

He stood up and looked at the body, glancing back and forth at the cell door and at the barred window set high up in the wall. Judging by the wound, the dart—or whatever it was—had struck Falko from behind and slightly above; from the way the body had fallen, it probably came from the window. The window was too high for Tarrel to reach, but his mirror showed him that it led directly outside, with nothing but a sheer wall. Standing where he judged Falko had been, he looked out of the window along the most likely path of the projectile. There was nothing in sight, as he expected.

A cursory glance around the cell turned up nothing else. Tarrel put his tools away and peered out of the cell to where Solly stood on the corner. Everything seemed quiet. He left the cell, locking it again behind him, and quickly repacked his tools.

"Let's get out of here," he said to Solly.

"But I just talked us in past all those people," said the changeling. "What do we tell them on the way out?"

"Easy," replied Tarrel. "The high-ups took one look at me and decided I'm the wrong guy. Now, you've got to take me all the way back to the Palace of Justice."

Solly groaned. "They'll never believe it," he said.

Tarrel chuckled. "If I know bureaucracy, they will."

● ● ● ◉ ● ● ●

"Stop here." Mordan kept his rapier pressed against Hintram's neck. He brought the wagon to a halt in a darkened alley. There was no one about.

"What do you want?" he asked. His voice still had the nasal whine that Mordan had known as a child.

"I want you to talk to a friend of mine," Mordan said, "about the Vedykar Lancers."

Hintram tried to conceal a start of surprise. "Never heard of them," he said. Mordan chuckled unpleasantly.

"We'll see about that," he said. "Though I must say, you're looking pretty good, considering."

"Considering what?"

"Considering you're supposed to be dead in the Mournland." Hintram twitched his neck uncomfortably. A trickle of blood was running down from where the rapier made contact.

"I'm telling you," he protested, "you've got me mixed up with someone else!"

"Of course I have," said Mordan, in a low and dangerous voice. "You're just an honest dealer in stolen zombies and equipment, trying to make a living in our brave new age of peace. You can talk to me, or I can take you to the Ministry for a little chat. I'm sure they'd love to know about your little arrangement with Dabo. Your choice."

Hintram shifted uncomfortably on the driver's bench.

"Just get that thing out of my neck," he said. "I'll tell you whatever you want."

"I think I'll leave it there for now," replied Mordan. "Do you know where the Black Dragon is?"

"Yes."

"Good. Drive there, and don't attract any attention. Oh, and you know the friend I want you to talk to? He's a cleric of the Blood of Vol, and he can talk to the dead. So the only one who needs you alive—is you." It was a lie, but it would keep Hintram co-operative.

Hintram flicked the reins, and the horse walked on. The rapier-point pricked his neck as the wagon jerked into motion, and he flinched.

Something heavy landed on top of the wagon. The canvas cover ripped from its frame, enveloping Mordan. As he struggled to free himself, he caught a glimpse of Hintram running down the street with a speed born of sheer panic. Behind him, and gaining fast, was a dark shape—vaguely humanoid but impossible to identify in the darkness. Hintram ran down an alley, and the shape followed. A second later there was a scream, and then silence.

Wrestling himself free of the canvas, Mordan jumped down from the wagon and ran after the two. When he got to the alley, it was deserted.

❦ ❦ ❦ ❦ ❦ ❦ ❦

"Well, that was a good day's work," said Mordan. "Falko's dead, his warehouse has burned down, and I caught Hintram and then lost him."

He and Tarrel were sitting over dinner in his usual booth at the Black Dragon. Solly had left, saying that he had to attend to some other business.

Tarrel nodded as he speared a pickled radish with his fork. "What do you think chased him?" he asked.

Mordan shrugged. "Something heavy, strong, and fast. Beyond that, I have no idea."

Tarrel finished his meal and dropped some coins on the table. "We're not at a dead end yet," he said.

Several minutes later, the two of them stood in Tarrel's rented lodgings in the merchant district. A large trunk lay open beside the heavy oak table in the center of the room, and Tarrel was assembling a spirit burner. On the table, a round glass flask stood on an iron tripod. In the flask was the cutting Tarrel had taken from Falko's hair, containing the dark resin.

"I think this came from whatever killed him," he said. "If we're lucky, it's some of the poison."

Mordan stared at the alchemical apparatus, his arms folded. "And what will that tell us?" he asked. "Who killed him?"

"Maybe," said Tarrel.

Mordan frowned. "But you don't even know how the poison was delivered," he said.

Tarrel looked up. "Not for sure," he said, "but I've got some suspicions. I'm thinking it was a blowgun dart made of ice, with the poison frozen inside. The dart melts, leaving no evidence. Easy enough to make with a simple freezing spell. We're looking for a professional." He added a few drops of a blue liquid to the flask and started to heat it.

"Does that get either of us any closer to the people we're looking for?" asked Mordan, a little peevishly.

"I don't know yet," answered Tarrel, "but it's all we've got, so . . ."

He never finished the sentence. The windows imploded with a crash, and a dark shape flew in, knocking over the table and sending both of them sprawling. Mordan felt hands close on his shoulders in a vise-like grip, pinning his arms by his sides. He struggled but couldn't break free. There was a blur of motion, and he found himself flying through the broken window, still in the thing's grasp. They hit the ground outside . . .

An orange flare shredded the darkness. The creature released its grip on Mordan, and he struggled free, drawing his rapier. He found himself facing a tall woman, dressed in a ragged uniform under a dark cape. Her face was twisted in a mask of pain and rage, but he recognized her—she was the red-headed woman Solly had impersonated in the Black Dragon, just the day before.

She struck him with a back-handed blow, snapping his head around and throwing him backward. Dizzy and weak, he dragged himself to his feet and brought his rapier up to the guard position. Then Tarrel appeared in the doorway of the building; the night lit up orange again, and a beam of light struck the woman in the back. She staggered, and Mordan's rapier caught her in the arm. Her skin smoked where the sword went home, and she howled in pain—not like a woman, but like a wounded animal. She turned and started to run, but Tarrel leaped on her back, one arm clamped round her throat as the other reached over her shoulder in a stabbing motion. She gasped and fell to the ground.

Mordan limped to where Tarrel stood over the fallen woman. He kept the length of his rapier between them, but she didn't move. She didn't even seem to be breathing—and then he saw the wooden stake sticking out of her chest.

"Now you know what that wand does," said Tarrel. "Come on, help me get her inside!"

Along the street, faces were beginning to appear at windows. He put one of the woman's arms over his shoulder, and Mordan took the other.

"What's goin' on?" A short, stocky woman stood in the doorway of the lodging house, dressed in a nightgown and cap. She stood with her hands on her hips, looking at the three suspiciously.

Tarrel gave her an apologetic smile. "Nothing," he said. "These are friends of mine. They were out celebrating, you see, and it seems the young lady had a little too much to drink."

The landlady glared at the woman's sagging form. Her cloak had fallen forward, hiding the protruding stake.

The landlady stumped back to her apartment, muttering about foreign ways and some people's lack of consideration. Tarrel ran back to his room and reappeared a few minutes later with a large bag.

"Well," he whispered to Mordan, "it looks like we're going to your place."

● ● ● ⊙ ● ● ●

"She's secure," Tarrel announced, standing up. Mordan had called in a favor with some business contacts and gained them the use of a waterfront basement. A trapdoor gave access to the river; it was normally used for smuggling.

The woman hung by her wrists over the trapdoor, with her feet tied together and the stake still in her chest. Tarrel had hung a silver chain around her neck, with a pendant in the form of a crescent moon. In one hand he held a holy symbol of the Silver Flame.

"Things are about to get noisy," he said, "so I'll make the introductions now. Allow me to present the Honorable Captain Brey ir'Mallon, of Flamekeep in the fair land of Thrane."

Mordan raised his eyebrows and gave a low whistle.

"So that's why your client can afford expensive locating spells," he said. "She's related to the General?" General Valtar ir'Mallon was a war hero, respected even by his enemies.

Tarrel nodded. "Only child," he said.

Mordan grimaced. "He's not going to be happy, is he?"

Tarrel did not answer.

"Hold her steady," he finally said. Mordan held his left arm across her chest, keeping the rapier in his right. Holding the symbol of the Silver Flame in front of the woman's face, Tarrel reached forward with his free hand and pulled out the stake. Mordan released her and stepped back.

Her eyes flew open, and her mouth twisted in a snarl, revealing sharp white teeth. She struggled, and then saw the Silver Flame. A riot of emotions played across her face: rage, fear, despair, and finally anguish. She gave vent to a great howl that echoed off the earthen walls. Tarrel backed off a couple of paces, still holding the Silver Flame in front of him. Breathing heavily, the woman tested the strength of the ropes that bound her hands. Tarrel stood by the winch that secured the other end of the rope.

"Lady ir'Mallon," he said, sounding a great deal more assured than Mordan felt, "you might like to look down before you do that." The woman shot him a glance of unmitigated hate, snarling like a cornered animal.

"That's the Cyre River under your feet," Tarrel went on, slightly louder. "And with this winch I can drop you right into it. I know you don't like running water." To illustrate his point, he let the winch slip a little. The woman's lower body dropped through the trapdoor, leaving her waist at floor level and her feet inches from the sluggish river. She continued snarling.

"Oh," continued Tarrel, "I almost forgot. That amulet round your neck stops you shapechanging, which is probably the next thing you'll think of. You're stuck in human form for now."

The woman looked down at the silver moon pendant for an instant, then closed her eyes in concentration. Nothing happened.

"Now," said Tarrel, "I'm—"

The woman cut him off. "I know who you are," she said, her voice rasping and heavy with loathing, "and I know what you want. That's why you couldn't find me. I'm not going home. Kill me if you want, but I won't let my family see me—like this."

"Your father had a spell cast," Tarrel went on. "A very powerful, very expensive spell. He was trying to locate your body so he could have it brought back to Thrane for burial. Instead, the spell showed you were in Karrlakton. Whether you go back to Thrane or not, I'm going to have to tell your father something."

"No!" Brey shouted. "You can't! The truth would kill him! Just leave me alone!"

"Easy—easy!" said Tarrel. "Now, my guess is that you're on the trail of whoever did this to you. We can help you with that. It's not strictly the job I signed up for, but I think it's what your father would want. If he knew."

Brey considered this for a moment. "No," she said. "This is between me and them."

Tarrel ran one hand through his graying hair. "You may want to think that over, my Lady," he said softly, "because if I go back to Thrane now, your father's just going to send some-one else. Maybe another inquisitive. Maybe an exorcist. Or maybe he'll come himself. You know he won't give up."

Brey's head drooped onto her chest, which shook with sobs. When she raised her head at last, tears of blood were running down her cheeks.

"Untie me," she said, her voice flat, "and we can talk. I won't hurt you if you don't hurt me." Her eyes went from Tarrel to Mordan and back again.

Tarrel winched her back up through the trapdoor. "I'll be keeping my Silver Flame close to me," he said.

Brey made a sound that was neither a sob nor a laugh. "Keep it," she said, "and may it bring you comfort and pro-tection. As it no longer does for me."

When her feet were clear of the trapdoor, Mordan closed it, then backed away with his rapier at the ready as Tarrel untied the young woman. Then the half-elf stepped back, with the Silver Flame in one hand and his wand in the other. Brey reached for the silver chain around her neck.

"I'd just as soon you kept that on for now," said Tarrel, gesturing with the wand. "Just until we're done talking."

Brey shrugged and dropped her hands to her sides. "So who are you?" she asked, looking at Mordan. "And why are you looking for the same people that I'm looking for?"

"Just a war veteran looking for some soldiers who didn't come back," he said.

Brey examined her jerkin where the stake had pierced it. She dipped a finger in the blood and put it to her mouth.

"Worthy enough, on the face of it," she said, licking her lips. "Do you know what they were doing?"

Mordan shook his head. "I was hoping you could tell me," he said.

A PALADIN'S TALE
CHAPTER 8

Vult 11, 993 YK

Enemy!"

Captain Brey ir'Mallon turned away from the Cyre River. On the ridge above the floodplain, outlined against the pale gray sky, stood at least a score of Karrnathi lancers.

"Flame!" she exclaimed. "Corus, if you were asleep at your post, I swear I'll—" But she knew her lookout was dead.

"To horse!" she yelled, waving her sword in a circle above her head and running to Thalin. The great white war-horse was jerking his head and whinnying, as if trying to raise the alarm himself. She leaped into the saddle and rode off at a gallop, heading west along the riverbank with her rangers behind her. She sent up a silent prayer of thanks that they had spotted the Karrns in time—lightly armed rangers would not have stood a chance against a wedge of lancers charging down that slope.

Their orders were to avoid contact with the enemy. The Inmistil Rangers were deep behind enemy lines, scouting potential crossing-points for a planned invasion.

She glanced backward. The rangers were riding flat out. The Karrns followed along the top of the ridge, but were slower with their heavier armor and equipment. Around the next bend, she knew, was a gentle slope that would lead them up and away from the river. They should be able to outdistance their pursuers.

Then she saw the undead. Formed up in a block, a couple of dozen armored zombies stood between the Thranes and escape. Another glance backward told Brey that the lancers were not far behind. They would have to break through the undead quickly.

Thalin didn't slacken his pace as she let go of the reins. Steering him with her knees, she held her sword aloft in one hand and her Silver Flame pendant in the other as she began the incantation. Flame willing, it should put some of the zombies to flight and disrupt their formation enough for the rangers to overrun them. Around her, rangers were drawing their shortbows and nocking arrows, still at full gallop.

She screamed the final syllable, but nothing happened. Not one of the zombies fled; this had never happened before. At least a few always broke in fear of the Flame.

A few dozen yards away, the lancers had stopped. Their lances were upright, not set for a charge. At the center of their line, a pennant fluttered from one lance: a letter V, surrounded by a wreath, over a pair of crossed lances. She made a mental note of it, for the report she would make if she survived.

Something was very wrong here. She had assumed that the zombies were meant to delay her rangers so the lancers could cut them to pieces, but now it seemed that the lancers had simply herded the Thranes into contact with the undead. Still, she thought, that gave them a chance. Even though she had failed to turn any of the zombies, her troops had the advantage of being mounted.

The rangers' arrows rattled off the zombies' shields as they galloped ever closer. In uncanny unison, the undead dropped their shields, and each raised an empty hand. A strange light flared briefly from beneath their armor, and bolts of dark energy filled the air.

The double impact caught Brey by surprise. Gasping in pain, she looked down at her chest; two holes penetrated her breastplate just below the sternum, but there was no sign of the missiles that had caused them. She heard cries of pain and anger from the other rangers. Her mind reeled—she had fought Karrnathi undead before, but these were using magic. How could that be?

Something small flew through the air, falling to the ground in front of the charging rangers. A pall of gray-green smoke blossomed out from it, briefly obscuring their view of the undead. Some of the horses shied, but they were moving too fast to stop. Brey put a hand on Thalin's reins, but his pace didn't waver.

She held her breath as she entered the cloud, but it was no use. The foul, stinging vapors filled her eyes and nose, making her head swim. Thalin coughed, whinnied in alarm, and began to slow down. The couple of seconds she spent inside the magical vapors seemed like an eternity. When she broke through at last, she slowed Thalin to a trot and looked around.

The spell had done its work. Although some of the rangers had resisted the effects of the stinking cloud, about half of them were leaning forward in their saddles, retching uncontrollably. Many of the horses had pulled up short, and were coughing and shaking their heads, threatening to dislodge their riders. The charge had been broken.

The zombies loped forward like wolves—faster than any zombies she had ever encountered—and Brey guessed they aimed to push the rangers back into the cloud. She couldn't understand why they hadn't drawn their weapons. Here and there, rays of coruscating light stabbed from their bony fingers, striking those rangers who were not incapacitated by the cloud. One struck her in the chest, and suddenly her whole body felt heavy. She could barely raise her sword as one of the zombies lunged for her with outstretched arms.

Weak as her blow was, it was effective. Her sword struck home, and a flare of silver light singed the zombie's hide. It dropped back into a crouch. Thalin reared to trample the foul creature, but the zombie caught his forehooves in mid-air, holding horse and rider back with incredible strength. There was a brief impasse, and then the undead twisted to one side, throwing Thalin to the ground.

Brey leaped from the saddle, hit the ground and rolled to her feet. Her sword and armor felt like they were made of lead. She was vaguely aware of similar struggles going on all around her, but she kept her eyes locked on the zombie as it loped toward her. For the first time, she noticed that its hide, where it was visible between the plates of its armor—had been tattooed with strange-looking symbols. She murmured a prayer to the Silver Flame and waited for the attack.

A beam of black energy slammed into her chest, dropping her to her knees. She looked up in surprise to see another zombie standing behind the first with one arm outstretched. Her sword fell from her hand; she tried to stand but couldn't. Then something heavy hit her from behind, and she lost consciousness.

● ● ● ● ● ● ●

"She's coming around!"

Rangers gathered round as Brey struggled to sit up. Like them, she had been stripped of her armor and weapons. Even her Silver Flame pendant was gone. She and her rangers were crowded together in a small rock-hewn cell, separated from a larger chamber by a wall of stout iron bars. The only light came from a flickering brazier in the outer chamber.

"Egen," she murmured. Her second-in-command leaned over her.

"Captain," he said. "Drosin and Neskus are dead, but everyone else is alive. Talandro's in a bad way, though."

Brey struggled to her feet. Her neck and shoulders ached where she had been struck from behind. Talandro lay at the back of the cell, pale and scarcely breathing. Focusing her thoughts on a mental image of the Silver Flame, she knelt over him. With one hand on his head and the other on her chest, she began to pray. After a moment, his eyes fluttered, then opened.

"Captain?" he said, weakly. She placed a finger on his lips.

"Save your strength," she said. He nodded feebly and closed his eyes again, lapsing into a deep and peaceful sleep almost immediately. She turned back to Egen.

"Where are we?" she asked.

"As far as I can tell, we're still in Cyre," he replied. "At any rate, we didn't cross the river. We marched for about three hours—I couldn't tell the direction because they had us blindfolded—and that's all I know."

"So the Karrns have a base in Cyre," Brey said, half to herself. "Have you seen any troops other than the lancers and those undead?"

Egen shook his head. "What are those things, anyway?" he asked. "Zombies don't use magic."

"I don't know," she replied. "Some new Karrnathi abomination."

A door banged in the outer chamber, and they turned to see a slender, robed elf enter the room, flanked by two zombies. With a shock, they recognized the faces of their dead comrades, Drosin and Neskus. Branded into their flesh was a badge of some kind—a skull with the numbers six and one. They glowered malevolently at their former comrades.

"No!" Brey half-shrieked, gripping the bars. The elf gave her a nasty smile.

Brey glared at him. His skin was pale even for an elf, and his eyes set deep within dark rings. The embroidery on his robes was in the Aerenal style, which surprised her. Elves found in the company of Karrns were usually Valenar mercenaries. He produced a ring of keys.

"You stay where you are," he ordered Brey. "The rest of you, against the back wall, with your hands on your heads!" At a gesture from him, the zombies drew their swords.

"We are prisoners of war!" shouted Egen. "We have rights!"

The elf chuckled dryly. "We don't worry much about the Articles of War here," he said. "And you should know that anyone who fails to comply will be forced to watch their comrades die—very slowly, and very painfully. And then"—he gestured at Drosin and Neskus—"they will rise like these two, and tear you apart."

Brey held up a hand.

"Do as he says," she told the rangers. Reluctantly, they backed away from her. The elf unlocked the door and motioned her out of the cell. Drosin and Neskus stood each side of her as the elf turned to lock the door again.

"Flee before the wrath of the Silver Flame!" Brey screamed, throwing her arms in the air. The zombies did not even flinch. Something was very wrong here.

"I'm afraid not," said the elf. "We have been working on correcting that weakness—among others." Drosin and Neskus each took hold of one of her arms. She struggled, but their grip was unbreakable. They were much stronger than they had been in life.

As they marched Brey through a succession of stone-walled passages, she saw several other elves, and even a couple of half-elves and humans. They all had the same unhealthy pallor as her captor. Zombies shuffled to and fro, apparently on various errands.

At last, they came to a heavy wooden door bound in black iron. The elf unlocked it with another of his keys, locking it behind them. On the inside of the door, painted in red and black, was a demonic face, its mouth opened to reveal an array of jagged teeth.

"The Blood of Vol!" she breathed.

The elf smiled again. "Among others. The master has many such arrangements," he said. "We like to think of ourselves as open-minded in religious matters."

They came into a high, vaulted chamber, dominated by a huge stone sarcophagus on a stepped plinth. Around the edges of the room were several semi-circular apses, each holding a smaller coffin. Torches flickered in iron wall-sconces, casting fluid shadows on the dark velvet draperies, and on the pale figures that gathered around her. They wore a kind of uniform, but it was made of a nobleman's silks and brocades rather than the leather and canvas of a soldier. Their eyes had a reddish tinge, matching their mouths, and they looked hungrily at her.

"Stand back!" ordered the elf. "This one is for your captain!" Hissing and cursing softly, the pale figures drew back. Brey could see their fangs clearly.

She jumped as a hand landed on her shoulder. The zombies relinquished their grip, and she found herself staring into a man's face. It was hard and cruelly handsome, its hair and beard trimmed and oiled, and its eyes—she blinked and shook her head, turning away to avoid further eye contact.

"What have you brought me, Kylaer?" he said. "This one looks tastier than our usual fare."

"A present from the master," replied the elf. "A paladin from Thrane."

The vampire threw back his head and laughed. "You must give him my thanks," he said, "and my compliments on his wit!"

Brey struggled in vain. Strong hands held her fast as the fangs penetrated her neck. She prayed to the Silver Flame to take her soul.

* * * ⊙ * * *

Brey awoke in a small, dark space, her head throbbing and her whole body burning with a raging thirst. Summoned by her cries, a pale crowd lifted her out of the coffin and carried her gently to a couch where a terrified peasant girl lay trembling in chains. The others whispered that her former life was over, that the Silver Flame had abandoned her because of what she had become, that they were her family now. When she renounced them and reaffirmed her devotion to the Flame, they laughingly sent for her pendant. To her horror, she found she could no longer look at the holy symbol, and when she tried to touch it, it burned her flesh. Brey prayed and prayed, but the hunger was too strong; weeping red tears of shame and revulsion, she fed.

The months that followed were a waking nightmare. As much as she could, she fought the dark impulses that were growing within her, but when the bearded vampire commanded her, she was powerless to resist. She wore the same uniform as the others, with that same badge, and she went out with them by night and did unspeakable things.

They were a military unit in the army of Karrnath, she was told, under the command of the bearded one, whose name was Wultram. The complex where they rested by day—where she and her rangers had been brought as prisoners—was a laboratory, dedicated to the creation of new and more powerful undead troops for the Karrnathi cause. The vampire spawn were but one avenue of research; another had produced the spell-casting zombies that had captured her, and still other projects were under way. Overseeing everything was the one Kylaer had called the master—an elf whose name was Marbulin Dravuliel, a necromancer who had sold his services to King Kaius and his defilers of the grave.

When they were not carrying out their atrocities, the vampire spawn were kept in the vaulted room, which Brey learned was the base of a tower. Above them was a ruined Cyran fortress, now abandoned. Only Wultram habitually left the chamber, apparently to confer with Dravuliel and receive his orders. She tried to sneak out—with the vague idea of escaping, or finding her rangers, or both—but was always stopped by the Blood of Vol symbol on the inside of the main door. Apparently it had the same effect on her new comrades as well, though Wultram seemed immune.

Wultram himself took great delight in tormenting her. He would order her to do the most humiliating and demeaning things, and she was unable to resist his commands. He ordered her to curse the Silver Flame, and her heart rebelled even as her lips spoke the words. But as she came to the name of her deity, she found herself unable to pronounce it, despite repeated orders and a savage beating. She wondered why, as she lay scratched and bloodied in her coffin that day. Was she unable to speak the holy name because of her fallen condition, or was it that, somewhere deep inside her, a spark of devotion had proven stronger than the vampire's hold on her?

She suspected that Wultram was trying to break her will and make her a more cooperative subordinate, but she swore to herself that she would never be a willing party to this abomination; he would have to force her to carry out every order. Even if it was true that the Flame had abandoned her because of what she had become—and the others told her so often enough—she vowed that she would never abandon the Flame. Even though she could no longer speak its name or look upon its image, she would remain faithful in her heart. The alternative would be to give in to the red madness.

One night, Wultram told his spawn that they had been summoned to attend a great ritual. For the first time since she had arrived, Brey was able to see parts of the complex outside the vampire's chamber. Although Wultram kept a close eye on her, she looked for any sign of her rangers, fearful of what might have been done to them. But she saw no familiar faces on the way to the cavernous temple to Vol where the ritual was to take place.

The temple was laid out around a huge, bloodstained stone altar. The smell of blood—both new and old—was so strong in the air that Brey's stomach twisted with hunger, and her fangs ached with longing for the fluid of life. Looking around, she could see that some of the others were looking restless. Only Wultram seemed unaffected, and he curtly ordered them to be still.

In addition to the vampire spawn, the temple was thronged with zombies, and the pale, cadaverous assistants who served Dravuliel. To one side of the altar was a vast orrery made of silver, gold, and precious stones; it did not reflect Eberron and its moons as Brey knew them, and it was too far away for her to make out the markings on its various spheres.

When Dravuliel entered, Brey realized that although she had heard his name spoken almost daily, this was the first time she had actually set eyes on him. He was tall for an elf, towering over even the half-orc zombies that flanked the arched doorway through which he entered. He was thin, too, even for an elf. She wondered for a moment if he might be a lich. His robes were exquisitely embroidered with symbols that made her shudder, and cut in the style of Aerenal. This puzzled her. She had always been told that the Aereni venerated life rather than death, and that their revered Undying were beneficent creatures, and not the product of foul necromancy.

Her thoughts were interrupted as Dravuliel mounted the steps to the altar and began to speak.

"This night is one of great significance. Tonight, you will all become stronger and more capable than you have ever been. Tonight, the power of Mabar itself will be yours!"

His cadaverous assistants applauded, and he paused for a moment to acknowledge their adulation.

"Tonight, we shall create a link with the Endless Night, a permanent link that will not weaken with the shifting juxtaposition of the planes. Its dark energy will flood this temple, and flow through all of you! You will be transformed!"

Though her body remained rigidly still in accordance with Wultram's orders, Brey's heart quivered. During her training at the Temple of the Silver Flame she had learned something about the different planes of existence, and Mabar was one of the darkest and most dangerous. She had already seen how Dravuliel's necromancy had strengthened the zombies, and she shuddered to think of the horrors he could perpetrate with this new power at his command. She tried with all her will to move, to do anything to disrupt the proceedings, but her body would not respond. She had been commanded to be still.

As Dravuliel went over to the orrery, his disciples began a low chant. He set the machine into motion, and the gemstone spheres began to rotate around each other in a complex, shifting pattern. The air in the temple seemed to become thicker, cold, and heavy like a winter fog. Above the spinning orrery, the air shimmered and darkened. The chant rose in pitch as the darkness coalesced, sinking into the orrery itself and hiding it from sight. The candles and torches that lit the temple flickered, their flames leaning toward the darkness as if blown by a strong wind. A deep sound below the range of hearing vibrated the floor and walls.

Dravuliel stood in rapt contemplation of the darkness as the chanting continued. It expanded steadily, seeming to drag the light out of the chamber. The vibration intensified. Suddenly a tendril of pure darkness shot out and wrapped around Dravuliel's body. He screamed in surprise and struggled as it lifted him off the floor.

For a moment, no one in the temple moved. Then the cadaverous disciples stopped their chanting and hastened to help their master. Wultram leaped forward, drawing his greatsword and calling on his spawn to follow him. Like ants attacking a rat, they swarmed around the darkness, assaulting it with spell and blade. Brey joined them as she had been ordered, although she longed to leave the elf to his fate.

More tendrils erupted from the sphere of darkness, lashing across the temple and scattering whatever creatures they touched. Wultram fought his way to Dravuliel's side and hacked at the thing with demonic ferocity. At last, he severed the tendril, and Dravuliel fell to the floor, gasping for breath. Wultram stood over him, leaning down to help him to his feet. In that instant, one of the thrashing tendrils struck the vampire on the back of the neck. His head snapped back with such force that it was torn from his shoulders, flying across the chamber with its mouth open in a silent scream. His body tottered, turning black before it crumbled into dust. Nothing was left of Wultram but his clothes and his greatsword.

A wave of nausea swept over Brey, and she struggled to keep her feet. She could move again; her body was her own. With the master vampire destroyed, the spawn were free. Most continued fighting, but she backed slowly away. In the chaos, no one noticed.

❂ ❂ ❂ ❂ ❂ ❂ ❂

Over the years that followed, Brey the vampire wandered the night, learning to use her new powers and struggling against the savage nature that came with them. Always in the back of her mind was the thought that Dravuliel might have escaped, that others might be doing similar work for the blasphemous king of Karrnath. She devoted herself to uncovering and destroying the undead troops and those who made them.

She was in Karrnath on the Day of Mourning, resting in her coffin under a low bluff not far from Fort Zombie. She gained control of a minor functionary there, a supply clerk who could tell her where the fort's undead troops came from. When she awoke that night, she could sense the change in the world. She learned from her mortal pawn that some terrible disaster had occurred, and before dawn she stood on the banks of the river, looking across the darkness at the strange gray mist that enveloped the neighboring land. Surely, she thought, some terrible judgment had been wrought on Cyre.

At the war's end, she considered returning to Thrane. Perhaps there would be someone in the Temple of the Silver Flame who could help her atone for the crimes she had committed under the control of Wultram and Dravuliel. But she knew in her heart that it was a futile hope. The thing that she had become was abhorrent to everything the Church stood for; she would be hunted down by the Church's exorcists and destroyed as an abomination. She knew, as well, that she could not control her dark and violent impulses indefinitely. She had restricted herself to feeding on enemy combatants, trying to limit the evil that she did, but now that the war was over she needed to find her unholy sustenance where she could.

As she realized that her faith could no longer save her, she clung to the one thing she had left: vengeance. She had long since torn the foul badge of Karrnath from her clothing, but she remembered it clearly enough. She remembered, too, the emblem of the Karrnathi lancers involved in her capture. That was where she would start, and she would not stop until she had killed everyone who had played a role in making her what she was, or until she herself was destroyed.

BLOOD ON THE WATERFRONT
CHAPTER 9

Olarune 19, 999 YK

So what have we got?"

It was a little before dawn as Brey and Tarrel sat in Mordan's rented room above the Black Dragon. Mordan himself was pacing around the room. He counted off the facts on his fingers.

"The Vedykar Lancers were active—and alive—in Cyre before the Day of Mourning. They were associated with a secret facility making superior forms of undead, probably for the Ministry. It was destroyed in a magical accident—no word on how many survived, or where they might have gone."

"And I'm willing to bet that Falko was taken to the Ministry for questioning because he asked about the badge of that secret facility," said Tarrel.

"He said he had a contact in the Ministry," said Brey.

Mordan and Tarrel looked at her sharply.

"What?" she said. "I talked to him, like you did. He didn't know anything more than he told you."

"He didn't mention that you'd been asking," said Mordan.

"That's because I told him to forget—about me and the badge," Brey answered. She no longer wore the silver moon pendant.

Tarrel raised an eyebrow. "Told?" he asked.

Brey shrugged. "You told the changeling not to tell me about you," she said.

"You talked to Solly as well?"

"I talked to everyone Tarrel talked to," said Brey. "I knew he was asking about me, and I wanted to know what he'd been told."

"So," said Mordan, "you came to Tarrel's room tonight to—talk—to me? That didn't work out too well for you."

Brey made a sour face.

"And I'm guessing," he went on, "that it was you who interrupted my—talk—with Hintram earlier? What did he tell you?"

"Not much," she said. "He left after the accident. He was there undercover, and he went back to the Emerald Claw."

"The Emerald Claw?" said Mordan. "The King had them disbanded. Did he say how they're involved in this—or where they're based?"

"I didn't ask," said Brey. "He didn't know anything more about the undead makers, so . . ."

"So you killed him?" Mordan interrupted.

"I was hungry," said Brey. "Besides, there's always your cleric friend."

"What cleric friend?"

"I heard you tell him you knew someone who could speak to the dead. I kept the body, so you can ask him whatever you like."

Mordan sat down. "That was just to keep him co-operative," he said. "I don't know any clerics."

Brey snorted. "How was I to know that?"

"You still have the body?" Tarrel asked. "If you turn him into a vampire he'll be under your control, right?"

Brey shook her head. "I don't do that." She bridled under Mordan's questioning glance. "I didn't want what was done to me, and I wouldn't do it to anyone else—ever."

Mordan shot Tarrel a glance. "Do all Sharn inquisitives know as much about vampires as you do?"

"I knew I was coming to Karrnath," Tarrel replied, "so I did some reading on undead. To be honest, I expected to see more of them around."

"Brelish propaganda," said Mordan. "I heard some of it—all Karrns worship the dead, drink blood, and spit-roast babies for dinner."

"I've seen Karrns do bad enough things," said Brey.

"How about this Blood of Vol cult?" asked Tarrel. "I heard it's powerful in Karrnath. Any chance you could find a cleric to talk to Hintram's corpse after all?"

Mordan shook his head. "I'm not a member," he said, "and I don't know anyone who is. Besides, you can't just drag a body into a temple unannounced and ask if they'd mind having a word with it."

"Hmm," said Tarrel. "More propaganda, I suppose." He sat in thought for a moment, then looked sharply at Brey. "You said you still have the body?"

❊ ❊ ❊ ◉ ❊ ❊ ❊

"This is never going to work," said Solly.

"You've always said you can be anyone," answered Mordan.

The changeling was standing with Tarrel and Mordan in a dark attic above a fish shop near the waterfront. Slim fingers of sunlight reached in through gaps in the roof, dappling the wooden coffin where Brey was sleeping. At their feet was the pale and battered corpse of Berend Hintram.

"You don't understand," Solly said. "There's more to it than the face and the clothes! I don't know how he moves, how he stands—and then there's the voice."

"I can help you with the voice," said Mordan. "He talked through his nose, kind of whiny."

Solly snorted. "You have no idea, do you? A true impersonation is a work of art!"

"We're not looking for a work of art," said Tarrel, "just good enough to fool his two goons and get into that warehouse. They don't look too bright."

"But . . ."

Mordan cut him off. "You could pretend to be sick or something. That would take care of the voice. Keep your cloak wrapped round you, sneeze occasionally—they'll never know."

"No!" said Solly. "It's madness. It can't possibly work. They'll see right through it, and then I'm dead!"

Mordan laid a comforting hand on the changeling's shoulder. "Don't worry," he said, "we'll be right there. Tarrel and I can take care of the muscle if it all goes wrong. And you haven't seen what our new friend can do. You'll be as safe as if you were in the Black Dragon."

"Your half-orc lawman was pretty good," Tarrel reminded him.

Solly brightened slightly. "Well, yes, but I've been working on that one for weeks," he said. "This is completely new, and it's someone I've never even met"—he glanced down at the body—"alive, that is."

"Solly," said Mordan, "it only needs to work for a couple

of minutes. Are you saying you can't fool a couple of cheap dockside thugs for a couple of minutes?"

"I—that is—I mean . . ." faltered Solly. He looked at Mordan earnestly. "Just a couple of minutes?" he asked. "And you'll be right there?"

Mordan smiled. "I'll never let you out of my sight," he promised.

Solly sighed. "If anything goes wrong . . ."

"What can go wrong?" asked Mordan, lifting Hintram's body so that a ray of sunlight illuminated the face. "Let's see you work your magic."

◈ ◈ ◈ ◈ ◈ ◈ ◈

"Got her!"

Rolund looked up from the rat he was eating. He and Aeren had entered Karrlakton undetected and established themselves in a dusty mausoleum in one of the city's older cemeteries. The elf stood before a tall, highly-polished mirror, but instead of reflecting their dismal surroundings, it showed a wooden coffin lying in a dark attic. Not far from the coffin itself, three figures were crouching over what appeared to be a dead body.

"Where?" Rolund knew that he would get no sustenance from the vampire woman, but he was eager to feed on her mortal lackeys. He had made do with rats and pigeons since entering the city, and hunger was gnawing at his vitals.

"I'm working on that," Aeren turned to face him revealing a face as gray and tight-skinned as Rolund's own. "It will take another spell."

"Then hurry," said Rolund. Their best plan would be to kill them before sundown; then she would be helpless in her coffin.

"Be patient," said the elf, rummaging in a bag.

Rolund snarled, and went back to chewing on his rat.

＊ ＊ ＊ ◉ ＊ ＊ ＊

"There it is," whispered Tarrel, pointing into the darkness. "The one at the end, with all the canvas."

Mordan squinted. "I can't see it," he said.

"Of course you can't," said Tarrel. "By the time your weak human eyes could see it, we'd already be there! Solly, can you see it?"

Solly pushed back the hook of the rough cloak, revealing Hintram's face. He peered into the gloom. "No," he said. "We'll need to get closer." Tarrel raised his eyes heavenward.

"I can see it," said Brey, "and the half-orc outside it. Why don't you just let me deal with him?"

"Because dead bodies are suspicious," said Tarrel. "Even here. Let's stick to the plan. Now, there should be another one around the back. Do you think you can keep him quiet?"

Brey grinned, her teeth glinting in the twilight.

"I think so." She turned to leave.

"But remember," said Tarrel.

Brey finished the sentence for him. "I know. Don't break him, because he might know something." She disappeared into the shadows.

Solly looked nervously at Mordan and Tarrel. "You'll be close by if anything goes wrong?"

"We'll be watching you every step of the way," said Mordan. He and Tarrel hung back as Solly set off along the waterfront.

The changeling shook himself a little as he walked, trying to focus on his performance. The others had told him the face was good enough, but he still wasn't sure about the walk and the voice. He experimented with a long, slightly wide stride, as might befit a soldier and former cavalry officer, but decided it was too much. Eventually he settled for a generalized human walk, with slightly hunched shoulders and a heavy step.

He coughed loudly as he approached the semi-ruined warehouse at the end of the row, but the half-orc was already looking at him. As he was trying to think of something to say, the lookout gave him a curt nod of recognition, and he returned it without a word. Lifting up a flap of canvas, he went into the warehouse.

* * * ⊛ * * *

At the back of the building, the guard turned to look at the newcomer. She tottered unsteadily along the alley, humming an old marching song between hiccups. Red hair spilled out from beneath the hood of her cloak.

"Hey, there!" she slurred, stopping a little short of the guard. "I think I'm lost! May—maybe you can do me a favor!" The guard grinned, thinking of a favor that was probably not what she meant. He went to take a step forward, and suddenly she was right in front of him, pinning his arms to his sides with a grip of iron. Her eyes burned into his, and he felt his will melt away. He would do whatever she asked.

"Go to sleep," she said.

* * * ⊛ * * *

Inside the warehouse, Solly headed for the back and waited. His heart leaped as he heard a low muttering outside the back door, then he recognized Tarrel's voice. The door opened, and his three companions came in. Tarrel was putting away a scroll.

Mordan lit a lamp, and they looked around. The warehouse appeared to be empty; there were no zombies, weapons, or anything else to be seen, just a few empty crates and general debris.

"Look at this," said Tarrel, pointing to a paper pinned to the wall. "It looks like a calendar." The others gathered round. Some dates had been circled.

"Do you suppose these are the deliveries?" asked Mordan. "The first one was a couple of days ago."

"That fits with the weapons and the zombies arriving," said Tarrel. "When's the next one?" He ran his finger along the line.

"Not for almost two weeks," said Mordan. He thought for a moment. "That makes sense. It's five or six days by river, then a few hours overland to Fort Zombie. It would take a couple of weeks to get there, load up, and come back again."

"So how are they covering up the zombies that go missing?" wondered Tarrel. He turned to Brey. "I don't suppose you asked?" he said.

She shook her head. "Maybe we should go there and find out," she said.

"Now wait a minute," said Solly. "I may have fooled the goon outside with this act—for a couple of minutes in the dark, remember—but I'm not going all the way to Fort Zombie to try it again! Besides, I hate boats!"

"Easy," said Tarrel. "You won't have to. For one thing, they're expecting our boy to stay here and take care of business. If he shows up at the other end, they'll know something's wrong. We need another approach."

Solly didn't have time to reply. There was a strangled cry from the half-orc outside, and then something flew in through one of the high-set windows. It broke on the floor with a sound like crockery, and suddenly everything went dark.

Mordan became aware of the sounds of fire and the smell of smoke. He heard several more crashes as he groped in the magical darkness, trying to find a way out. He headed in what he thought was the direction of the back door, but tripped over something and fell into a pile of burning debris. By the time he had beaten out the flames on his clothes, he had no idea where he was. From the noise and shouting around him, he surmised that the others were in a similar predicament.

There was a splintering sound from above him, and the noise of more debris hitting the floor. He hoped that the roof wasn't caving in, and continued to grope for an exit. Eventually he found a wall, and felt his way along it. His eyes stung from the smoke, and each breath was torture. He found that the smoke was less dense closer to the floor, and started to crawl on his hands and knees.

He found a break in the wall, covered by some smoldering canvas. He threw it aside and half-jumped, half-rolled over the stump of the wall, sucking in a huge lungful of comparatively smoke-free air. He wiped his eyes with his sleeve; there was more light outside the burning warehouse, but his eyes were watering so much that he couldn't see any more than he had been able to in the darkness. Then there was a dull twang a little way off, and something ricocheted off the wall beside him. He knew the sound—a crossbow.

He rolled aside, running away from the sound in a low crouch. He kept the stump of his left arm in contact with the wall, and as soon as he found a corner, he ducked round it and pulled his elven cloak over his head. It took another couple of seconds for his vision to return.

When his eyes cleared, he found himself close to the open back door of the warehouse. Smoke was pouring out through the door, and through the high-set windows where the incendiaries had been thrown in. Watching the door were three dockside thugs, obviously waiting to attack anyone who came out. By some miracle, they hadn't seen him—the combination of the twilight, the smoke and his elven cloak had worked in his favor.

Mordan threw his cloak back and leaped forward, drawing his rapier before he hit the ground. The three thugs were taken by surprise, and one was down before the others could turn to face him. A flick of his rapier and a second thug was backing away, leaving his sword on the ground and clutching a deep gash in his arm. Mordan adopted a fencer's pose, his blade pointed directly at the heart of the third ruffian, and waited. For a long moment, the two looked at one another, then the thug swung his weapon. Mordan spun out of the way, delivering a back-handed slash to his opponent's neck before he was half-way through delivering his blow. Blood fountained across the alley as the thug fell to his knees, then pitched forward on his face. The wounded one stared for an instant, then turned and ran.

From the corner of one eye, Mordan saw a blur of motion, and spun to face it. He found Tarrel in front of him—or rather, at his feet—coughing and choking helplessly. Looking up, he saw Brey's dark shape leaping to the roof, which had already begun to burn. A second later, she returned with Solly. Hintram's features rippled in disturbing spasms as the changeling coughed, his distress interfering with his disguise.

Brey motioned to the front of the warehouse and held up three fingers. Mordan nodded, and indicated that he would go counter-clockwise around the burning building. Brey went the other way; they would attack from both sides.

Reaching the front of the building, Mordan peered

around the corner. Two more thugs waited, both armed with swords. There was no sign of the third Brey had indicated; the crossbowman must be under cover, waiting.

The two thugs stepped back as a sudden gust blew the smoke towards them. It roiled round their feet for a moment, and then billowed up to head-height, coalescing into a human shape; Brey stood behind them. She seized one grimy neck in each hand, lifted them off their feet, and smacked their heads together with sickening force. They fell to the ground like rag dolls.

A crossbow bolt caught her in the shoulder, and she turned with a feral snarl, ripping the bolt out of her flesh and throwing it to the ground. Mordan was already running as a figure burst from the shelter of the crumbling jetty, dropping a crossbow and diving into the river. Brey stopped on the bank, spitting with rage; Mordan sheathed his rapier and dove in. He surfaced close to his quarry, who was swimming hard but gracelessly away from the fray. A few powerful strokes brought Mordan level; then he grabbed hold of the man's thrashing legs and dived toward the bottom.

The thug kicked and struggled, pulling a knife from his belt, but Mordan released his legs and grabbed his wrist, wrapping his left forearm around his neck in a choke-hold. Then, kicking upward for air, he put his full weight on his opponent and forced his head back under the water. He repeated the process three times before the man stopped struggling and dropped his knife, then he towed the choking and exhausted thug back to the docks.

Solly and Tarrel, now mostly recovered from the smoke, helped drag Mordan and his prisoner from the water. Brey was standing where he had last seen her, looking impotently down at the slow-flowing river.

"Nice work," said Tarrel, " but we don't actually need this one. I brought one of Brey's two around, and he told me everything." Mordan turned to the thug, who was bent double, vomiting brackish river water. Their eyes met for an instant.

"Get out of here," growled Mordan. Water dripped off him as he stood. The thug looked briefly from him to Tarrel and Brey, then limped off into the night.

"They're the same crew that burned Falko's place," said Tarrel. "Your crime lord somehow found out we were onto Hintram and decided to get rid of the evidence."

"Why did it go dark in there?" asked Mordan. "Magic?"

"My guess is, those fire-pots had something in them—a pebble, maybe—with a darkness spell cast on it. When the pot broke, the darkness was released along with the fire."

Mordan grimaced. "Nice," he said. "Since I let that one go, he's going to know we survived."

"We were an added bonus," Brey said. "They weren't expecting anyone but Hintram to be home. And don't worry about him—I let my two go as well."

Mordan stared at her.

"They're just lackeys!" she said, a little defensively.

"And that makes it a good idea?" he asked.

"I don't kill unless I have to," she said.

"They would have been happy to kill all of us," Solly pointed out. He was back to his usual form, and shaking a little now that the danger was over.

Brey put a hand to her forehead. "I may not be a paladin any more," she said, "but I still try to do the right thing. As long as I can hold back from killing, I know there's still part of me left; I'm not completely taken over by this"—she indicated herself vaguely—"this. I'm still in control."

"So what now?" asked Tarrel.

Mordan took off his cloak and wrung it out. "You do what you want," he said. "I'm going to get into some dry clothes, I'm going to pack a few things, and I'm going on a little trip before the Fat Man decides to feed me to the fish."

"I hear Fort Zombie is lovely at this time of year," said Tarrel. "What about you, my Lady?"

Brey snorted.

"Just call me by my name," she said. "I'm not a general's daughter anymore. Not here."

"If you say so," said Tarrel. "Though I'll still have to figure out something to tell him."

"Solly?" Mordan asked,

The changeling answered Mordan's question with a shake of the head.

"I'm staying here," he said. "This is the only place I know. Beside, the hired help didn't see me—they saw your dead soldier. I'll be fine."

Mordan shook his pale, long-fingered hand.

"Good luck," he said. "Meet at Brey's in half an hour."

"Fine," said Brey, "but I may be a few minutes late. A couple of things to take care of before I leave. You go on up, though. I, uh—told—the landlady that you're allowed."

CHAPTER 10

Oralune 19, 999 YK

From the outside, the boat looked like a perfectly ordinary sailing barge, broad and low in the water, with a single mast, a heavy rudder, and a low cabin rising above the stern. She was tied to a massive iron bollard, and a movable gangplank was hoisted up into a vertical position.

The creature that greeted Mordan, however, was far from ordinary. Its eyes blazed red, and the lights of the waterfront reflected dimly in its black hide. It looked something like a dog—if a dog was made of spiked iron plates and animated by magic. It stood on the boat's rail, glaring menacingly and working its jagged iron jaws. A warning hiss issued from its mouth.

"Decker!" yelled Mordan. "You there?"

He stood still and waited. The iron defender watched him, unmoving.

Heavy footsteps sounded from within the cabin, and a large masculine-looking warforged came out onto the deck, with a wrench in one hand and a wand on the other. He looked

114

down at Mordan, then put the tools in the heavy leather tool-belt that he wore like a bandolier.

"You again," he said. While his voice lacked the subtle tones of human speech, it carried a hint of weariness. As if picking up on his mood, the iron hound hissed again.

"Give me one reason why I shouldn't skin you and use your hide for a sail," said the warforged.

"You've already got a sail," said Mordan. "Look, Decker, I'm sorry about the Metrol business, but . . ."

The warforged held up a massive, three-fingered hand. "Whatever it is, the answer's no."

"Well, can I at least come aboard?" Mordan asked. "Five minutes—that's all I'm asking."

Decker thought for a moment, then let down the gangway.

"Back, Fang," he said. The iron defender came to his side, but it still glared and hissed as Mordan boarded the boat.

"Patrol," said Decker. With one last malevolent glace at Mordan, the beast padded off across the deck.

The warforged motioned Mordan into the cabin. Cogs, screws, and other mechanical parts were scattered across the single table. Decker cleared them away with surprising delicacy, given the size of his hands. Mordan sat down opposite his host.

"It's just a simple trip upriver," said Mordan. "Two passengers, a couple of crates—nothing to it."

"Forget it, Mordan." The warforged fixed him with an unblinking stare. "I'm still in trouble from your last little escapade. I suppose you know Ikar's put a price on your head?"

"You worry too much," Mordan said with a grin. "I already took care of Slarn and his boys. If Ikar were really upset he'd have sent someone better."

"Wonderful," said Decker. "If he wasn't upset before, he will be now. He can't let people get away with killing his messengers—you know that."

"Well, then," said Mordan, "supposing Ikar does send some more trouble to Karrlakton, wouldn't you rather be somewhere else?"

"I'd rather be wherever you're not," said Decker. "Whatever you're planning, I don't want to know."

Mordan reached into his jerkin and pulled out the paper Tarrel had given him. Unfolding it carefully, he put it on the table in front of the warforged. Decker's eyes swiveled toward it briefly—then he turned his whole head and leaned closer. A pair of lenses flipped down from beneath his metal eyebrows.

"Is that real?" he asked.

"Of course," Mordan replied. "It's a genuine House Kundarak bearer bond, and it's all yours for a couple of days' work."

The lenses flipped back into their housings, and Decker pushed the paper away.

"Not a chance," he said firmly. "Nothing pays that well unless it's suicide. I'm not letting you drag me back into the Mournland, and that's final."

"Who said anything about the Mournland?"

Decker looked at Mordan, then at the paper, then back at Mordan.

"Where did you get this?" he asked

"A Medani inquisitive with a rich client."

"And he hired you?"

"Not exactly," Mordan replied. "Let's just say we have a common interest."

Decker made a grinding noise deep in his chest.

"That welds it," he said. "If he's as crazy as you are, I definitely don't want to know." He pushed the paper back across the table to Mordan and folded his arms across his massive chest. The greenish light in his eyes faded to black.

"Look, Decker," Mordan pleaded, "it's for a good cause."

"I'm not listening," the warforged replied, swiveling his head in the opposite direction.

"Someone is stealing military undead and selling them into slavery."

Decker's eyes brightened, almost imperceptibly. He swiveled his head slowly back. "Slavery?" he repeated. Mordan nodded. Decker's eyes lit fully. "Where?" he grated.

"So far, we've traced one shipment to a construction site in the old town," said Mordan, "but we don't know how many others there are. All we know is, they're coming from Fort Zombie."

"And that's where you want to go?"

"Right."

"Not the Mournland?"

"You can hug the near bank all the way."

The light in Decker's eyes flickered briefly.

"Let me see that paper again," he said.

* * * ◉ * * *

Groping through the darkness, Mordan hit his head on a low beam and sat down with a curse.

"Can't we have some light in here?" he asked.

"You're the only one who needs it," Tarrel responded, and chuckled.

"That's right," said Brey. "Why don't you just sit there for now? Just be careful getting up."

"Well," said Mordan. "I've got a boat to take us to Fort

Zombie. Are you two ready to go?"

The others made noises of assent.

"Just one thing," said Brey. "It's getting near dawn, so I'm going to have to take to my coffin for the day. Can I trust you two to carry me?"

"We're definitely going to need some light, then," said Mordan. "If I can't get in here without knocking myself out, I'll never make it outside carrying a coffin."

Tarrel laughed. "Pathetic," he said. There was a brief pause, and he tossed a glowing pebble on the floor. It cast a dim light over the attic. "I've got a hand-cart outside for the luggage," he went on. "There should be room for the coffin. As long as you don't mind a few things stacked on top?" He raised an eyebrow at Brey.

"Do what you need to," she replied. "Just as long as you keep the thing shut."

Their conversation was interrupted by a heavy thump on the roof. Before they had time to react, a pale fist punched through the rotting shingles, and as it withdrew, something dropped through the opening, hitting the floor with a soft thump.

The thump was followed by a high-pitched buzzing, and Mordan saw the object was a sack. It was moving as though something alive were inside.

"Don't touch it!" warned Tarrel. As he did so, the sack sagged to one side, its mouth falling open. Out poured a dense cloud of insects, almost completely filling the room. The air filled with a carrion stench.

Mordan slapped at his skin and found a pale mosquito crushed on his palm in a smear of blood. Others were swarming around him, getting into his nose and mouth. Hurriedly he threw his cloak over his shoulder, so that it covered his lower face.

The attic filled with reddish light as flames jetted from Tarrel's outstretched fingers. He moved his hands in a circle, burning the insects around him. Mordan dodged with a muffled curse as the magical fire swung his way, setting light to the edge of his cloak. He stamped it out.

Brey reacted to the insects in a completely unexpected way. Her face distorted, her eyes rolled back in her head, and she started flailing her arms through the dense swarm, scraping the creatures off in their dozens and cramming them into her mouth. She seemed to be in a frenzy.

Mordan snatched up a piece of cloth—an old curtain, by the look of it—from the attic floor, and lit it from Tarrel's magical flame. By whirling it around his head, he was able to keep most of the insects away. His forearms were covered with blood, and he guessed the same was true of any other exposed skin; he was starting to feel a little weak.

Glancing up at the hole in the roof, he saw a pale face. Its lips were moving, although he couldn't hear the words above the buzzing of the mosquitoes and the sounds of fighting. A pale hand stuck through the hole, pointing at Tarrel.

Not waiting for the spell to be cast, Mordan grabbed the hand by the wrist and pulled down with all his strength. There was a crash and a muffled cry as the hand's owner found his shoulder slammed into the roof above, and then the shingles gave way and the attacker crashed through, his spell uncast.

Standing over the prone figure, Mordan drew his rapier and struck. He rolled the body over and found it was an elf—unusually pale and slender, with parchment-thin skin tight over a skull-like head, but an elf nonetheless.

He didn't have time to reflect on what this meant. Something heavy struck him from behind, almost knocking him to the floor. It was cold, whatever it was—not the normal cold of a winter's night, but something far, far worse. It grabbed his neck in an iron grip, lifting him choking from the floor, and threw him across the room. He cannoned into Brey, and they both hit the ground.

Tarrel turned his burning hands on the new attacker. By the flaring reddish light, it looked like a figure from a nightmare. It was—had once been—human, but its pale skin and cadaverous aspect hinted at something worse. It wore the rags of a uniform, but was unarmed and unarmored. An unholy hunger gleamed in its eyes as it leaped forward. Ignoring the flame, it dealt Tarrel a back-handed blow that slammed him into a low beam; he slumped to the floor and stayed still. The mosquitoes crowded thickly around him, settling like an unholy snow.

Mordan held his rapier in front of him as he tried to get back on his feet. From the corner of his eye, he saw Brey begin to move—and then she was locked in a death-grip with the creature.

It was almost as strong as she was, and for a few moments they wrestled each other ineffectually. Mordan's burning cloth had gone out, and he wrapped it around his head to ward off the cloud of mosquitoes. Tarrel was barely visible beneath the swarm; their pale bodies were slowly turning pink. Mordan hesitated for a moment, unsure whether to help Brey with her opponent or carry the inquisitive to safety.

The wight lifted Brey off her feet, trying to crush her chest with a powerful hug. She hissed like a wild cat, tearing at the creature's neck and chest with her teeth. Breaking free for a second, she struck the wight a powerful blow in the face, twisting its head around violently. It let her go and reeled for a moment, coming within Mordan's reach.

He lashed out with his left arm, striking it with the stump of his wrist as the dragonmark flared on his shoulder. To his surprise, the creature didn't even flinch—in fact, he saw some of its wounds close, as if healing. It fixed him with a malicious grin and raised a clawed hand to strike.

Brey struck the wight from behind as Mordan's rapier pierced its chest. The sword was torn from his grasp, its hilt jutting in the air as the vampire pulled the wight backward. Throwing it on the ground, she dropped heavily onto the creature, slamming her knees into its chest as she reached for the weapon. Mordan heard ribs break with the impact. It was then that he noticed the tattoo on the thing's shoulder—a skull with the number sixty-one.

With a furious snarl, Brey grabbed the rapier's hilt and twisted it savagely. The wight screamed in pain. Grabbing her head in both its hands, it butted her in the face, pushing her off it with hands and feet. Mordan threw himself onto the pinned creature, but it threw him off like a rag doll, wrenching the rapier from its chest and throwing it across the room. Then, with a powerful leap, it launched itself through the hole on the roof and was gone.

Brey leaped after it, but recoiled with an agonized cry. As she hit the floor, the side of her face was red and peeling, as if seared by a hot iron. Glancing up, Mordan could see that the sky was turning pale.

"Help Tarrel!" Brey snarled, and then limped into her coffin and slammed the lid down. All was quiet except for the buzzing of the mosquitoes.

⊙ ⊙ ⊙ ⊙ ⊙ ⊙ ⊙

"What happened to you?" asked Decker. The handcart with their belongings stood beside the boat, Brey's coffin obscured by various small crates and packages. Tarrel had dug out a healing potion from somewhere inside his coat but was still pale and unsteady on his feet. Mordan was bruised and scratched, his skin still seeping blood from the mosquito bites. He looked up at the warforged with tired eyes.

"We just got another reason to leave town," he said. Decker made no reply.

It took only a few minutes to load their baggage onto the boat. Brey's coffin was the last thing brought aboard. Decker looked at it suspiciously.

"Is this what I think it is?" he asked.

Mordan shrugged. "It looks enough like one."

Decker gave it an experimental heft. "Occupied?"

Mordan made an apologetic face and nodded.

"Two passengers with luggage, you said. You didn't mention another passenger being in the luggage." Decker put the coffin down.

"Friend or foe?" he demanded.

"Friend," Mordan replied, adding as an afterthought, "a friend of Tarrel's here."

Decker looked sharply at the half-elf, who had sat down on a hatch-cover.

Tarrel raised a weary hand in greeting. "Tarrel d'Medani," he said with a wan smile. "Pleased to meet you."

"Decker was in the navy during the War," said Mordan, trying to change the subject. "He's the best navigator this side of—"

"Stow it," the warforged interrupted, "and tell me exactly who—or what—you've brought aboard my boat." He took a step toward Mordan, looming over him.

"A vampire," said Tarrel. "That's the short answer."

Decker made a grinding noise deep in his throat. "And what's the long answer?"

"A friend," said Mordan. "At least, she's looking for the same things we are."

"A vampire," said Decker. "You expect me to sail with a vampire?"

"It's not like you have anything to worry about," Mordan said. "We're the ones taking the risk."

Decker considered this for a moment. "Any sign of trouble," he said, "and I mean *any* sign—and it goes into the river."

Mordan opened his mouth to protest, but Tarrel waved him to silence.

"Agreed," he said. "Now, it's been a very rough night, and if nobody minds I'd like to get some sleep." He got up and walked unsteadily into the cabin as Decker cast off the boat.

● ● ● ◉ ● ● ●

Clinging to the shadows, Rolund let the vampire and her friends escape. He had expected this job to be an easy one. Now Aeren was destroyed, Rolund was badly wounded, and he needed time to think. Without the undead wizard he couldn't contact the master for further instructions, but he knew that failure was not an option—not if he wished to go on existing himself. As silent as a shadow, he followed his quarry to the docks. He watched them board the boat with the big warforged, cast off, and head upriver. Rolund turned back toward the town. He was weakened by his wounds and needed to feed.

The house where the vampire had been hiding was in uproar. People were running to and fro in their nightclothes, putting out the small fires that had been started by the half-elf's fire spell and asking each other what had just happened. The few surviving bloodmotes had dispersed.

Rolund waited in the shadows, watching until there was only one human in the doorway. Then he struck. Two long strides took him across the street, and his sinewy arms swept up his surprised victim before he had a chance to cry out. A slap to the side of the man's head left a gray mark on the flesh, and Rolund felt the thrill of life energy flood his body. Another blow rendered the man unconscious, and Rolund dragged him up the stairs to the attic, to feed at leisure. He piled debris over the trapdoor; not enough to stop it being opened, but enough to give him some warning when another soft-bodied meal approached.

When at last he threw the drained husk aside, his eye was caught by another body lying on the floor. It was dead, and therefore no use to him, but the face was familiar. Stepping over to the corpse, he examined it for a while, and then a slow, vicious smile spread over his face. He leaned over the body, and tore the head from the shoulders with a single heave. Wrapping it in a scrap of scorched cloth he found on the floor, he picked up Aeren's corpse and made his way back to the old mausoleum where they had established their base. He left the head there, with a scribbled note explaining how he had found it. When Aeren failed to report back, the master was sure to send someone after them.

Rolund set out toward the river again, taking care not to be seen. He was somewhat refreshed by his kill, and he could regain his strength by hunting along the way.

❖ ❖ ❖ ◎ ❖ ❖ ❖

It was dusk before Tarrel emerged from the cabin, but when he did so he was looking better. Shielding his eyes with one hand, he looked around at the landscape and then back at the boat's **V**-shaped wake. Then he walked over to where Decker was leaning against the sternpost, with Fang curled up at his feet. The iron defender raised his head briefly, then settled back down.

"Nice boat," Tarrel said. "Elemental?"

"No," said Decker. "Mechanical, mostly. Built it myself. I won't enslave an elemental just so I can get around."

Tarrel raised his eyebrows slightly. Elementals were a major source of power in Eberron, used in everything from airships to armor.

"I know what it's like, see," Decker went on. "During the War, I was the property of the Royal Karrnathi Navy, bought and paid for. Instead of enlistment papers, I came with a receipt. Might as well have been a capstan or a catapult. You ever talked to an elemental?"

Tarrel shook his head. It was obviously the answer Decker expected, and Tarrel could tell that the warforged was just hitting his stride.

"No, of course you haven't," he continued. "None of you fleshies ever do, except to give 'em orders. Well, I have. After the War, I worked for House Lyrandar for a while. They taught me Aquan so I could help with the elementals. Sometimes, when everyone was asleep, I'd talk to them. They're smart enough to know what's happening to them, you know, and smart enough not to have an opinion about it. I made up my mind when they gave me my freedom—I'll never live at the expense of another thinking creature."

"So that's why you built this boat?" Tarrel asked.

"Mostly," answered Decker. "It's nearly as fast as a Lyrandar boat, too," he added proudly.

Tarrel nodded in appreciation. "And Fang there—did

you build him as well?"

"Standard pattern," said Decker. "All I had to do was follow the instructions. I've got some ideas for upgrading it, though."

"It?" asked Tarrel.

"That's right—it," said Decker. "I know you like to call things him and her, and that's up to you. Me, I like to keep the distinction between thinking creatures and simple machines."

"How did you fall in with Mordan?" he asked.

Decker made the same grinding noise he had heard earlier. "Don't ask," he said. "All I'll say is, I'm still regretting it."

"So why are you carrying us now?" The pale green light in Decker's eyes intensified slightly.

"He says you're chasing some slavers." Seeing the surprise on Tarrel's face, he leaned in close to the half-elf. "Was he lying?"

"You could look at it that way," replied Tarrel, a little nervously. "Someone's stealing undead from the Karrnathi military and selling them . . ."

"As slaves," Decker finished his sentence. "That's what Mordan said. You're the one he got the money from?"

"It's my client's money," said Tarrel. He wasn't at all sure where this was going. Decker leaned back against the sternpost, and Tarrel relaxed a little.

"Well, then," said the warforged, apparently to himself. "Maybe he was telling the truth after all."

"Where is he, by the way?" asked Tarrel, looking around. Decker made a soft grinding noise that might have been a chuckle.

"Down in the hold, with that vampire of yours," he replied. "I told him, that's where he's bunking down or over the side it goes." He gave Tarrel a significant look. "I've been caught looking after boxes for him before."

Tarrel decided to steer the conversation back to safer topics. "So how does the boat work?" he asked.

Decker gave him a penetrating stare. "You got any artificer training?" he asked. Tarrel shook his head. "Then I'll keep it simple," Decker went on. "Basically, the whole thing's a construct. It's not that different from a golem, really, except it's boat-shaped rather than shaped like you and me."

Tarrel looked suitably impressed. "And it's as fast as a Lyrandar elemental ship, you said?"

"Almost," replied Decker, "and I'm working on some upgrades. That's where the money from this trip will be going. Took a little more work than just summoning and binding an elemental of course, but I reckon it's worth it."

The shadows moved slightly, and both Tarrel and Decker looked up. Brey was standing beside them, looking over the starboard side of the boat with an urgent expression.

"I know this place," she said. "We've got to stop."

CHAPTER 11

Olarune 20, 999 YK

I was here," said Brey, once Decker had brought the boat to a stop. "I know it. See the that tree there, and the rock outcrop over to the left?"

Mordan shook his head. He couldn't see a thing in the darkness.

"I know it," Brey continued. "This is where I reached the river after I escaped. That means that the place where they held me"—she pointed across the river, toward the dead-gray mist of the Mournland—"is in there!"

"I'm not going in there," said Decker, although no one was listening to him.

"Listen," said Mordan to Brey, "I believe you. But that doesn't mean anything. Inside that mist, everything's different from what it was. Whole buildings—whole neighborhoods—in Metrol have been moved around, like the city was cut into pieces and shuffled. There's no guarantee that place is still where you left it."

"Besides," Tarrel put in, "didn't you say it was destroyed?"

"Yes," said Mordan, "and even if it wasn't destroyed when you got out, it must have been on the Day of Mourning."

"You're guessing," said Brey.

"And you're not?" asked Mordan.

"I don't care," Brey snapped. "I know something is still in there, and I've got to find it. What if someone survived?"

"What if that thing they summoned is still there?" wondered Tarrel.

"Thing?" asked Decker.

Nobody answered him.

"Look," said Mordan, "Fort Zombie is the only solid lead we've got—and we don't have much time. Once they get word that their friends in Karrlakton are out of business, they'll . . ."

"They'll just send someone else," Brey interrupted, "or they'll start shipping the zombies to different markets."

"I wouldn't be so sure of that," said Tarrel.

Everyone looked at him.

"If the Ministry found the swords in Falko's place," Tarrel continued, "they'll be able to guess what's going on—even if he didn't tell them himself."

Brey snorted. "So what could he tell them? He bought some swords from Fort Zombie. So? They don't know about the undead!" She shot Tarrel a piercing glance. "Do they?"

Tarrel shrugged.

"What did you do?" she demanded.

"Well," said Tarrel, "I was in the Sivis office sending a report back to my client"—he held up his hands defensively as Brey reacted to this news—"I only told him I'd confirmed you were in Karrlakton, you'd apparently moved on, and I was trying to track you."

"Never mind that," snapped Mordan. "Answer the question."

"Well," said Tarrel, "I sent an anonymous tip to the Ministry telling them to look into that construction site."

"You did what?" Brey's face was beginning to change. Tarrel backed away from her a little.

"Good for you!" Decker gave the half-elf a clap on the shoulder that nearly knocked him down. "So they'll go and release the undead slaves?"

"And they'll realize they came from Fort Zombie," Mordan continued, "and they'll get to Fort Zombie just as soon as they can."

There was an uncomfortable silence. Everyone stared at Tarrel.

"I had it all figured," he protested. "We could still get there first, and if things went wrong, we'd know the cavalry was right behind us!"

"That settles it," said Mordan. "We can't take the time for a detour—especially to a place that might not even be there any more."

"Well," said Tarrel, "It might take them a few days to track down the zombies. If your fat man is worth his weight as a crime lord, he probably has someone on the inside to tip him off. He'll simply hide the zombies and . . ."

"No," said Brey, "he won't. I killed him before we left." Her voice was perfectly even; she might have been discussing last night's dinner. "What?" she said, realizing that all eyes were now on her. "You expected me to sit and polish my nails while you two were out doing—whatever you did?"

"So we have to get to Fort Zombie first," Mordan said. "Decker, can you make this boat go any faster?"

"Maybe," said the warforged, "but we'd have to stop while I made alterations."

"Never mind that," said Brey. "I know where that place is.

I know your Lancers were there, and I know for damn certain the people I'm looking for were there. What if they still are? What if there's some clue to where they've gone?"

"That's too many 'what ifs,' " said Mordan, "We know the smugglers are working out of Fort Zombie, and we know Hintram . . ."

"All we have," Brey interrupted, "is one man—now dead—linking one of the two units with undead smuggling." Her eyes bored into his, a red light stirring in the back of them.

"We—have—to—go—in—there," she said.

"Save it for the enemy," said Mordan. "I'm not that easy to control."

"Meaning you're too pig-headed." Brey sulked. Mordan opened his mouth to reply, but Tarrel broke in.

"How about this?" he asked, trying to sound reasonable. "Brey goes and looks for the base, you carry on along the river, and we meet up at Fort Zombie?"

"I'm not going in there," said Decker.

❀ ❀ ❀ ❀ ❀ ❀ ❀

"Well, this isn't so bad," Brey said. "Whatever else that mist does, it keeps the sun off. I could keep going all day." She stopped and looked back at Mordan and Tarrel, who were struggling through the shattered terrain. Both looked exhausted.

"You speak for yourself," said Mordan. "We're going to need some rest at some point."

Brey shot him a sarcastic smile. "What's the matter, soldier? Can't keep up with a girl?"

"This had better be worth it," said Mordan. "I can't believe I let you two talk me into this."

They crested the ridge and looked out over the weird

landscape of the Mournland. The ridge itself was a wave of glassy-green rock, frozen in time. Below them lay an undulating plain of the same color, circled and criss-crossed with smaller ripples. Atop one small wave, a bare tree struggled to thrust its branches into the gray sky, like a drowning man holding up his arms. Out of the middle of the plain rose a great reef of jagged black rock, topped by a fortified tower that drooped to one side like an unwatered flower.

Things moved on the plain—things that were too small to see, or too far away; things that cast feeble shadows in the wan gray light. Overhead, the dead-gray mist arched like a canopy, covering the Mournland above as it surrounded it on all sides. There was no sun, no wind, nothing that spoke of nature—just still, dead air and pale, gray light. Following Brey, they made their way down the glassy slope and set out across the plain.

Water—or something like water—collected in the hollows of the plain, but they did not stop to drink. Nothing in the Mournland could be relied upon, and the pools might have been refreshing water—or even be imbued with magical healing properties—or they might have been deadly poison. There was no way to tell except by tasting them.

Passing in the lee of the leaning tower, they came upon a grove of crystals growing against the foot of the reef. On one side, the crystals were like the foam of a wave that breaks on a rocky shore, frozen in time like the glassy waves of the plain; on the other, they grew bright and jagged in small clumps, looking almost like plants. Their edges were razor-sharp, as Tarrel found out to his cost. Brushing carelessly against one leaf-like crystal, he tore open the side of his breeches and gashed his leg. The cut was long but not deep, and they stopped to bandage it.

A few miles further on, they came to a depression in the ground, shaped almost like an amphitheater. It was hundreds of yards across, and in the middle they saw a strange battle taking place. A cloud of pale green light was rolling around the lower edge of the depression like a marble in a bowl, as if it lacked the strength to climb out but was unable to stop moving. Wherever it rolled, armed skeletons burst forth from the ground, swords in hand. The cloud was pursued by a white haze of ghosts, which attacked the skeletons as soon as they appeared. There was no telling how long this battle had been going on; it might have been a ghastly re-enactment of some battle between living forces that took place before the Mournland was created.

They skirted a forest whose trees, blackened and dead, all seemed to have been pulled up by the roots and replanted upside down. Dark shapes moved between the trunks and branches, and skittered along the tops of the spreading roots. The nearest of the trees bent toward them, although there was no wind. They took care to stay out of reach of the clawing roots and branches.

At last Mordan and Tarrel had to rest. They stopped by a ruined farmstead that seemed largely intact. One end of the house had sagged like melted wax, but the barn was secure and free of dangerous creatures.

Brey stood guard as the two mortals slept, but their sleep was not restful. The unvarying gray light, and the noises that resounded across the weird landscape from time to time, made rest hard to find. After a few hours and a light meal, though, they were ready to move on.

After a few more hours' walking, Brey stopped and sniffed the air.

"Do you smell that?" she asked. Mordan and Tarrel both shook their heads. Brey shrugged and turned to go—and then turned back with a hoarse cry of alarm. Mordan and Tarrel had already begun to turn, in response to the sudden dimming of the ever-present gray light. Towering above them was a horrific apparition. Taller than a house, it was red, with no apparent form. Shapes came and went across its surface, some looking like tortured faces crying for release. It was ready to fall on them like a rockslide.

Tarrel fell back and drew his orange-tipped wand. Mordan drew his rapier and stared at the thing, wondering what he could do against a creature that size, with no apparent weak spots. Brey stood beside them; the smell of blood had grown stronger since she first noticed it, and it was beginning to affect her. Her fangs lengthened, and a snarl distorted her face as her fingers spasmed into claws.

The abomination flowed forward. Mordan judged its speed, and was about to suggest they could outrun it when Brey leaped forward. She tore into the creature with claw and fang, ripping and snarling like a wild beast, but its translucent red body closed round her, apparently undamaged.

Mordan slashed at the thing, hoping to cut Brey free, but the cuts sealed themselves as soon as they were made. It lashed out at him with a pseudopod, and he flung himself aside, rolling back to his feet. He looked helplessly at Tarrel; they could see that inside the body of the thing, Brey was still fighting.

A ray of brilliant golden light shot from Tarrel's wand, striking the upper part. As Mordan's eyes recovered from the flash, he saw that a huge chunk of scarlet protoplasm had been blown away and lay on the ground beside the thing, writhing weakly. The wound was blackened around the edges, and the creature stopped moving momentarily. Then, as they watched, the charred wound became translucent red again.

"Again!" screamed Mordan. Tarrel pointed the wand, but nothing happened. Mordan cursed; he knew from experience that magic was unreliable in the Mournland. His rapier was little use against the formless creature. The two looked at each other for a moment, then back at Brey, whose struggles were growing weaker. Tarrel's magic was their only hope. Tarrel raised the wand again, and this time it loosed another beam of searing light. The air filled with a foul burning smell; the horror stopped, its body wracked by violent ripples, and then it collapsed, splashing the two of them and soaking slowly into the ground.

Mordan leaped forward, reaching out a hand to pull Brey out of the mess. Her hair and clothes were caked with drying blood. To his surprise, she flung him aside with a vicious back-handed blow; her hand was so cold it seemed to burn him. Before he could get to his feet she was on him, kneeling on his chest and pinning his arms to the ground. With a snarl, she bent back his neck—and then stopped.

Tarrel was beside her, holding the silver flame pendant in front of her face.

"Easy now," he said gently. "He's a friend. Just try to relax." Her red eyes lost a little of their fire, and she looked down at Mordan again, as if seeing him for the first time. She relinquished her grip and climbed slowly to her feet, backing off a little way from the holy symbol. Her clawed fingers gradually relaxed, and the lines of her face softened. After a few moments, she held up a hand.

"I'm sorry," she said, sounding tired. "It must have been the smell of the blood."

Mordan climbed to his feet, and picked up his rapier. Tarrel still held the holy symbol in one hand, and his wand was in the other. For a long moment, the three looked at each other.

Brey wiped a hand across her face, and looked at it for a moment. "I need to clean up," she announced. Her matted hair swung like a wet mop as she turned around and walked away for a few paces. Then she seemed to dissolve. For a few moments, there was nothing in her place but a smoky cloud, and then the vapors coalesced into her form again, as Mordan had seen them do on the waterfront. That seemed like a long time ago. When she turned back, her hair, skin, and clothing were completely free of the red stain.

"A little trick I picked up," she said, as the two mortals stared in amazement. "And didn't your mothers ever tell you it's rude to stare at a lady when she's changing?" Neither of them had the strength to laugh.

For Mordan and Tarrel, cleaning up wasn't so easy. They couldn't waste the water they had brought with them, and Mordan insisted that any water they found in the Mournland was not to be trusted. So it was a foul and bespattered pair that trudged alongside the vampire woman as they continued on their way.

"What was that thing?" wondered Tarrel.

Mordan shook his head. "Never seen anything like it," he said.

"I think it was made of blood," Brey said, without looking back. "It certainly smelled like it."

They walked a little further in silence, then Tarrel turned to Mordan again.

"So how well do you know Decker?" he asked.

"Well enough," replied Mordan. "Why?"

"Do you think he'll wait for us at Fort Zombie like he said?"

Mordan shrugged. "He'll wait, but I don't know how long. How long do you think we've been traveling?"

"At least a day," answered Tarrel, "though it's hard to tell without light and dark."

"It took me a day and a half to reach the river after I escaped," said Brey, "so we must be getting close."

"Assuming it's still there," said Mordan, "and not wiped off the map—or moved to a different part of it."

"I know what I'm doing," replied Brey. "A lot has changed, but I've been recognizing things here and there. I'm pretty sure we're on the right track."

Mordan gave a noncommittal grunt. "I just hope you can get us back again," he muttered.

The ground began to rise gently, and after a while they saw a rounded hilltop ahead, crowned with the ruins of a fort. Brey quickened her pace.

"I think this is it," she said. Ignoring the protests of her companions, she broke into a run.

They struggled after her, and when they caught up, she was kneeling over a dead body. Many tales are told of the Mournland, mostly by those who have never been there. One of the most common reports is that the bodies of the fallen refuse to decay, and in this case it seemed that the stories were true. Although hideously wounded, the young man's corpse looked as fresh as if he had died a minute ago.

"There!" cried Brey triumphantly, pointing to the dead man's shoulder. His arm was almost severed, but there on his tunic, somehow clear of the dried blood, was a shoulder patch bearing the insignia of the Vedykar lancers: two crossed lances beneath a letter V, enclosed in a wreath.

Tarrel reached inside his coat and pulled out a cylindrical bundle wrapped in leather. Unrolling it, he selected a crystal lens from the array of tools inside and started to examine the body carefully.

"Anyone you know?" he asked.

Mordan shook his head. "Not the one I'm looking for," he replied.

Brey stood a few paces away, looking up at the ruins. Mordan left Tarrel to his work and went to join her.

"Well," he said quietly, "you can say 'I told you so.' "

"Of course," Brey said, "I don't know how much is left. Have you decided what you're going to tell your family yet?"

Mordan looked at her narrowly.

"That's my guess," she went on. "Tarrel's funding this trip by himself, so I doubt you have a rich client like he does. Yet you've spent months—maybe years—trying to track down these Vedykar Lancers. You've taken dangerous jobs in the Mournland to survive, and you've never given up. Got to be a relative if you ask me." She paused, her face suddenly dropping. "Or a sweetheart," she said, softly.

Mordan thought of his brother and chuckled bitterly. "It's not a sweetheart," he said. He turned back to Tarrel, who was getting back to his feet and stowing his tools.

"Not much to say," said the inquisitive. "Violent death, extreme forces—just about every bone in his body is broken—and no sign the body's been tampered with since it got here. If I had to guess, I'd say he hit the ground hard—maybe he fell from a great height, or maybe he was thrown a long way."

Mordan jerked his head in the direction of the ruins.

"Like from way over there?" he asked.

Tarrel shrugged. "It's possible," he said. "Though it's hard to tell when the evidence has been disturbed by a magical cataclysm."

THE FORT
CHAPTER 12

Olarune 21, 999 YK

They climbed the hill to the fort. It had originally been a strong, square structure with battlemented walls linking its four towers. Now the walls were rent with gaping holes, and only one of the towers stood more than a few feet high.

Against one wall was a huge pile of corpses. They approached it carefully, half-expecting the bodies to rise up and attack, but nothing happened. There were all races and nationalities, thrown together in a heap by some unknown force. The only thing they had in common were round holes all over their bodies, as if they had been struck by a large number of heavy spears.

They picked their way across the rubble-strewn interior of the fort, toward one of the ruined towers. All that remained were a few courses of stone, blackened on the inside as if by fire.

"Here," said Brey, pointing. At her feet, half-hidden by fallen stone, was a stone staircase leading down. She picked up a stone slab almost as big as she was, and tossed it aside.

Mordan and Tarrel put their shoulders to another block, pushing it out of the way. Within a few minutes, there was enough of an opening to squeeze through.

A sudden noise made them look up. Something was coming, and it sounded big. Mordan threw his elven cloak over himself, while Brey and Tarrel crouched behind a mound of rubble.

The thing was immense—almost as tall as the blood-creature that had attacked them, but hunched and massive. It looked something like a warforged—they had all seen the terrifying power of the huge, barely sentient warforged titans on the battlefields of the Last War—but it had a pair of three-fingered hands instead of the great axes and hammers with which those awesome killing machines were normally armed. Its segmented carapace was covered with spikes, and they knew at once where the piled corpses had come from. There were fresh bodies all over the thing, impaled like insects.

They watched as the great construct stumped over to the corpse pile. It began picking the corpses off its carapace, adding them to the heap. When the last body had been removed, the thing turned and marched off the way it had come. Creeping to the shelter of a broken wall, the three watched it until it was out of sight. Mordan looked at Brey.

"You didn't tell us about that," he said.

"I never saw it before," Brey answered.

"Well," said Tarrel, "I guess that's how they got the raw materials for their necromantic research."

Brey scowled into the distance. "One of the ways," she said. "They needed living subjects to make vampires."

"There's something I don't understand," said Tarrel, standing up and taking in the ruins with a sweep of his arm.

"This is—was—Cyre. What's a Karrnathi research establishment doing here? Surely the Cyrans would have found it?"

"This part of Cyre was pretty much anybody's," Brey said, "at least, when we were captured. We'd been behind the lines for more than a month, and we'd seen more Karrns than Cyrans in that time. My guess is, this operation moved around, following the front lines. Living or dead, they needed fresh materials."

They gathered round the staircase.

"Ladies first," said Mordan.

* * * ⊙ * * *

Decker hummed to himself as he tinkered with the boat's inner workings. All around him were strewn cogs, pistons, springs and other things; he had taken off one of his hands and replaced it with a long, thin metal probe, which was currently thrust deep into the bowels of the mechanism. A greenish-yellow light flared from within the apparatus, keeping time to his tune. It wasn't anything a human would have recognized as music, but he liked it.

There was a sudden thump up on deck, and he heard the scrabble of Fang's metal claws. Sticking his head up through the hatch, he saw the iron defender facing down a pale, humanoid-looking figure dressed in a worn and ragged uniform. Fang leaped, and was swatted aside like a toy, skidding across the deck and crashing against the base of the mast.

"What's this?" Decker shouted, hauling himself up through the hatch. The figure froze, turning to look at him with burning eyes. Fang clattered to its feet, hissing in rage, and stood at Decker's side. The figure tensed to spring, but relaxed as Decker raised the probe attached to his arm and let off a warning jet of fire.

For a long moment, the two looked at each other in silence. Then the creature spoke.

"Vampire," it croaked. "Where is the vampire?"

"They've gone," Decker replied, keeping the torch in front of him.

"Where?"

Decker jerked his thumb over his shoulder, in the direction of the Mournland.

"There," he said. The creature glanced briefly at the dead-gray mist across the river.

"Take me," it demanded.

"No," replied Decker, as still as a metal statue.

The creature appeared to think. It gave Decker one more long, appraising look, and suddenly dashed to one side. A couple of steps took it to the boat's rail, and it dove overboard without breaking its stride. Fang arrived at the rail too late, and stood hissing, glaring at the widening ripples where the creature had entered the water.

Decker called the iron defender back and cast a professional eye over it. A couple of plates were bent, but there was no serious damage. He detached the probe from his wrist and re-attached the hand. Then he knelt beside the metal hound, with one hand resting lightly on either side of its body, and muttered a brief incantation. When he straightened up again, the construct was as good as new.

"Patrol," he said, and Fang trotted off to resume its circuit of the deck. Decker went below again.

● ● ● ◉ ● ● ●

Dravuliel unrolled the note and read it slowly, an unpleasant smile spreading across his thin, pale face.

"Show me," he said, and the cadaverous elf reached into

142

the bag, bringing out Hintram's severed head by the hair. Dravuliel looked at the dead features for a moment. "Ah, yes," he said at last, "I remember this one. A member of our esteemed Karrnathi lancers, was he not? Bring him closer."

The elf approached Dravuliel's throne, and he reached out a bony hand to touch the dead man's forehead. He murmured briefly in a strange, sibilant language, and after a second or two the dead eyes flickered open.

"What was your name?" Dravuliel demanded. Stiffly, the jaws of the severed head began to move.

"Berend Hintram." Its voice was no more than a hoarse whisper.

"You were a lancer, were you not?"

"Yes."

"And when did you leave us?"

"After the ritual—the Mabar ritual."

"Ah, yes," Dravuliel said. "That was most unfortunate. Where did you go?"

"To the Crimson Monastery."

Dravuliel raised an eyebrow. "So you were the one reporting on our activities?" he asked.

"Yes," said the head.

"I see," he said, waving his assistant away. The elf replaced the head in the bag.

"You also recovered Aeren's body?" Dravuliel asked. His acolyte nodded.

"Good." Dravuliel sat back in his throne and steepled his long fingers in thought.

"Revive Aeren," he said at last, "and prepare the wheel of pain. I wish to discuss his disappointing performance with him."

The elf bowed.

"Yes, master," he said. "And this?" He held up the bag containing the head.

"Keep it," Dravuliel answered. "I may have more questions later. Oh, and assemble his fellow lancers. I am sure they will be eager for news of their erstwhile comrade."

He chuckled, a sound like the scratching of wind-blown twigs against a tomb door.

● ● ● ◉ ◉ ● ● ●

Sergeant Kraal stood rigidly at attention, staring at the wall behind the desk. On the wall was a map of Karrlakton, and beside it a smaller-scale map of the whole of Karrnath. Colored pins dotted each map. He fixed his gaze on one of them.

In front of him—and below his line of sight—stood a richly-carved desk on a wooden dais. Behind the desk sat a gnome; his mouth was smiling, but his watery blue eyes were not.

"You found none of them?" the gnome asked, in a slightly wheezy voice. His tone was one of casual enquiry, but Kraal knew he was deadly serious.

"One headless body, human, male," said the officer. "Another body, human, male, intact, cause of death uncertain. Neither one matching the description of the fugitives."

The gnome picked up a brass letter-opener and began casually cleaning under his nails.

"So tell me, Sergeant . . . Karl, is it?"

"Kraal."

"Kraal, yes. Forgive me. Tell me, Sergeant Kraal, where do you think they went?" He looked up at the sweating officer, wearing an expression of polite curiosity. Kraal cleared his throat, playing for time.

"Can I get you a glass of water, Sergeant?" the gnome asked.

Kraal swallowed hard. "No," he replied. "Thank you."

There was a moment of silence that seemed to stretch on forever. Finally Kraal spoke. "Our inquisitives picked up a couple of trails," he said, "but they couldn't track them to a conclusion. On account of the foot traffic that had passed over them in the intervening time."

The gnome put down the letter opener, and treated the officer to an ingratiating smile.

"Well," he said, "I hesitate to mention this, because I'm sure you and your fine officers have already considered it—and, no doubt, found a good reason to eliminate it from your investigation—but do you think they might have gone to Fort Zombie?"

"Fort Zombie?" asked Kraal.

"Of course." The gnome spread his empty hands, "I am not a professional investigator like yourself. I lack your training and experience. But still, it makes me wonder. The weapon dealer Falko was known to have masterwork swords from Fort Zombie in his possession. He was killed before he could tell us anything. His premises burned down, and shortly afterward an unused warehouse on the waterfront also burned down. Then, all in one night, three things happen. We receive an anonymous message about a construction site where stolen military zombies are being used as workers. Leonus Dabo, whom we know is involved with that same construction site, is murdered in his own home. And finally, a cheap lodging-house catches fire, and two bodies are found inside, one of them without a head. Would you like to know what I think, sergeant?"

Kraal looked down at the gnome, who sat back in his deep-buttoned leather chair and took a sip of wine. Then he continued, in the modulated tones of one who is explaining something complicated to a small child.

"I think our friend Dabo was smuggling stolen zombies from the fort, or perhaps simply buying them from the smugglers. They require no food or rest, so they are ideal unskilled workers—and much cheaper than living employees. It was fortunate that Falko came to our attention—fortunate for us, that is, and not so fortunate, of course, for Falko himself. One of his customers eluded your officers during that arrest, did he not?"

Kraal swallowed again.

"Yes," he answered.

"In any case, it seems to me that Falko was murdered while in custody to prevent him from naming the smugglers from whom he obtained the swords. The destruction of his warehouse may be an attempt to destroy the evidence. The anonymous tip and the murder of Dabo indicate that someone was opposed to the smugglers, as, quite possibly, does the burning of the second warehouse, if that is where the illicit goods were landed."

The sergeant's brow writhed as he tried to follow what he was hearing.

"So you think they're all connected?" he said at last.

The gnome beamed happily. "You see, my dear Sergeant," he said, "how everything fits together! I am so glad. As to the rooming house, I am sure your investigation will arrive at the truth, but I would not rule out a connection. I think that, having dealt with Dabo and the undead smugglers here in Karrlakton, our unknown suspects will not be satisfied. Would you be?"

"Um—probably not." Kraal wasn't sure, but he thought it better to agree.

"No," continued the gnome, "they will almost certainly take the logical next step—to go to Fort Zombie and discover the root of this operation."

"Will they?" Sergeant Kraal said hopefully. He still didn't quite follow the gnome's logic, but he knew that Fort Zombie was safely out of his jurisdiction.

"Thank you for your report, Sergeant," said the gnome. "It will be of incalculable help to my own investigation. And, as always, the Royal Swords can count on the full support and co-operation of the Ministry of the Dead. Please be sure to give my warmest regards to your commissioner. Now, unless I can be of any further assistance to you?"

Sergeant Kraal seized the chance to escape.

"No," he said. "Thank you." And he turned and left the office as quickly as he could.

The gnome smiled after him, and then picked up a brass-bound speaking tube from the rack at the side of his desk.

"This is Haldin," he said. "I will need an airship to Fort Zombie immediately. Alert our people there, but tell them to do nothing until I arrive. That is all."

❂ ❂ ❂ ❂ ❂ ❂ ❂

Brey kicked a loose stone across the floor of the cell.

"This is where they held us," she said, "before . . . Before." She closed her eyes.

"What happened to the others?" asked Tarrel. He was kneeling, looking at something in the dust.

"I don't know. I never saw any of them again. I guess that means none of them became . . ." She faltered, and leaned heavily against the metal grating that fronted the cell. When she raised her head, crimson tears were trickling down her cheeks.

"There's no telling what other atrocities were committed in here," she said, between clenched teeth. "The vampires, those spell-casting zombies—they could have done anything to them."

"Can you find the place where the vampires were kept?" asked Tarrel.

"I think so," Brey said. Then she turned to the inquisitive with a resolute expression. "I want to know what else was done here. I want the world to know. I want you to give my father every scrap of evidence. He should know what happened to me—to all of us."

Tarrel said nothing. Brey led the way out of the cell. "It was down this passage," she said.

Tarrel eyed the cracks in the walls nervously but followed her. They came to the doorway she had seen before; the heavy wooden door lay on the ground, torn off its hinges by some unknown force.

The vaulted ceiling had partially collapsed, and one side of the chamber was strewn with rubble. The stepped dais was still in the center of the room, but a stone slab had come down on Wultram's sarcophagus, breaking it in two. The coffins in the surviving niches looked intact.

"Think anyone's home?" asked Mordan, eyeing the coffins cautiously.

"No," said Brey. "Once Wultram was destroyed, I'm sure the others got out of here as fast as they could, just like I did." But she still flipped the lids open, one by one. Tarrel was sketching a map of the chamber, and making notes here and there.

They left and explored the rest of the complex. The barracks area was deserted, but there was plenty of evidence that the Vedykar Lancers had once been quartered there. A huge banner hung askew on the wall, bearing their insignia, and in the adjoining stable-block they found the Lancers' badge on several abandoned pieces of tack, as well as branded into the hides of two dead horses. The broad ramp leading from the underground stables to the surface was choked by rubble and impassable.

"What's behind here?" asked Mordan, indicating a pair of double doors that they had passed several times, but not opened. Brey seemed to be avoiding them.

"That's the temple," she said. "On the other side of it are the staff quarters, I think. But I don't know if the thing they summoned is still in there."

Tarrel put his ear to one of the doors. "It all sounds quiet," he said after a moment. "Do you think it would have stayed in there when it has all the Mournland to choose from?"

"I'm not sure it could get all the way through the gate," Brey said. "It might still be on the other side, waiting for someone to come within reach."

"One way to find out," said Mordan, opening one of the doors before Brey could protest.

The temple area was devastated. The wreckage of the orrery was strewn about the chamber, scattered among the undecomposed bodies of those who had died defending their master from the hellish tendrils of the beast. The altar was shattered, reduced to a heap of fragments as fine as river gravel. There was no sign of the magical gate, and all was quiet. Tarrel began sketching again, stooping now and again to pick up something.

"This one's still alive!"

Brey and Tarrel looked round sharply at Mordan's cry.

"Impossible!" Brey declared. "It's been years . . ."

Mordan was bending over a small mound of corpses. An arm poked out of the mound, its fingers twitching and clutching at the empty air.

"Be careful!" Brey warned, but it was too late. Mordan grabbed the arm and gave a mighty tug—only to fall over backward as the severed limb came out of the charnel heap more easily than he expected. On the other end of the arm, instead of a body, was a creature the size of a large dog, chewing on the exposed muscle and tendon and making the fingers twitch. It was as surprised as Mordan was, and landed on his chest with a thump, snarling down into his face.

Apart from its size, the creature was more like a rat than a dog—although it wasn't very much like a rat. Its long tail was hairless, but its elongated jaws held a double row of sharp, conical teeth. Bony spines erupted all along its back and from the joints of its four limbs, and a crimson mane on its shoulders contrasted with its black, greasy fur. Blood and spittle dripped onto Mordan's face as it growled.

Mordan slid his left arm beneath its jaw and pushed up, forcing the thing's jaws shut and preventing it from biting. With his right hand, he reached for the dagger in his belt. He had almost reached it when Brey strode over and dealt the beast a savage kick. It flew across the room, hitting a wall with a sickening crunch and a yelp of pain. Then it ran off into the darkness.

"There's nothing alive here," Brey said, pulling Mordan to his feet. "At least, nothing human."

Tarrel had reached the door behind the altar—the door through which Dravuliel had entered at the start of the disastrous ritual.

"What's through here?" he asked.

"I don't know," said Brey. "Let's find out."

DISCOVERIES

CHAPTER 13

Olarune 21, 999 YK

Beyond the door was a large open chamber, hewn out of the rock. A broad crack ran up one wall and across the ceiling, but this area was relatively intact. Luminous crystals set into the ceiling provided an illumination almost as bright as daylight.

The middle of the chamber was occupied by rows of wooden tables, each with a small workbench beside it. Most of the tables were bare, but corpses were laid out on a few of them, bearing similar wounds to those the three had seen in the charnel heap above ground.

Tarrel examined the nearest workbench. It bore a clay pot of dried earth, a large inkwell, a selection of iron needles, and a parchment scroll. Unrolling the scroll, he found a schematic diagram of a humanoid body, covered with glyphs and mystical patterns.

"What do you make of this?" he asked, holding up the scroll.

Brey came over to him and looked at the patterns. "The zombies that captured us were tattooed," she said. "The patterns look similar." Tarrel pulled a small sack from a pocket inside his coat, and dropped the scroll into it.

The workbench was fitted with two drawers. In one, Tarrel found a number of black, glassy stones; in the other, a lot of short bones that he recognized as finger-bones. He put a couple of each in his sack.

"Look at this," called Mordan. He was standing at the far side of the chamber, where a series of stone vats stood against the wall. Each was the size and shape of a sarcophagus, and each had a thick layer of foul-smelling sludge at the bottom. Three of the vats contained bodies, almost unrecognizable beneath the muck that coated them.

Roughly in the middle of the row of vats, a set of sturdy wooden shelves stood against the wall, crowded with jars and bottles of all shapes and sizes. Tarrel examined them, noting down the writing on their labels. Finding a long-handled iron spoon, he carefully ladled some of the sludge from the nearest vat into an empty jar, stoppered it tightly, and dropped it into his sack.

"Alchemy," he said at last. "I'd guess they were working on ways to make the zombies tougher—maybe slower to decay, as well. The other things are probably spell ingredients. I know a couple of experts in Sharn who can tell for sure."

Two doors led deeper into the complex. Listening at one, Tarrel gestured the other two to silence.

"I hear it," said Brey. "It sounds like chanting."

Tarrel put his sack down and pulled his mirror from a pocket inside his coat, holding it in one hand as he opened the door a crack. They all winced at the slight creak it made, but the chanting continued unbroken. Sticking the mirror through the crack, Tarrel cast a rapid glance over the room beyond. Then he withdrew the mirror and put it away.

"Looks like some kind of ritual," he whispered. "They haven't heard us."

> *Anglau men hethluc guelltho,*
> *Marlath men buyluth guelltho,*
> *Trannuch men gledach guelltho,*
> *Trengi beo.*

The chant repeated over and over, a guttural drone with no beginning and no end. Tarrel listened intently. "That's elven," he whispered at last.

Mordan looked at him questioningly. "Doesn't sound like Valenar," he commented.

"It's not," said Tarrel. "I think it's Aereni—maybe an archaic form. Something about peace in pain, life in death, birth in"—he searched for a word in the common tongue—"in dying. Something like that."

"How many of them?" whispered Brey.

"Three," Tarrel replied, "plus some kind of sacrificial victim." He drew his orange-tipped wand and looked at the others.

"Ready?" he asked. When they nodded, he kicked the door open.

Brey leaped into the room, sticking to the ceiling like a spider. Mordan dove in, rolling to his feet with his rapier drawn. Tarrel stood in the doorway, holding his wand in both hands.

"Anglau men hethluc guelltho," the chant continued without a break.

In the center of the room, the dead body of an elf hung from its hands, which were nailed to an upright post of black wood. Dried blood stained the post, running down to a brownish puddle at the base. In front of the post, with their backs to the doorway, three zombies stood before a lectern of carved bone, chanting tirelessly. They did not even look around as the three entered.

The fight was over quickly. The zombies maintained their chant until the first of them was attacked, and two were destroyed before they had time to react—one by the searing light from Tarrel's wand, and another by Mordan's enchanted rapier. Brey felled the third as it turned toward her, crushing its chest with a stamp of her foot. The three looked nervously up at the inert figure on the post, but it did not move.

Having retrieved his sack from beside the door, Tarrel examined the book that rested on the lectern.

"Instructions for the ritual," he said after a few moments. "The chant's in here—apparently the one on the post is supposed to cross over from life into undeath."

"Doesn't look like it worked," said Mordan, looking up at the motionless elf corpse. Are you saying he was alive when they nailed him up there?"

"Most likely they nailed him to the pole before they raised it," answered Tarrel. "See how loose it is in its socket? It was probably made to be taken up and down."

Mordan winced. "Bad way to die."

"Something doesn't add up, though," said Tarrel. "I think the zombies were just providing the chant. There should have been someone else to conduct the ritual." He added the book to his sack, which didn't appear to be getting any more full.

Brey laughed. "He probably ran like the rest when the accident happened," she said. "I bet they've been chanting here ever since, just because nobody told them to stop. Just like that thing outside, collecting the dead."

"Let's get him down," said Tarrel. "I'd like to take a look."

Somewhat reluctantly, Brey and Mordan held the elf's legs while Tarrel climbed up the pole and pulled out the nails with a pair of pliers.

"Look at these," he said, dropping to the floor. He held out his hand, and the others could see the arcane symbols carved into the heads of the nails. Reaching inside his coat, he pulled out a small lens and peered through it at the nails.

"Some kind of enchantment," he said, dropping the nails into his sack. He bent over the body.

"No wounds other than the nail-holes in the hands," he muttered, half to himself. "The shoulders have dislocated, probably because of hanging there for so long. I'd say when he died, there was no one around to complete the ritual and bring him back."

Mordan came back into the chamber from a short side-passage.

"All clear here," he called out. "A lot of small rooms with desks and supplies. Looks like some kind of living quarters, except there are no beds."

"Zombies don't need to sleep," Brey pointed out, "and whatever this one was supposed to become, that probably doesn't need to sleep either. Dravuliel had a whole crowd of them as servants and assistants—all elves, and all undead. They were smarter than zombies, though—just as if they were still alive. A lot of them could cast spells."

Tarrel looked up. "Not zombies and not vampires," he said. "Could he have found a way to make wights?"

Brey shook her head.

"I don't think so," she replied. "They were smarter than wights, too. Maybe they were some kind of lich."

Tarrel shook his head in puzzlement. "Another question for the experts," he said. He looked down at the body for a long moment.

"You're not going to put that in your sack?" asked Brey.

Tarrel grinned and shook his head.

"No," he said. "Too big. I'm just making sure there's nothing I've missed."

"Look at this," called Mordan from across the room. He had pulled back a tattered hanging to reveal a large and solid-looking door. Prominent among the carvings was a large elven rune.

"Interesting," commented Tarrel. "My Aerani's kind of rusty, but I think that says 'Master.' Wait!"

His warning came too late. Mordan swung the door open, took half a pace into the passage beyond—and stopped in mid-stride. Brey and Tarrel stared for a few moments, but he didn't move. He didn't even look as though he was breathing.

"It's probably trapped." Tarrel finished tonelessly, looking at Brey with a gesture of despair. Standing as far from the doorway as she could, she grabbed Mordan by the neck and dragged him back into the room. He was as stiff as a statue. She laid him down on the stone floor; his forward foot stuck incongruously into the air, frozen before he could finish his step.

Tarrel examined him, then breathed a sigh of relief.

"Looks like he's only paralyzed," he said. "With luck, he'll come round in a minute or two." He searched the ground just beyond the doorway, and held up a pinch of dirt between finger and thumb.

"This was on the floor," he said, "marking out some kind of glyph until our brilliant colleague disturbed it." Brey was looking down at Mordan in concern.

"Are you sure he'll snap out of it by himself?"

"Not completely sure," said Tarrel, "but most magical paralysis doesn't last too long. I'll give him till I've looked over those rooms he found down the passage. If he isn't moving by then, I've got a scroll that ought to fix him up."

"You seem to know a lot about magic," said Brey. "Did you train as a wizard?"

"No," Tarrel replied, "but I've made a study of scrolls and things. If I can figure out how something works, I can usually use it."

"Like the wand?" Brey asked. Tarrel trotted off to examine the rooms Mordan had found earlier.

As Tarrel had predicted, Mordan's paralysis did not last long. After a minute or so his heel dropped to the floor. He blinked and sat up, surprised to find himself prone.

"What happened?" he asked Brey.

"According to Tarrel, you walked into a trap," she replied. "Next time, be more careful—you could have been killed!"

"I didn't know you cared," he said, climbing to his feet. Brey gave him a sour smile. "Where is Tarrel, by the way?"

"Checking out those rooms you found," said Brey, pointing to the passage. Just as they reached it, Tarrel emerged, with his sack slung over his shoulder.

"You were right about the spellcasting," he said. "There's not much in those rooms, but I did pick up a few spellbooks. Mostly necromancy, by the look of them."

"Makes sense," said Mordan.

"Well, then," said Tarrel briskly, "time to see the master's quarters." He strode toward the doorway.

"Watch out for that trap," warned Mordan.

Tarrel grinned back at him. "Nothing to worry about," he said. "You took care of it when you set it off." Mordan scowled and drew his rapier, following Tarrel through the doorway into a short passage.

At the end of the passage was a round chamber with a domed roof. It was dominated by a stepped dais supporting an ornate throne, which was apparently made of fused bones. Skulls decorated the back and the ends of the arm rests. Tarrel looked at it through his crystal lens.

"It's not magical," he said. The three looked around the chamber. There were two doors, one on each side of the throne. Between the doors, the walls were decorated with weird tapestries depicting scenes of life, death, and undeath.

Tarrel examined the doors. The one on the left was carved with the symbol of a fanged, demonic face, its mouth open as if to devour all who dared enter.

"I know that sign," said Brey with a shudder. "The Blood of Vol."

The second door, on the right of the grisly throne, was marked with the same elven rune that they had seen before.

"The master's chamber?" wondered Mordan.

Tarrel approached the door with caution, examining it carefully through his crystal lens. Then he dropped to a crouch and looked at the floor immediately in front of it. Putting on a thick leather glove, he turned the iron handle and pushed the door. It swung open with a faint creak.

"After you," said Mordan. Tarrel stepped cautiously through the doorway, and the others followed.

The room beyond was smaller than they expected. There was scarcely enough space for the plain wooden bed and tall cupboard. The walls were completely bare.

Inside the cupboard, Tarrel found a few changes of clothing, including a couple of richly worked ceremonial robes, which he stuffed into his sack. Mordan, meanwhile, was examining the bed but found nothing except a ceramic chamber-pot.

"I guess he wasn't undead," he said, holding the pot up. Tarrel suppressed a laugh; Brey just averted her eyes and muttered something about boys.

The mood was more somber, though, when they returned to the antechamber and looked again at the demonic face inscribed on the other door.

"Allow me," said Brey. She shattered the door with a powerful kick, sending splinters flying into the space beyond. The demonic face was destroyed.

Inside, it was too dark for Mordan to see anything. Trampling the fragments of the broken door, Brey and Tarrel went in, while Mordan reached into a pocket and pulled out the glowing pebble that Tarrel had given him. Holding it over his head, he saw a small room with a stone altar at the back, and other objects ranged around it.

The walls were black, and covered with a fine arcane script written in something brown and powdered. Tarrel was looking at the script and making notes, while Brey scratched off some of the brown pigment with a fingernail and sniffed it cautiously.

"Blood," she said, to no one in particular.

Tarrel looked up from his examination of the script. "Blood of Vol," he replied. "Your former employer had his own private chapel." He turned and examined the altar.

The altar was a block of dark green stone the size of a small table, flecked and veined with scarlet. A depression in the top held more dried blood, and flanking the bowl were two candlesticks made of bone. They had a skeletal hand at each end: the burnt-down nub of a rune-inscribed candle was clutched in the fingers of the upper hand, while the lower one stood on its spread fingertips like a weird spider. Tarrel began sketching.

Standing in front of the altar was a prayer-stand of black wood, inlaid with elaborate patterns in bone. On its rail, a book lay open. Brey glanced at down and flinched, instinctively making the sign of the Silver Flame. She picked the book up, and tore it in half down the spine.

"Hey!" called Tarrel, turning at the sound. "Don't do that! That's evidence!" He laid a restraining hand on Brey's arm and noticed that she was trembling.

"It's a blasphemy," she said between clenched teeth. "It must be destroyed, in the name of the—of the . . ." Her voice tailed off; she still could not pronounce the name of her deity.

"Silver Flame," said Tarrel gently, finishing her sentence. Brey winced at the sound, but gave him a wan smile. "I'll make you a deal," Tarrel continued. "Just for now, let me put it in my sack, where it can't do any harm to anyone. When all this is over, I'll give it back to you—or I'll take it to Thrane and hand it over to the Church—and then it can be destroyed with all the ceremony, and righteous wrath, and anything else you want." He looked at Brey, holding the mouth of his sack open. Slowly, she relaxed her grip on the two halves of the book.

"Don't read it," she said, fixing him with an urgent gaze. "It's . . ."

"Don't worry," said Tarrel. "I won't. But I would like an expert to look it over—with proper magical and religious precautions, of course. It could tell us something about what we're up against—maybe even give us some idea of a weakness." There was a moment's pause, and then Brey dropped the pieces into the sack. Tarrel closed the top quickly.

"What's the matter?" he asked after a moment. Brey was still shaking a little.

"I'm not sure," she said. "There's something about this room. I feel good being here. Too good. Does that make any sense?"

"Like when you've just . . . eaten?" With a worried expression, Brey nodded.

"It's probably negative energy," he said. "If this chapel's been dedicated to Vol with the right spells, it will be flooded with negative energy. That makes necromancy more powerful, and undead stronger."

Brey's head sagged a little, and she closed her eyes.

"That makes sense," she said. "It feels—I feel—stronger, but not so much in control. Like the monster is trying to take over."

Mordan looked up in alarm. He had seen Brey in a blood-frenzy before.

"Listen," he said, "if you'd rather step outside . . ."

Brey shook her head. "No," she said. "I've been fighting this ever since—ever since I got my will back. I can handle it. Besides, I have to see this. Know the enemy, like Tarrel says."

After a moment, she asked, "Are you finished with the altar?" Tarrel glanced at her uncertainly, but nodded.

"Good," she said grimly. Striding forward, she swept the bone candle-holders aside and gripped the carved stone at each end, hoisting it above her head with a massive effort.

"Get out of the way!" she screamed, her face distorting and her fangs beginning to show. Mordan and Tarrel flattened themselves against the wall as she hurled the altar with all her might. It shattered against the far wall of the chapel as if thrown by a giant; the two mortals ducked and covered their faces as shards of stone ricocheted around the room.

"That felt good," Brey snarled, looking down at the wreckage. A small crack had opened in the rock where the altar had struck the wall. With a soft grating noise, it began to widen, spreading rapidly. At the same time, the ground began to vibrate—slightly at first, and then more violently.

"What did you do?" yelled Mordan above the rising noise. Dust and small chips of stone were beginning to fall from the ceiling. Without another word, the three turned and fled.

Brey took the lead as they entered the necromantic workroom, hurling the heavy wooden tables to aside as she ran to clear a path for the others. Larger fragments of the ceiling had started to fall; in the main temple she hit Mordan with a flying tackle, knocking him aside as a piece of stone the size of a horse missed them by a hair's breadth. Rolling to her feet, she shoved him through the doorway into the main passage. The floor was rolling like a ship's deck in a storm as they zigzagged their way along it.

By a miracle, the staircase was still largely intact. They scrambled up it and out into the ruins of the fort, beneath the gray light of the Mournland. The rubble-choked grass of the fort's interior was heaving; concentric ripples spread across the hilltop like the surface of a lake disturbed by a falling rock, or by the motions of some huge creature barely submerged. Then a hole opened up, widening rapidly. The remains of the fort toppled into the expanding void. The whole interior of the hill was caving in.

"Run!" screamed Brey, close behind her two companions. She had slowed her pace to match theirs, determined not to leave them behind. An earth-ripple as tall as a man swept beneath their feet partway down the hill, sending them tumbling and rolling to the bottom in a shower of dirt and stones.

A cloud of dust enveloped them as they reached the bottom of the hill, mingled with dirt and debris. They could no longer see the top—or even tell if it was still there. Coughing and cursing, they struggled through the dust—and found themselves staring at an immense pair of metal legs.

CHAPTER 14

Olarune 21, 999 YK

The cadaver collector towered over the three of them, peering down with small, luminous green-white eyes. Then it looked up at the top of the hill—or rather, at the place where the top of the hill had been. Finally, it looked down at them again.

"Run!" screamed Brey.

Mordan hurled himself aside as an immense clawed hand reached for him, but he was a fraction too slow. The metal claws struck him a glancing blow, sending him cartwheeling across the ground. A beam of light stabbed out from Tarrel's wand, striking the monstrosity directly in the face—and bouncing back to hit Tarrel himself, knocking him off his feet. Ignoring the fallen half-elf, the construct lumbered over to Mordan, picking him up in its massive fist. As he writhed in its grasp, it lifted him over its head, directly above the blood-encrusted spikes on its back.

"No!" With a cry, Brey leaped onto the creature's back, swinging from spike to spike like an acrobat. Bracing her feet against the metal carapace, she reached out for its wrist—a column of metal and stone as thick as a tree-trunk—and pushed upward with all her strength. For a moment, she held the limb back, but a long, jagged spike was only inches away from Mordan's body. He struggled in the thing's iron grasp but could not free himself.

Tarrel struggled to his feet, smoke rising from a charred hole in the front of his coat. He clutched his chest, his face distorted in agony, and staggered a few paces toward the great construct. He stared at the impasse between construct and vampire, as if dazed and unsure of what he was seeing.

Brey had begun to shake with the strain of resisting the thing's titanic strength. Its other arm was reaching over its back, trying to find her, but she was protected for the moment by the spines and corpses around her. Mordan's struggles were becoming weaker as the metal fingers slowly crushed his chest. Brey's lips drew back in a snarl of determination as she fought to hold the huge arm, but Mordan's body was inching closer to the tip of the spike, a hair's-breadth at a time.

Tarrel heard the sound first—or rather, he felt it before he heard it. It began out of the tremors of the collapsing hill, and rose in pitch until it became a rumbling, grinding sound like a rockslide. Then it struck.

The ground at the huge construct's feet heaved and split, and a rushing column of debris vomited up from the earth, slamming into the cadaver collector with the force of an avalanche. The metal beast swayed backward and was forced to lower its arms to steady itself. Its fingers opened, dropping Mordan to the ground. Brey flung herself from the creature's back and scooped up the wounded Karrn as the two huge beasts squared off.

The earth had taken a rough form: two stubby legs

supported a thick body with no discernible head. It flailed at the construct with massive arms made of earth, stone, and bone. Pieces of the work-tables from the underground laboratory stuck out of its hide, along with stonework and even fragments of the dead bodies they had found there.

Brey and Tarrel backed away as the two titanic beasts flung themselves at each other. The earth shook with the fury of their battle; neither gave ground as they traded massive blows. The corpses on the construct's back were quickly reduced to pulp, and the spikes upon which they had been impaled were bent or broken. Still the metal giant fought, ignoring the dents in its carapace from its opponent's rocky fists. With every crashing blow of its metal claws, it rent a little more material from the fabric of the earth-creature's body, but that did nothing to lessen the force of its attack.

Tarrel looked over Mordan's battered and unconscious body, telling Brey with a nod that he was still alive. She slung the Karrn over one shoulder and pointed questioningly at the Brelander's injured leg. Speech was impossible above the din of the battle. Tarrel limped a couple of paces, and evidently Brey did not think that he was going quickly enough, for she unceremoniously flung him over her other shoulder and set off at a run, away from the ruined hill and the fighting monstrosities.

When her untiring stride had put a few miles behind them, Brey set her companions down beneath the shelter of a fallen tree. At least, it looked like it had once been a tree, but now it was a massive, roughly cylindrical rock, crowned with an eruption of slim and jagged crystals. Mordan was still unconscious, his breathing ragged; Tarrel was stiff and sore from his injuries, but could limp around well enough. He dug around in his sack and pulled out a small clay jug. He uncorked and slowly poured a deep red liquid down Mordan's throat.

A few seconds went by, and for a moment Tarrel feared that it was too late. Then the Karrn coughed, his face contorting in pain as his chest spasmed over broken ribs. His eyes fluttered open, and he tried to sit up. Brey pushed him down, gently but firmly, and he went to sleep.

Tarrel raised the jug to his lips and took a swig. Through the hole that the spell had blasted in his clothing, Brey saw his charred flesh knit together a little, though it remained inflamed.

"What were those things?" she asked at last. Her voice was low and strained; the events of the last hour had taken their toll even of her undead constitution. Tarrel shook his head in bewilderment.

"I have no more idea than you do," he replied. "That thing with the corpses was some kind of construct—the biggest I've ever seen. It turned the spell from my wand back on me somehow—I didn't know anything could do that. The thing that attacked it looked like some kind of earth elemental, but its body was made out of the wreckage of that base. It's as if the whole place just came alive."

Brey looked over at Mordan's sleeping form and back at the half-elf.

"Do you have any more of that healing potion?" she asked.

"That's goodberry wine," he said, "made by Brelish druids. Trouble is, you have to wait a few hours before you can take another dose. There are a couple of regular healing potions in the luggage, but we're on our own till we get back to the boat."

Brey frowned. "How fast do you think you can walk?" she asked.

Tarrel grimaced. "Faster than I could before I took a drink," he said, "but still not very fast. How long do you reckon it'll take us to get back to the river?"

* * * * * * *

Rends Flesh hauled the corpse into a sitting position and chewed around the flesh of the neck. It was not the best part of the body; the meat around the neck-bones was sweet enough, but it was stringy with tendons. But it wasn't the neck meat he was after.

A few bites and a tug separated the head from the body, and another quick bite under the chin severed the helmet-strap. Discarding the helmet, the ghoul carried the severed head to a rounded rock he had noticed earlier, and raising it high above his head in both hands, brought it crashing down onto the rock with all his strength.

A couple more blows and he could see a break in the skull through the torn flesh and matted hair. Rapidly peeling the scalp away, he got his strong nails into the crack and pulled. With a dull crack, a hand-sized piece of the skull came away, revealing the sweet, sticky brain inside. He sat down beside the rock, set the broken skull in his lap, and began scooping out the brain with his hands.

This had been a good find. There were at least a hundred fresh corpses strewn across the rocky slope, and only a few carcass eaters to chase away. The spiny beasts snarled and threatened as the ghouls approached, dodging the stones thrown by the ghoul pack, but they withdrew after Smells Strong caved in their leader's head. A few of them still loitered around the edges of the find. Now and then, one would dash in to bite a chunk of flesh off the nearest corpse, running back into the rocks to eat it. Mostly, though, they sat and watched, waiting for the ghouls to eat their fill and move on.

Sucks Marrow had picked up a leg-bone discarded by one of the others, and Rends Flesh followed her to see what she would do with it. The smaller ghoul was weak but smart, and she was healthy and well-fed despite only being allowed to eat what the others discarded. He watched as she picked up a rounded stone the size of her two fists; carrying it in one hand and the bone in the other, she went over to a flat rock. She put the bone down on the rock and then raised the stone over her head, as he had done earlier with the skull. She hit the bone with the stone, over and over again until finally it splintered. With a dexterous twist, she pulled something long and soft from inside.

Before she had a chance to eat her prize, Rends Flesh loped over and snatched it from her hand. He silenced her whine of protest with a back-handed blow to the head and a tooth-baring snarl of dominance; still whining, she slowly backed off as he began to eat. It was some of the sweetest, softest flesh he had ever tasted, and he probed the inside of the bone with a finger to see if there was more. He picked up the rounded stone and hit the bone again, but finding no more of the sweet meat inside, he gave up and wandered back to the corpse he had been eating. He would have to keep watching her, he thought.

Nobody saw the stranger appear—not even Chews Ribs, who was supposed to be on watch. The first anybody knew was when his body came crashing down in the midst of the corpses and feeding ghouls, and lay still.

The stranger did not look like them. His skin was pale, and he had hair on his head like a living one. He wore clothes like they did. The ghouls sniffed in his direction, but could not smell the warmth of life upon him. He stood and waited, a challenge in his fierce eyes.

Smells Strong got to his feet and walked slowly toward the stranger. As the leader of the pack, it was his place to answer the challenge. The other ghouls gathered a little way behind their leader, watching to see what would happen. The stranger began to walk forward as well.

The two stopped when they were a few paces apart. Smells Strong snarled to display the keenness of his teeth, and stretched to show his size and strength. For a moment, the stranger stood still, not responding to the display. Then, keeping his eyes locked on his opponent, he took a deliberate ‑tep forward. This was too much. Smells Strong charged with a mighty roar.

As fast he was, the stranger was faster. He stepped aside from the raking claws, striking a blow to the jaw that sent his opponent reeling back, spitting out splintered teeth. Smells Strong shook his head and snarled again, bracing as the stranger leaped forward. A crushing blow smashed his chest, sending him sprawling. As he climbed back to his feet, the others could see broken ribs sticking out through his skin.

Smells Strong stood unsteadily, glaring at the stranger as he circled slowly around him. He picked up a long bone from the ground, and wielded it in both hands like a club, waiting for the stranger's next move.

When that move came, it was almost too fast to see. Grasping the bone club in one hand, the stranger lifted Smells Strong off his feet. He drove his hand into the ghast's midsection, ripping it open. Smells Strong stood for a moment and then collapsed, the light fading from his eyes.

The ghouls huddled together, preparing to fight if the stranger attacked them. Instead, he reached down to the ghast's body, pulled off his head with a single wrench, and threw it to the carcass eaters that were skulking on the edges of the site.

One of them picked it up in its wide jaws, and trotted off among the rocks.

Then the stranger looked down at the ghouls.

"I am your leader now," he said in a dry, rasping voice.

❧ ❧ ❧ ❧ ❧ ❧ ❧

"Well, *that* wasn't here before."

Mordan, Brey, and Tarrel stood and looked down into the chasm. It plunged for hundreds of feet, and a faint glow of molten lava could be seen at the bottom. Sulfurous fumes wafted up from the depths. It was only about forty feet wide, but it extended as far as they eye could see in either direction.

"That's the Mournland," said Mordan, "always changing." Another draught of the goodberry wine had revived him, but he was still pale.

"I could get across," said Brey, "but I don't know about you two." Tarrel dug around in his sack, and brought out a long coil of rope.

"There's nothing to tie it onto," said Mordan. He was right; the ground on each side of the chasm was strewn with boulders, but there were no trees or anything else that could be used to anchor a rope.

"Don't worry," replied Tarrel. "I've got that covered." He uncoiled the rope and offered one end to Brey.

"Just a minute," she said. She closed her eyes and concentrated, and her form shifted. Her arms and legs grew shorter. Her chest broadened, and her fingers extended, growing thin membranes of skin between them. A huge bat crouched on the ground where the woman from Thrane had been standing.

The bat took the rope in its taloned feet and launched itself into the air, crossing the chasm with a few beats of its powerful wings. Once on the other side, it changed back into Brey. She took the rope in a firm grip and signaled that she was ready.

Tarrel wrapped the other end of the rope around his body and tested the ground with his heel until he was sure he had a secure footing. Then he turned to Mordan.

"Whenever you're ready," he said.

"How are you going to get across with no one to hold the rope?" asked Mordan.

Tarrel grinned. "Trust me," he said, leaning backward to take up the slack.

Mordan hooked his left elbow around the rope, held on with his right hand, and swung his legs up and over. Tarrel leaned back further to take his weight, and gave him a nod of encouragement. Slowly, Mordan began to inch his way along the rope. He'd done it often enough as a cadet at Rekkenmark—although he'd had both hands then—and it wasn't long before he reached the other side. He dropped to the ground beside Brey, and saw Tarrel straighten up.

"So what's he going to do now?" he wondered.

As if in answer, Tarrel shouted across to them. "Get ready to pull!" he called.

Mordan and Brey looked at each other, then Mordan took hold of the rope.

"Ready?" yelled Tarrel. Brey waved an acknowledgment. Then, to their surprise, the half-elf ran toward the edge of the chasm and threw himself off.

Instead of dropping like a stone, Tarrel floated gently down. Brey and Mordan pulled on the rope, reeling him in. His feet hit the side of the chasm a few feet below the edge— much more gently than if he had fallen at normal speed—and they hauled him up the rest of the way.

"How did you do that?" asked Mordan when they had pulled him up. Tarrel grinned and folded back the lapel of his coat. Stuck into the back was a small gold pin, cast in the shape of a feather.

"These are popular in Sharn," he said. "It is the City of Towers, after all—and falling all the way from Palatinate can ruin your entire day."

Mordan didn't have time to reply. With a screeching cry, a pack of ghouls burst from hiding behind the rocks. Standing on one of the higher rocks was a figure they recognized—the same wight who had attacked them in Karrlakton.

"Kill the woman!" he shouted, and the ghouls crowded around Brey, clawing and biting. She scattered them right and left with powerful blows of her fists, but while she was occupied, the wight leaped from the rock and advanced on the two mortals.

Mordan drew his rapier. From the corner of his eye, he saw Tarrel pull out his wand, but there was no beam of searing light. Tarrel cursed, and Mordan's heart sank: The wand had expended all its energy. Tarrel drew his shortsword and the two of them watched their enemy approach.

The creature lashed out at Tarrel, but Mordan blocked the attack with a flick of his rapier. The enchanted blade cut a deep gash in the wight's arm, and he drew back with a snarl.

"You'll pay for that!" he spat, and struck at the Karrn with a bony fist. Mordan barely dodged in time; this thing was even faster than he was.

A clawed hand struck his right wrist, sending a numbing chill through his whole body and knocking the rapier from his hand. He fumbled for the dagger in his belt, knowing he wouldn't reach it in time.

Then something dark flew through the air, landing on top of the creature and knocking it to the ground. Brey had launched herself from the midst of the ghouls, somersaulting high in the air and dropping down onto the wight. They both rolled to their feet.

"Cover my back!" yelled Brey. Mordan picked up his rapier and moved to guard her as the ghouls ran to the attack. Tarrel came to his side.

There were a half-dozen of the creatures, hairless, dressed in rags, and with blotched purple skin that looked like one huge bruise. One fell right away, clutching at the hole Mordan's rapier had made in its belly. Tarrel cut savagely at another, which fell back with a deep cut in its shoulder. Mordan slashed a third across the neck, and the others hesitated momentarily. He risked a glance back.

Brey and the wight were locked in a deadly embrace, each holding the other's arms. They were testing each other's strength, and the first to falter would be the first to die. Brey kicked her opponent savagely in the groin, but he didn't flinch. They continued to grapple.

The ghouls had regrouped, and rushed at Mordan and Tarrel in a mass.

"Don't let them touch you!" yelled Tarrel. Mordan nodded—he had heard that these things could paralyze the living. Sometimes they even started eating them before they were dead.

His rapier flicked out, and another ghoul dropped to the ground, clutching at a gash in its belly. Tarrel stabbed another through the throat, and it fell back. Mordan dodged a slashing claw, and impaled its owner with a savage thrust. The two remaining ghouls retreated; now that the odds were even, they weren't so brave—especially as one of them was badly wounded. Mordan made a mock charge, and they turned and fled.

The two turned to see Brey and the wight still locked in combat. He tore one hand free and clawed her viciously across the face; she drove her knee into his midsection, striking him between the shoulder-blades as he bent over. Then, before he could straighten himself, she seized his head in both hands and twisted savagely.

Instead of resisting the torque, the wight rolled with it, lashing out with a foot and tripping Brey. Mordan and Tarrel rushed forward, but she was already back on her feet. The wight looked at the three of them.

"We'll meet again!" he snarled, and turned away, leaping over the rocks with unnatural speed and grace.

"Oh, no!" Brey snarled back. "This ends here!" She dropped to all fours, shifting into the shape of an immense, red-coated wolf. Within a couple of strides she was upon the wight, her jaws clamped onto the back of his neck. The wight tried to dislodge her, but she wrestled him to the ground, shooting an urgent glance to her two companions.

Mordan ran over, rapier in hand, and stood over the two struggling forms for a moment—then thrust hard between the wight's ribs, twisting his blade in the wound. The creature howled in agony, writhing and clutching at the elven sword, but the wolf-Brey had his throat in a crushing bite and he could not escape. His struggles became gradually weaker, and at last they stopped altogether.

Brey shifted back to human form. Her cheek still bore the wounds from the wight's claws, but as the two mortals watched, they faded and vanished, leaving no trace of a scar. She stared down at the body of her foe for a moment.

"That was no ordinary wight," she said.

"Nothing from this unit is ordinary," replied Mordan. He had sheathed his rapier, and was kneeling beside the creature's body. Its shoulder was tattooed with the badge of the mysterious Unit 61, and he set about cutting the skin off with his dagger.

"Souvenir?" asked Tarrel, raising an eyebrow.

"Evidence," replied Mordan, "for the next time some-one tells me this badge doesn't exist. Oh, and you know that feather pin of yours? Magic doesn't always work the way it's supposed to in the Mournland. Remember the blood-creature, when your wand stopped working for a moment? You were lucky this time, but a non-magical backup plan is always a good idea."

Tarrel looked back toward the chasm, and Mordan chuckled as the three resumed their journey.

CHAPTER 15

Olarune 22, 999 YK

Stopping in her tracks, Brey cursed under her breath. Her two companions stopped and looked questioningly at her through the dense gray mist.

"Sunlight," she said. "I can feel it. We must be near the edge." She backed away a few paces into the mist.

"You two wait here," said Mordan, and loped off into the mist without waiting for a reply. He returned a few minutes later, with a smile.

"The river's only a few hundred yards," he said, "and it looks like we're only a few miles from where we left the boat."

"You're sure?" asked Brey.

Mordan nodded. "Positive," he said. "I've been up and down this river a lot in the last few months."

"How long till sundown?" Brey asked.

"About four, five hours," he replied.

Brey thought for a moment. "You two go ahead," she said. "I can't go out there till dark, and I'll need to hunt as soon as the sun goes down. I'll catch up with you tonight."

"I'll wait with you," offered Tarrel.

Brey shook her head.

"I spent a lot of time looking for you," he said. "How do I know you won't just disappear on me?"

Brey grinned. "You don't," she said. "But here's something you *should* know: I haven't fed in a long time."

Tarrel's eyes widened a fraction, and he got up to leave. "Since you put it that way," he said. He slung his sack over his shoulder, and set off into the mist with Mordan.

"So have you decided what to tell her father yet?" Mordan asked, after the two had walked a little way in silence.

Tarrel shook his head. "Maybe she's right—it would have been better if I'd never found her," he said. "I can see why she doesn't want to go back to Thrane—the Church of the Silver Flame isn't as forgiving about undead as you Karrns are, even ones who were originally paladins. It'll be hard on her family if she goes home, and hard if she doesn't."

"They wouldn't be the first parents to be cruelly disappointed in their offspring," said Mordan. Tarrel looked at him, expecting a cynical smile, but the Karrn's face was set. He stared at the ground in front of him as he walked.

"It's not like it was her fault, you know," Tarrel replied.

Mordan kept his eyes on the ground. "I've never known that to make a difference," he said.

Then they came to the edge of the mist.

Tarrel blinked. Even though it had been getting lighter as they approached the edge of the dead-gray mist, he was still unprepared for the sudden sunlight. They stopped at the river-bank and looked across at Karrnath.

"We left Decker a few miles back that way," said Mordan, pointing to his left.

"Do you think he'll still be there?" asked Tarrel. "He didn't seem like your greatest fan, and he wasn't happy about having a vampire on his boat. Would he take the money and run?"

Mordan shook his head with a slight smile. "No," he said. "He'll be right there, working on that mechanical engine of his."

"How can you be so sure?" asked Tarrel.

"Because I know him," Mordan replied, "and because I haven't paid him yet."

* * * * * * *

They found the boat a few miles downstream, moored under an overhanging tree. Fang was pacing the deck but seemed not to see them. It was more than an hour before they caught sight of Decker, and another ten minutes of shouting before he noticed them. He waved them to wait, and after a few minutes, the boat crossed the river toward them.

Once aboard, they told Decker what they had seen in the Mournland, and he proudly showed them the engine. It looked a little more complicated, but neither of them could have said what was new—or even what most of the wheels, shafts, and pistons were supposed to do. When Decker got the boat under way, though, they both noticed an appreciable increase in speed. The boat traveled about as fast as a trotting horse.

Tarrel went below and changed his clothes. Dusk was beginning to fall when he came back up with a couple of healing potions. He found Mordan sitting moodily at the stern, staring at nothing in particular. Mordan accepted the potions with a nod of thanks, but although his color improved, his mood did not.

Tarrel sat down beside him. "Want to talk about it?" he asked.

Mordan looked sideways at him. "About what?"

"About whatever it was that wasn't your fault."

"No."

They sat in silence for a minute or two.

"You know," said Tarrel, "I don't know why you're so hard on her. She saved your life back there."

Mordan looked up sourly. "I'll have to buy her some flowers."

"What is wrong with you?" Tarrel said. "You'd be meat on the back of that metal thing right now, if she hadn't arm-wrestled it for you!"

Mordan looked at him with a tired expression. "I'd be at Fort Zombie right now if she hadn't dragged us in there! And what did we find? Nothing."

"Nothing?" echoed Tarrel, looking at his sack. Although it still only looked half-full, it contained almost enough to fill a cart.

"And then she smashes that damned altar and brings the place down on our heads! And for what? Religion? What good is her religion to her now? She can't even say its name!"

"And whose fault is that?" said the Brelander. "Or have you forgotten how she got that way? You're lucky she hasn't killed you just for being a Karrn."

"I'm sure she'll try," Mordan shot back, "just as soon as I stop being useful."

Tarrel stared at him.

"Look," said Mordan, with quiet intensity, "She's not the only person bad things ever happened to in a hundred years of war. There are no losers, no winners—just survivors. And she's just another survivor."

"She's entitled to some justice."

"Justice?" Mordan's laugh was hollow. "Everyone is entitled to justice—but how many are going to get it?"

"She will," vowed the half-elf, "if I have anything to say about it."

"Oh, of course!" spat Mordan. "Because her father's a general and can afford to hire a fancy Medani inquisitive!"

"No," replied Tarrel, his voice dangerously quiet, "because what happened to her shouldn't have happened to anyone. Because someone chose to do this to her—and because . . ."

"Because you're getting paid," said Mordan. "Admit it!"

Tarrel clenched his fists for a long moment, then forced himself to relax them. "Whatever you say, hero boy," he grated. "You can sit here and contemplate the unfairness of life as long as you like. I'm going to get some sleep." He got up, and went below deck.

Mordan leaned his head back, looking at the stars as they appeared. After a few minutes, Decker stuck his head out of the cabin.

"What was all that about?" he asked.

Mordan let go a long, hissing breath. "Human stuff," he said. "It's hard to explain."

"Hard to understand, too," muttered the warforged.

"Hey, Decker?"

"What?"

"Do me a favor. He's got a wand—fires some kind of light. I think it ran out of power. Once he's asleep, could you take a look at it?"

"Sure," said Decker. "And maybe you should get some sleep, too—I've noticed you fleshies get unpredictable when you need it."

● ● ● ◉ ● ● ●

When Mordan awoke, the boat was no longer moving. He sat up, rubbing his eyes, and looked out to find they were moored at a jetty on the edge of Flumakton. Cursing, he went up on deck. Fang was pacing along the landward side as usual, and Decker was sitting on the roof of the cabin, looking intently at the iron defender.

"How long have we been here?" Mordan asked.

Decker swiveled his head to look at the human. "A couple of hours," he replied. "I didn't wake you because I thought you needed to sleep. You were a bit erratic before. Your lady friend came back before dawn—she's asleep in her box now. Oh, and I looked at your friend's wand. I couldn't do anything with it, but I think I know someone who can."

There was a pause as Mordan absorbed the stream of information. "Where is Tarrel?" he asked.

"He went off into town as soon as we got here. Didn't say where he was going."

"Thanks," said Mordan. His stomach grumbled. "I don't suppose you've got any food on board?" he asked.

Decker looked at him blankly. "Food?" he said. "No, no food."

Mordan headed down the gangplank. "If Tarrel comes back before I do, tell him to wait," he said.

Decker went back to staring at Fang.

Like Karrlakton, Flumakton had seen better days. During the war, it had been a base for the powerful fleet that protected the Karrnathi side of the Cyre River, as well as the main river port serving Fort Zombie and the rest of the southern frontier. The river fleet was still here, although much reduced in strength. Its purpose now was to patrol the river and deal with anything that came out of the Mournland.

The massive fortifications of the fleet harbor still dominated the southern end of the town, showing the marks of a century of war, but the boats moored there were fewer and smaller. The stormships had been moved north to Scion's Sound and Karrn Bay, to deter any future attacks from Thrane and Aundair if the fragile peace should fail.

The commercial port, at the northern end of the waterfront, was better kept up than its counterpart in Karrlakton, but this had more to do with civic pride than economic reality. Flumakton had been hit just as hard by the collapse of river trade, but its citizens held on stubbornly in the hope of better times to come. Even so, some of the wharves were abandoned, and grass grew up in the cracks between the cobblestones.

Most traffic to Fort Zombie used the lightning rail from Korth and Atur in the west. However, the single road out of Flumakton led to the fort, almost fifty miles away, and was still used for those goods that were too bulky or too unimportant to travel by lightning rail.

Mordan kept an eye out for Tarrel as he made his way through the commercial district, but he had other business in mind. A few minute's walk from the waterfront, he came to a large two-story building with a large pair of wooden gates. Hanging over the gates was an oversized wagon wheel, painted bright yellow. Opening a door set into one of the gates, he went inside.

The building was constructed around a large courtyard. Built lean-to fashion around the yard were a stable-block, coach-house and smithy, along with tack stores and the other facilities required by a coaching line. The only thing missing were feed bins; this was because the Golden Wheel Coach Company used undead horses, skeletal beasts decommissioned from the Karrnathi armed forces.

As Mordan entered the courtyard, a burly dwarf in a leather apron came trotting out of the smithy, wiping his hands on a rag. His smile faded as he recognized his visitor.

"Oh," he said, "it's you."

Mordan gave him a broad smile.

"It's good to see you too, Balnark," he said. The dwarf held up a stubby hand.

"You needn't think I'm giving you another wagon to take across the river," he said. "Not until you've paid for the last one." Mordan held out his empty hands in a gesture of innocence.

"I wouldn't dream of it," he said. "All I'm looking for is a ride to the fort, for two passengers, one large crate, and a few pieces of luggage. And if this job goes well, I just might be able to settle up with you over that other business."

The dwarf looked at him with distrust, his narrowed eyes almost invisible behind his lowered eyebrows.

"I'll believe that when I'm counting the gold," he snorted. "It'll cost you twelve galifars each to the fort, plus ten for the crate. In advance."

"I only need one way," said Mordan.

"And that's what you'll get," retorted the dwarf. "But I've still got to bring the coach back from the fort, whether you're on it or not. Besides, you're a bad risk. Thirty-four galifars, take it or leave it."

Mordan considered.

"I should haggle you down to twenty," he said, "but I haven't got all day. I'll give you thirty, plus two hundred for the wagon and horses I lost in Metrol. All in House Kundarak bearer bonds. What do you say?"

Balnark's eyebrows twitched—it was the first time Mordan had ever seen him surprised.

"In advance," he said. "And I'll know if they're forged."

"In advance," Mordan conceded. "And they're genuine. Let me just round up my associate."

The dwarf snorted again and stumped off toward the smithy.

* * * ● * * *

It was dusk when they arrived at Fort Zombie. Although living horses could trot faster for a short time, the undead animals pulling the coach were tireless and kept up a pace that would have killed a normal team. Their driver said nothing all the way to the fort, but his eyes were never far from his two passengers; evidently Balnark had told him to be careful of them.

Mordan and Tarrel rarely spoke on the way, either. They were still uncomfortable after their last conversation on the boat, and to make things worse, Tarrel had refused to cover the debt that Mordan owed Balnark. It had taken him almost an hour to bargain the dwarf down to forty galifars—six more than the price he had quoted Mordan—plus a refundable deposit of ten as a surety of the Karrn's good behavior. They cooperated to load the crate holding Brey's coffin onto the roof of the coach but ignored each other for most of the journey.

At last, the fort's ramparts became visible on the horizon. The fort was a rambling structure with a high wall linking many towers. A sleek airship was moored to the top of one of them. As the coach came closer to the fort, they could see the collection of buildings that surrounded it: the lightning rail station, the small Ghallanda inn, and a number of small stores and taverns selling goods shipped in from Korth and Vedykar at inflated prices. Over everything lay the smell of death—the same smell they had noticed on the waterfront at

Karrlakton, but stronger and all-pervading. Tarrel booked them into the guest-house, and after their luggage was unloaded they watched the coach pick up another load of passengers and head back toward Flumakton.

Inside the inn, braziers of incense and bunches of dried herbs hung from the rafters, somewhat masking the smell of the zombies. A fire burned cheerfully in the grate, and the halfling staff was friendly and welcoming. When they had finished a helping of spiced hardhead stew accompanied by Plains flatbread still warm from the oven and several mugs of warming tal, they were both in a considerably better mood.

"So," said Tarrel, laying down his spoon, "now we're here, what do you plan to do?"

"Look for more Vedykar Lancers," Mordan replied, "and find out who Hintram was doing business with. You?"

"I'm going to see what happens to undead who come here for demobilization," said Tarrel. "If I know the procedures, I can figure out the most likely way that the smugglers are skimming them off."

"Isn't anyone going to ask me what I'm going to do?"

They jumped at the sound of Brey's voice. Neither one had noticed her approach.

"I'm not sure I want to know," said Tarrel.

Brey laughed. "Don't worry," she said, "I won't kill anyone. Unless they truly deserve it." A halfling waiter brought a chair for her, and she sat, graciously declining the offer of food.

"Just remember," said Mordan, "the fort is still an active military establishment. They're not going to let just anybody in." Tarrel produced a sheaf of documents with a grin and spread them out on the table.

"Meet Ivello Ebinor, of the *Korranberg Chronicle*," he said. "I've got identification papers, a selection of clippings representing my best work, and a letter of introduction. My assignment is to cover the withdrawal of undead troops from active service, and tell the world how much Karrnath's gesture means for continuing peace."

Mordan cast an eye over the papers. "These are pretty good," he said. "Where did you get them?"

Tarrel smiled. "A Sharn inquisitive doesn't disclose his sources."

Mordan turned to Brey. "I don't expect *you'll* have much trouble finding a way in," he said, "but be careful. They have people who are good at dealing with undead."

"They won't even know I'm there," she said with a smile. "I'll wake you before dawn and let you know what I've found out."

The three rose from the table and left the dining room—Brey to scout the fort by night, and the two mortals to get some sleep.

$\bullet \bullet \bullet \odot \bullet \bullet \bullet$

Mordan was awakened by a hand on his shoulder. Even through the blanket, it was cold. He opened his eyes to find Brey standing over him. It was still dark, but he could just make out her shape in the gloom.

"Not much to report," she said softly. "Just the usual guards. Everyone else is asleep. No sign of any lancers."

"They probably wouldn't be in uniform," Mordan said. "Hintram wasn't."

He could feel Brey's eyes on him in the darkness. He sat up in bed.

"But you'd know them by sight?" she asked.

"Some of them," he said, "not all."

"Were you one of them?" she asked.

He shook his head. "No," he said, "I'm just looking for one of them."

"What will you do when you find him?"

"Depends on what I find."

Brey was silent for a moment. "Listen, Mordan," she said. "Thank you for coming into the Mournland with us. I know you didn't want to."

He looked at her face, but it was too dark to make out her expression. "Have you been talking to Tarrel?"

"No," she replied. "Should I?"

He shook his head. "No," he said. "Anyway, you saved my life, so I guess we're even. Where is he, by the way? I thought the pre-dawn conference was for all of us."

"It is," Brey replied. "Right now, it's around midnight. I just wanted to talk."

Mordan groaned. "What about?"

"Who is it you're looking for?"

"None of your business."

"Maybe not, but it would be a shame if I accidentally killed him, wouldn't it?"

Mordan shrugged. "His name is Galifar ir'Dramon, last known rank lieutenant. Male, human, six feet two inches, build medium, hair blond, eyes blue, age . . . age now would be twenty-eight."

Brey took a moment to digest this. "Are you working for his family?" she asked.

Mordan nodded. "They told the families that the Vedykar Lancers were in Cyre on the Day of Mourning—they're missing, presumed dead. But they disappear from the records six months earlier."

"Which was before I encountered them in Cyre," said Brey.

"Right," said Mordan. "You're the last person I've found who saw them alive."

"Suppose they all died in the accident?" she asked. "Your government wouldn't want anyone to know about what was going on in that place, and the Day of Mourning wasn't that long afterward. It makes a very convenient excuse."

"I thought of that," said Mordan. "They were certainly there. But I didn't see enough bodies. And I didn't see the body of the one I'm looking for. Since Hintram's still alive—or was, till he met you—I'm thinking maybe some more of them are."

"What if you're wrong?" Brey persisted. "What if they all died in there, and we just didn't find the bodies?"

"What about our friend with the ghouls?" he replied. "He had their badge tattooed on his skin. He was undead. That says to me that someone from this Unit 61 got away. And the fact that he wanted us dead—that sounds like whoever got away doesn't want to be found."

"Do you think they're still working for the government?"

"I don't know," Mordan answered. "If they are, it would be a state secret, and we'd probably be arrested just for asking about it. You and Tarrel would, for sure—and the wartime penalties for espionage are still in place here. Even though we're at peace, I'm sure the King would love to have the diplomatic leverage of a couple of alleged spies from Thrane and Breland."

"But no one's tried to arrest us," said Brey.

"They tried to arrest me at Falko's," he said, "but I think it was just because I was there at the time. It was really Falko they were after. And that was right after I'd showed him your sketch of the Unit 61 badge, and he asked his contact at the Ministry of the Dead. Since then, people have tried to kill us, but nobody's tried to arrest us."

The door crashed in. Brey turned and hissed like a cornered animal. Mordan found the tip of a crossbow bolt pricking his throat; he kept his hands in plain sight and stayed still. He couldn't make out more than rough shapes in the darkness, but it seemed that at least three people had entered the room.

"I believe I can remedy that omission," said a polite, slightly wheezy voice from somewhere close to the door. "Please consider yourselves under arrest."

A FEW SIMPLE QUESTIONS
CHAPTER 16

Olarune 24, 999 YK

Mordan sat quietly in the chair as the gnome spread his belongings on the desk. He was only too aware of the two half-elf guards who stood behind him. He wondered where Brey and Tarrel were.

Eventually the gnome seemed satisfied. He sat behind the desk, placing a fist-sized carving of a dragon in front of him. It appeared to be made of sapphire. After muttering something in a language Mordan did not recognize, he looked up with a disarming smile.

"Please excuse my little preparations," he said, "and allow me to introduce myself. My name is Garro Haldin, and I work for the Ministry of the Dead."

"So you got Tarrel's message," said Mordan. He felt one of the guards shift slightly, and tensed himself—but nothing happened. Haldin gestured to the guards and they stepped aside a little. They were still close enough, though, and they loomed deliberately at the edges of his peripheral vision.

"Quite so," said the gnome, "although you had come to our attention some time before that." He looked briefly at a sheaf of papers on the desk.

"Kaz Mordan," he read from the top sheet. "A veteran of the Company of the Skull, five years' service on the Talenta Plains. I presume that this beautiful elven rapier is a trophy from your battles with the Valenar? Several commendations, discharge about six months ago"—he glanced up at Mordan briefly—"your left hand, ah yes. Since that time you have visited Vedykar, Korth, and Karrlakton, and in each of those places you have made enquiries about the Vedykar Lancers, through both official and unofficial channels. I notice from your accent that you are a native of that region, am I correct? And of the landed classes, unless I am very much mistaken."

Haldin waited for Mordan to speak, but the young Karrn held his gaze and said nothing. After a moment, he glanced back down at the papers.

"No records have been found previous to your enlistment— well, perhaps that is not so strange. The Company of the Skull is famed for its lack of curiosity regarding the backgrounds of its recruits."

The gnome looked up again, this time with an apologetic smile.

"In my profession," he said, "it is sometimes necessary to eavesdrop on private conversations. Deplorable, I know, but of great assistance in matters of national security. I'm sure you understand. While we were outside your room preparing to make our entrance, I heard you mention the name Galifar ir'Dramon to your charming companion. I found that most interesting."

"As I am sure you know," he went on, "Galifar ir'Dramon was a junior officer of the Vedykar Lancers. Like many of his comrades, he was a graduate of the Rekkenmark Academy, of good family, and with a distinguished record, both as a cadet and on active service."

"What I found even more interesting, though, is the fact that he had a brother—a young man of about your age, in fact—who deserted from the Rekkenmark Academy some five and a half years ago, apparently to escape court-martial for the murder of a fellow cadet. That would have been at about the time you enlisted in the Company of the Skull, would it not?"

Mordan sat still, and said nothing.

"The name of the missing cadet is Kasmir ir'Dramon, and it appears that he is still wanted in connection with the murder. A curious coincidence, don't you agree, between that name and yours? Kaz is a common abbreviation of Kasmir, I believe, and Mordan happens to be an anagram of Dramon." He chuckled softly.

"But you must forgive me," he went on. "I am afraid that I have the curiosity and weakness for speculation that is so often attributed to my race. And I am sure that a young man of your intelligence and talents would not have chosen such an obvious method of disguising his name. It cannot be anything more than coincidence—like the fact that his records show him to have an aberrant dragonmark similar to yours. Pure coincidence. The fugitive Kasmir ir'Dramon remains at large and has left no trace of his whereabouts."

"But now," he said, "to return to the matter at hand. I had the opportunity to speak with your unfortunate friend Falko—after his demise, sadly, which was most inconvenient. He was good enough to tell me that you were the source of a certain badge, which he showed to one of my colleagues in Karrlakton. May I ask where you got it?"

"From the young lady," Mordan replied.

The gnome's smile brightened. "Ah," he said, "how interesting! I must remember to ask her about it. I am looking forward very much to speaking with her."

"Another thing I learned," he continued, "is that you recognized the smuggler who sold him the swords belonging to the stolen zombies. He said that this individual was a former member of the Vedykar Lancers. I take it that you are sure of this?"

Mordan nodded.

"Unfortunately, Falko was unable to provide me with the name of this person. Do you happen to know it?"

Mordan thought for a moment. He was reluctant to give away what he knew, but he had also heard rumors about what happened to those who fell foul of the Ministry of the Dead. He decided to cooperate for now.

"His name was Berend Hintram," he said. "He graduated from Rekkenmark in the same class as Galifar ir'Dramon."

Haldin nodded and made a note. "Thank you," he said, with an ingratiating smile. "Now, for reasons that you will no doubt appreciate, the Ministry is anxious to find both the Vedykar Lancers and the other unit. So anxious, in fact, that I am authorized to offer you an exchange of information—subject to the preservation of state secrets, of course."

He noticed Mordan's look of surprise and made a small shrug of helplessness.

"It is all really most awkward," he went on, "but the unexpected death of a certain official has had an unintended and extremely inconvenient side-effect. This official was privy to certain information of a sensitive nature, which for reasons of security was never recorded. Among this information, which died with the unfortunate official, is the whereabouts of these two units."

Mordan's jaw dropped. "You *lost* them?" he said, incredulous.

"I know," said Haldin, with an apologetic smile, "it really is most unfortunate. And of course, I need not remind you that this is a state secret, revealed to you in strictest confidence, under penalty of treason. But since you have been so helpful in the matter of Berend Hintram, I feel it is the least I can do."

"So the story about the Lancers being lost on the Day of Mourning was a lie?"

The gnome's smile changed, from one of apology to one of amusement.

"Come now," he said, "I'm sure you already knew that. Although for what it's worth, only a very few people were ever privy to that knowledge."

"What about the undead smugglers?" asked Mordan. "Are there more Lancers involved?"

"I'm afraid that the investigation is not yet complete," Haldin replied, "although a few individuals are assisting the Ministry with its enquiries. So far, none of them has any known connection with the Vedykar Lancers. Based on what we have been able to discover so far, it appears that the smugglers are all members of the Order of the Emerald Claw."

Mordan thought for a moment. "I thought the King had the Emerald Claw disbanded," he said.

"You are quite correct," Haldin replied, "although you will forgive me if I do not go into details. However, we have been aware for some time that the order is still active, in defiance of the King's decree. It has gone underground, as you might say, and is involved in a variety of criminal activities. The theft and smuggling of military undead is only one such operation."

"So Hintram was a member of the Emerald Claw?"

"We have yet to establish that for certain, but it seems likely."

✦ ✦ ✦ ✦ ✦ ✦ ✦

High above the Cyre River, a patch of deeper darkness crossed the night sky. Its shape was indistinct, and it moved swiftly. No one on the ground would have noticed anything more than the momentary shadowing of stars as it passed, as if by a small and fast-moving cloud.

Marbulin Dravuliel gazed out over the rail of the flying ship, his keen elf eyes watching the countryside slip away below him. Build of darkwood, the vessel was more than a hundred feet long, her sleek lines broken only by the four great binding struts holding the ring of dark energy that girdled the vessel. Behind him on the afterdeck, one of his cadaverous servants manned a great wheel of wood and black iron, steering the ship through the night.

At his master's signal, the helmsman swung the wheel to the left, turning away from the dark river and the pale mist of the Mournland. Before long, the bluish flare of a lightning rail carriage could be seen on the ground far below; the ship turned south to follow it, keeping pace easily.

"How much longer?"

The necromancer turned to the tall figure beside him, and smiled indulgently.

"Patience, Captain," he said. "Your warriors will be in action soon enough."

The newcomer had the same wiry build and fierce eyes as the assassin Rolund, but he wore half-plate armor over a faded Karrnathi uniform. On his shoulder was a badge bearing a letter V with two crossed lances, surrounded by a wreath—the insignia of the Vedykar Lancers. His features were those of a typical Karrn, but paler. His hair was the color of ivory, and his eyes were almost completely white, with only a trace of blue. His skin, where it could be seen, was the color of parchment, and covered with tattooed symbols in dark ink.

"What of the vampire?" he asked. His master shrugged casually.

"There will be time for her later," he said. "We may yet hear from Rolund—and if not, she will continue with her quest to find us. After tonight's business is concluded, we can make sure she succeeds."

"Are your . . . men ready?" he asked, after a moment's silence.

The captain nodded. "We are always ready."

"That is good," said Dravuliel, "but you must be sure to wait until the gates are open. I would hate to see you incur any unnecessary casualties."

The captain grinned savagely. His teeth were white and sharp, like those of a great shark. "We are not afraid," he said proudly.

The necromancer smiled. "Of course not," he replied. "You have no reason to be. My motives are entirely selfish. I wish to save myself the trouble of re-animating too many of you after the battle."

"And we are free to kill?" asked the captain.

Dravuliel nodded. "I shall deal with the undead, but the living are entirely yours. Our objective is to wipe out the smugglers, and with them anyone who had contact with our prodigal comrade Hintram. Killing them all is easier than finding out who is a smuggler and who is not. And of course, if you see any suitable candidates for recruitment . . ."

The captain nodded. "We will make spawn of them," he said.

❃ ❃ ❃ ❃ ❃ ❃ ❃

Brey looked down at the silver manacles that secured her to the chair. She tensed one arm experimentally.

"Those chains are enchanted to resist even your strength," said the gnome behind the desk. "These precautions are unpleasant, but necessary. I do hope you will understand."

Brey gave him a thin smile. "What do you want?" she demanded. "If you're going to destroy me, just do it!"

"My dear young lady," replied the gnome, "I assure you that nothing could be further from my mind. If you will forgive me for saying so, Karrnath is more forgiving about these things than Thrane. That is your nationality, is it not?"

"It was," said Brey bitterly, "before this happened to me."

The gnome smiled sympathetically. "My name is Garro Haldin," he continued, "and I serve the Ministry of the Dead, which is part of the government of Karrnath. May I request the privilege of knowing your name?"

"Captain the Honorable Brey ir'Mallon, of the Inmistil Rangers," Brey said stiffly.

The gnome half-bowed.

"An honor, my lady," he said politely. "I have heard much of your illustrious father."

Brey clenched her jaw, and a tear of blood stole down her cheek.

"Please forgive my thoughtlessness," said Haldin solicitously. "I had no wish to distress you."

"Customarily my next question would be to ask what brings you to our country," he went on, "but I am aware that you have been enquiring after two of our military units. Given that Karrnath is still under martial law, it is my duty to ask you why." He looked at her expectantly.

"Because," grated Brey, "they made me what I am."

Haldin looked genuinely shocked for a moment, but quickly restored his expression of polite deference. "Then you were captured?" he asked.

"My whole troop was captured," she said. "Two of our casualties were turned into zombies. I never saw the others again."

"I see," said the gnome. "This is a very serious matter."

Brey laughed bitterly.

"I can imagine what you think, my lady," Haldin went on, "and I am aware of the vile propaganda spread by our enemies regarding our efforts in the development of undead troops. But I beg you to believe me when I say that all of our military was—and remains—bound by the Articles of War. What was done to you and your unfortunate comrades is unforgivable, and you have my personal guarantee that those responsible will be made to account for their actions." He looked directly into Brey's eyes as he spoke—something very few people had done recently. "To which end, I must ask you to tell me everything that happened. I will not insult you by compelling you to speak, but if that should become necessary . . ." He patted the blue dragon figurine that stood before him on the desk—the same one with which he had held her at bay in the guest-house.

● ● ● ◉ ● ● ●

Mordan and Brey looked up as Tarrel came back to the cells, flanked by two half-elf guards. The cell door clanged shut behind him.

"Pleasant little fellow, isn't he?" said Tarrel. "Likes to hear himself talk, though. Still, I've been interrogated by worse."

"What did he ask you?" asked Mordan.

"Not much," said Tarrel. "A few questions to check your

stories, did I know anything else about this place in the Mournland, things like that."

Brey snorted. "He's smart," she said, raising her arms. They were still bound by the silver shackles. "I don't know where he got these things, but I can't do anything with them on. I can't bend the bars, change shape, or anything."

"He's also powerful, behind that friendly face," said Mordan, "or that's what he wants us to think—I can't decide which."

"What makes you say that?" asked Brey.

"He didn't try to intimidate us," Tarrel interjected. "He wants us to think he doesn't need to. I was wondering about that myself."

They sat in silence for a while.

"Still," said Tarrel, "we learned a few things from him."

"He told us a few things," countered Brey. "We don't know if they're true or not."

"They're plausible, at least," said Mordan. "The Lancers were clearly sent on some secret mission when they dropped off the record—why shouldn't they have been assigned to this Unit 61?"

"Which somehow corrupts them, severs contact with the Ministry, and goes renegade?" asked Tarrel. "I don't know."

"Whether it's true or not," Brey put in, "I'm sure that's the story they'll tell if the truth ever comes out. Even in Thrane, we've heard of plausible deniability."

"It puts us in an interesting position, though," Mordan reflected. "If the Ministry decides to cover the thing up, we'd be very inconvenient to have around."

Brey looked up sharply. "Did you hear that?"

❋ ❋ ❋ ❋ ❋ ❋ ❋

Sitting astride his undead steed, Dravuliel watched the lancers disembark from the ship. She hovered just a few feet above the ground, with a loading-ramp lowered. The horsemen formed up by a small wood as the ship rose back into the air, quickly becoming lost against the night sky.

"Take your position, Captain," he said to their leader, "and wait for my signal."

The rider dipped his lance in acknowledgment and galloped away with his troops following him in ranks of three. Dravuliel watched them go, permitting himself a moment of satisfaction. They were fine troops, and their skeletal mounts were almost as fast as the prized Valenar horses, but completely tireless like their riders. They would have served Karrnath well if the War had continued. Now, they would serve him. He struck his heels against his mount's exposed ribs and galloped off after them.

It was less than an hour's ride to the fort. The necromancer dismounted half a mile away, hiding his steed in a small copse. He pulled an amulet from his robe—a piece of red gold worked onto the demon-faced symbol of the Blood of Vol—and cast a spell on himself. Then, keeping to the shadows, he approached the fort. The zombies on the parapets appeared not to notice him, which was good—but the spell did not hide him from the eyes of the living.

He quickly reached an area of deep shadows at the foot of a tower. He could sense that he was close to his goal. Hanging the unholy symbol of Vol around his neck, he knelt for a few moments in muttered prayer. Had anyone been watching, they would have seen him fade like the memory of a dream, becoming pale and translucent until he was barely visible. The prayer complete, he turned to face the base of the tower and walked right through it.

Within a few minutes he had found the barracks where the off-duty zombies were kept. Like the sentinels on the parapet, they did not react when he appeared through the wall. He dropped the spell with a word, and they turned to face him as he raised the gold demon-mask in front of him, but they made no move to attack.

"Go outside," he said softly. One of the zombies opened the door, and the others filed out into the passage. Within a few minutes, almost a score of zombies were assembled.

"Now," said the necromancer, "seek out and destroy all the other zombies in the fort. If anyone tries to stop you, kill them."

THE LAST CHARGE OF THE VEDYKAR LANCERS
CHAPTER 17

Olarune 24, 999 YK

Sergeant Dorn hated night duty. He hated zombies, he hated Fort Zombie, and above all he hated that the War was over.

He had always dreamed of being a bone knight like his father, and he spent his boyhood sharpening his weapon skills and studying with old Father Brand. When his acceptance letter came from the Order's training school at Atur, it was the happiest day of his life. Then, two weeks before he graduated, the War ended.

He'd pushed hard for a posting to Fort Bones, hoping to see action against the Valenar elves on the Talenta Plains, but they'd sent him here instead, to take charge of zombie units being moved to and from the frontier. They said that after a month or two you didn't notice the smell any more, but Sergeant Dorn did. It clung to him even when he was out of uniform. Skeletons didn't have that smell.

He heard a scuffling behind the door. It was probably rats—tempted by the smell, they would sometimes try to eat what they saw as dead meat, and the zombies would stamp them to a pulp. He was taken completely by surprise when the door flew open and zombies started pouring out.

"Halt!" he yelled, jumping to his feet and fumbling for his symbol of Vol. They ignored him.

"Halt!" he repeated, holding the symbol aloft. Still, they ignored him. This had never happened before. Cursing, he drew his longsword and clapped his skull-faced helmet on his head.

The zombies were heading for the guard room, which gave access to the other barrack blocks. Grabbing one by the neck, he tried to pull it out of the doorway. His eyes widened in surprise as a jagged sword was thrust through his back.

He fell to the floor, and the zombies stepped over him on their way out. The last thing he saw was an ancient-looking elf in a robe, following them out of the barracks. The elf turned and looked down at him.

❂ ❂ ❂ ❂ ❂ ❂ ❂

"Bring that," said Dravuliel. One of the zombies threw the dead bone knight over its shoulder, and followed the rest into the guard room.

The remaining guards were quickly overcome, and the zombies soon destroyed those of their fellows that could not be brought under the necromancer's control. The alarm was raised only when the undead troops poured out of the barracks and began attacking the zombies on the walls.

Taken completely by surprise, the defenders of Fort Zombie were thrown back initially, but quickly rallied. Bone knights and living troops formed up in the fort's central courtyard and began to cut down the undead with sword and spell. For a moment, it looked as though the undead revolt would be contained—but then more zombies entered the fray. These were the guards and others who had died in the barracks, and several of them wore bonecraft armor. As the skirmish continued, it became increasingly difficult to tell friend from foe; all wore the insignia of Fort Zombie, and the dead would rise up and attack the living. In the confusion many defenders were mistakenly slain by their own comrades.

No one saw the elf as he moved through the carnage, protected by magical invisibility. He stood at the edge of the melee, admiring his handiwork. Then he touched a nearby corpse and it, too, became invisible. Feeling for its skull, he gouged out an eye and pressed a black onyx into the socket; his chanted invocation went unheard in the din of battle.

"Open the gates," he said. Unnoticed by the living, footprints appeared with no apparent cause, heading for the gates of the fort.

* * * * * * *

Haldin the gnome hurried into the cell block, flanked by his two half-elf guards, who were carrying the three prisoners' belongings.

"Quickly," he said, "the fort is under attack!" His habitual smile was missing; he looked grim and purposeful. He was dressed in well-crafted half-plate armor and carried a repeating crossbow. Brey saw with a start that the emblem of the Silver Flame was inlaid into its stock.

Mordan buckled his rapier to his side and donned his elven cloak. Tarrel rummaged through his sack and other belongings, and then cursed.

"The wand!" he exclaimed. Then he stopped short and made a helpless gesture.

"It was out of power anyway," he said, half to himself.

Mordan suddenly remembered that he had asked Decker to examine it; it was probably still with him in Flumakton.

"Here!" cried Haldin, tossing a wand to the Brelander. Tarrel studied it for a moment, and nodded.

Brey was already out of the cell and looking out of a window into the courtyard. Her eyes were wide with surprise.

"Something has taken control of the zombies!" cried the gnome, in answer to her unasked question. "We need everyone's help, or the fort will be overrun!"

Weapons drawn, the six of them ran down the passage and out into the courtyard.

Everything was chaos; some of the bone knights had rallied the few zombies still outside the attackers' control and set them against the waves of undead that poured from the barracks. Elsewhere, several figures wearing the distinctive bonecraft armor of the bone knights shambled along with the attacking zombies. In the darkness and confusion, it was not easy to tell living defenders from those recently raised by the attackers.

"Get me into the middle of them!" yelled Haldin, shooting his crossbow as he ran. His two guards flanked him, cutting a path through the slaughter with their longswords.

Brey grabbed the nearest zombie by the neck and pulled it from the fray, breaking its back over her knee and leaving it flopping uselessly on the ground. It could have been an attacker or a defender; she neither knew nor cared. Her powerful fingers were bent into claws, and she displayed her fangs in a feral snarl.

Taking careful aim with his wand, Tarrel loosed a point of red light into the midst of a group of zombies that were still emerging from the barracks. It blossomed into a cloud of fire, destroying several of them and setting the rest ablaze. They lurched onward, ignoring the fire that spread over their clothing and bodies. The fire cast an eerie, flickering light over the scene, making it seem more than ever like a nightmare.

Mordan grabbed Tarrel's arm, and the two of them followed Haldin. A zombie tried to claw the gnome down from behind but fell to the young Karrn's rapier. As the two guards carved a path for their master, his former prisoners guarded his back.

At Haldin's signal, they stopped in the midst of the battle. Slinging his crossbow on his shoulder, the gnome raised something high over his head—the blue dragon statuette from his desk, Mordan noticed—and howled something in an arcane tongue. The Karrn winced as a bright blue-white light appeared above the carving, hovering there for an instant before shooting outward in all directions. An expanding ring of light shot over the combatants, and wherever it touched the undead, they fell like wheat before a scythe.

The defenders paused and lowered their weapons, half-unable to believe what had happened. Beyond the reach of the light, more zombies were lurching forward; there were scant seconds before the onslaught would be renewed.

"Form a line!" Mordan found himself with his rapier held high, shouting orders as he had done as an officer in the Company of the Skull. In the absence of anyone else taking charge, the defenders obeyed, drawing themselves into a rough order of battle and preparing to receive the next wave of attackers. Facing the barracks from which the zombies were coming, they did not see the fort's main gate opening.

❋ ❋ ❋ ❋ ❋ ❋ ❋

Standing invisible on the parapet above the gates, Marbulin Dravuliel also winced as he saw the sacred light sweep the zombies to the ground. He couldn't see the source of it, but he knew that someone in the midst of the battle had powers that he hadn't counted on. It was time for the next stage of the plan.

As he had anticipated, the defenders were focused on the zombie barracks, and had their backs to him. His sharp eyes watched the invisible zombie's footprints as they slowly made their way to the gates, and they went out of sight below him he heard the creak of the gates opening. He held a hand up and pronounced an ancient syllable: four globes of light streaked upward and hung dancing in the air more than two hundred feet above the fort. They would be visible for miles.

With the signal given, the necromancer turned his attention back to the fort's interior. The tide of the battle was turning in the defenders' favor; broken bodies littered the ground, and they were gradually pushing the remaining zombies back toward the barracks complex. A movement at the edge of the melee caught his eye, and he was pleasantly surprised to see a tall vampire woman crushing the skull of a zombie in her bare hands. Her long red hair, and the patched uniform beneath her cloak, told him that Rolund had failed in his mission.

"Never mind," he murmured to himself with a smile. "It's fitting that I should clear up this loose end . . . personally." Moving smoothly along the parapet, he pulled a small cloth pouch from a pocket in his robe, opening the neck and scattering a glittering dust into the air as he chanted.

* * * ◉ * * *

Somewhere, deep in the back of her mind, Brey was worried. As a paladin of the Silver Flame she had certainly never shied away from battle; she had even felt satisfaction in the destruction of Thrane's enemies. But this was different. For the first time, she had given free rein to the beast within her. She had summoned all the dark and violent impulses that she had spent so long resisting, and added her rage against her captivity and the thing she had become. She had hated the undead even before her captivity, but now her hatred was unquenchable.

She lunged, spun, tore, and ripped, scattering zombies before her like a whirlwind. The rhythm of combat became almost a meditation. One part of her being gloried in the destruction, drunk on the rage and violence. Another wondered if she would be able to regain control of herself once this was over. Deeper still, a third voice—one which sounded eerily like old Provost Jeffin, her confessor and personal mentor in the Order—pondered the ethics of using the weapons of evil in the cause of good.

Something washed over her like a cold wind, chilling her even though she had lost the ability to feel cold. The zombies in front of her crumbled into dust, and she felt dizzy. Looking up, she could see no visible cause for what had happened; shaking herself to throw off the strange chill, she loped over to the barracks, where the defenders were forcing the zombies back.

At the center of the defenders' line, Mordan found himself in command. No officer from the fort had challenged his authority, and the defenders looked to him for orders. Keeping the line tight, he advanced against the mass of zombies, enveloping them and pushing them back. To his left, Haldin was pulling back the lever on his repeating crossbow. Judging by the effect his bolts were having on the undead, Mordan guessed that the silver flame symbol on the stock was more than mere decoration. To his right, Tarrel was using the gnome's wand of fireballs to break up the zombies' ranks, disrupting their formation and making the combat easier for the fighting line. Haldin's half-elf guards stood shoulder to shoulder with the fort's troops, wielding their longswords to deadly effect. The battle had been hard, but it had finally turned in their favor.

❖ ❖ ❖ ❖ ❖ ❖ ❖

On the parapet, Dravuliel watched with surprise as the vampire shrugged off his spell. She had become more powerful than he had expected. Still, no matter. From the corner of his eye he saw a line of pale riders streaming toward the fort, whose defenders, still intent on destroying the last few zombies, had their backs to the gates. He moved to a good vantage point, his smile as invisible as the rest of him. He was going to enjoy this.

The Vedykar Lancers came through the open gates of Fort Zombie at full gallop, four abreast. Without slowing their pace, they shifted to a wedge formation and couched their lances, striking the rear of the defensive line like a thunderbolt. Troops perished beneath the hooves of their skeletal horses, and writhed on the points of their weapons. Fully half the surviving defenders were mowed down by the first charge.

With an eagle's feather tucked into his belt, Dravuliel threw himself off the parapet, soaring like a bird above the melee. The defenders were wavering; their line was disintegrating from the force of the lancers' charge. Reaching into a belt-pouch, he pulled out a small, smooth brown object about the size of an olive. He squeezed it in his fist, and drops of blood dripped out of it and sprinkled onto the defenders below.

Mordan had turned an instant before the charge struck, alerted by the sound of galloping hooves. Knocking a lance aside with his rapier, he dodged the thrashing hooves of an undead horse and struck out, severing a leg and bringing it crashing to the ground. Haldin whirled with him and loosed a bolt at one of the riders, knocking him—it?—backward out of the saddle. Tarrel aimed his wand, but the attackers were too close—a fireball would do as much damage to friend as to foe. Transferring the wand to his left hand, he drew his shortsword and waited.

Slinging his crossbow, Haldin raised his dragon statuette again and began to chant. Mordan stood behind him, his rapier flickering like silver lightning as he deflected lance-points and hooves from striking the gnome.

The riders looked very much like the creature that had attacked them in the attic in Karrlakton, and then again in the Mournland with the help of the ghouls. They looked as though they had once been human, but their parchment-pale skin was stretched tight over shriveled muscle and bony faces. Their teeth were sharp, and glittered in the light of the several small fires that had broken out in the courtyard. Most noticeable to Mordan, though, was the badge each of them wore on its shoulder—the V and crossed lances of the Vedykar Lancers. With the fury of their charge spent, they had dropped their lances and were drawing longswords.

They did not waver in response to Haldin's chanting, and Mordan wondered if he had failed—but then he noticed that several of the undead horses were bucking and rearing, as if trying to turn and flee. Their riders struggled to control them, and for a moment the attack wavered.

The break might have come too late. The defenders were

shaken by the unexpected charge, and several zombies were still fighting; they were beset on two fronts. As Mordan began shouting orders, he saw panic in the eyes of some. A few defenders broke and tried to flee, only to be cut down by lancers on one side or zombies on the other.

"Do something!" he roared at Haldin. If the gnome could turn undead, he could probably cast a spell to rally the troops. Haldin nodded, extending a hand in the direction of the most badly affected troops. A few words, and they shook off their fear, falling back into line.

Then something dark flew through the air, landing in the midst of the zombies. By now, the defenders had them pinned against the wall of the barracks complex, with barely room to move. Lithe as a cat, Brey landed on her feet in front of them, signaling Mordan to turn his troops around to face the new threat. He waved an acknowledgment and issued the order. Brey would take care of the zombies.

As the vampire woman set to work, the other defenders faced about and formed up, linking shields against the undead horsemen. But Mordan could see that they were tiring. They needed something to encourage them.

He somersaulted over the top of the line, landing beside one of the undead horses. A stab from his rapier dropped one rider to the ground, and he leaped into the saddle, holding his rapier in his teeth as he wrapped the reins around the stump of his left arm. He pulled the reins back and his mount reared; at the same time, he lifted his rapier high, shouting "Karrnath!" at the top of his voice. Even those defenders who didn't hear him could understand the symbolism of his action, and a ragged cheer went up from their line.

The lancers were fast and skillful—more so, Mordan suspected, than they had been in life—but they were no match for a soldier who had spend five years fighting the dreaded Valenar cavalry. He was well accustomed to undead mounts, too—the Company of the Skull used them extensively for long-range patrols on the Talenta Plains, matching their tirelessness against the superior speed of the living Valenar horses. This one, he noticed, was quicker, more responsive—no doubt Unit 61 had improved its horses as well as the undead troops is produced.

Dodging and twisting in the saddle, Mordan laid about him, stabbing and slashing at horses and riders alike. He fought with savage intensity, knowing that he could hold out for only a limited time against so many enemies. His horse reared and kicked as he fought, backing gradually toward the line of defenders. This was deliberate; he wanted to avoid giving the undead lancers space to surround him, and by giving ground, he was slowly drawing them toward his troops.

A lancer chopped at his horse's head with a longsword, nearly severing its neck. The animal staggered and regained its footing, but it was obvious that another such blow would kill it. A crossbow bolt whizzed past his head, burying itself in his opponent's throat; the shot would have killed a living man, but the undead lancer merely snarled. Mordan followed up with a thrust to the heart. The wight displayed its sharp teeth in a savage grin and raised its longsword.

At that moment, a great shout went up from the defenders. Inspired by their unofficial leader, they charged into the lancers with sword and spear, surrounding Mordan and his damaged horse. A lancer fell from the saddle scant feet away; the Karrn pulled his feet from the stirrups, crouching briefly on the saddle before jumping to the newly vacant mount.

The lancers withdrew abruptly, wheeling their horses and opening space between themselves and the defenders. Tarrel took advantage of their maneuver to launch a fireball into their left flank; a couple of the undead horses fell smoking to the ground, while their riders sprang from the saddle and rolled to extinguish their burning clothing. Mordan risked a glance behind him and saw that Brey had destroyed the last of the zombies and was making her way to the end of the defenders' line.

The two sides looked at each other. The defenders braced for another charge, raising their shields, setting spears, and readying whatever other weapons they had. But the charge never came. Instead, the lancers broke into two blocks, with an empty space between them. Riding down that corridor, at a sedate trot, came one who appeared to be their commander. Where his skin was visible, it bore elaborate tattoos. His armor gleamed, despite a couple of dints and buffets from the fight. He sat proudly in the saddle, flying the pennant of the Vedykar Lancers from the tip of his spear. Coming level with the front rank of his own troops, he handed the lance to a subordinate and drew a gleaming longsword. Still at a parade trot, he rode to within a few feet of Mordan, a savage grin on his face.

"Hello, brother," he said.

A FAMILY REUNION
CHAPTER 18

Olarune 24, 999 YK

Kaz Mordan stared at the apparition before him. It was hard to recognize his brother's features under the tattoos, and the shrunken flesh concealed his muscular build—but something in the tone of his voice gave him away. It was dry, like a man with a sore throat, but the familiar contempt was unmistakable.

"Gali?" Mordan breathed. "Dol Arrah, what's happened to you?"

Gali's grin widened, showing wickedly pointed teeth. "I could ask you the same question," he rasped. "What did you do after you deserted from Rekkenmark—run away and join the Company of the Skull under a false name? At least you lost that puppy fat"—he glanced down at Mordan's left arm—"and that's not all, by the look of it. Did someone get tired of that damned mark of yours?" He laughed. "I'm going to enjoy this." Bringing his longsword up to shoulder height, he tapped his mount's ribs with his spurs.

With a roar, the defenders swept forward to protect their

leader. Gali raised his left hand and barked a word. Before they had gone a couple of paces, a wave of dark energy swept over them. Mordan was rocked in his saddle, but unharmed—behind him, more than a dozen people fell to the ground, dead. The others faltered.

"This is a family matter," Gali said. "You shouldn't interfere." The remaining defenders drew themselves together into a tight knot, watching the two riders. He spurred his mount again and charged.

Mordan countercharged, rapier held forward. Ducking under the slashing longsword, he thrust at his brother's ribs. Gali's laugh turned into a yelp of pain and surprise. Turning their horses, they faced each other again. Gali raised his longsword in an ironic salute.

"Well struck, little brother!" he said. "I see you've learned to fight a little better since I last saw you." He dipped a finger in the dark blood that oozed from his side, licking it with a long, pointed tongue. "That's a very nice sword, too," he observed, pointing toward the elven rapier. "But it won't help you. I always win—remember?"

"Father thinks you're dead!" said Mordan. "You should see what it's done to him!"

Gali laughed again. "That's good, coming from you!" he sneered, then raised his voice to address the defenders.

"Your hero!" he cried. "The one you're hiding behind! Did you know he deserted from Rekkenmark rather than face a court-martial? He disgraced his family and foreswore his oath of loyalty! This is who you're following!"

"Besides," he added, lowering his voice, "I *am* dead."

Gali spurred his horse forward again. This time, he expected his brother's dodge, and Mordan was knocked from his horse by a sweeping blow that opened a deep wound in his left shoulder. He hit the ground hard but rolled back to his feet as Gali turned his skeletal mount again.

With a blur of motion, Brey was standing between them, glaring at the lancer.

"You're mine," she spat, "you and all your dead friends!" Behind her, Tarrel had raised his wand, and Haldin his crossbow.

Gali smiled. "Well, well," he said, "I never thought I'd see you again! The vampire experiment was terminated, by the way. Much too unreliable."

"As I said before," he continued, "this is between me and my little brother here. I must ask you not to interfere"—he raised his hand again in the direction of the surviving defenders—"or more innocents will suffer."

Their eyes locked. Slowly, Brey backed away. He gave Tarrel and Haldin a significant look, and they too lowered their weapons.

"But do keep a spot on your dance card open for later," Gali said to Brey. "I'd be delighted to destroy you after I've concluded this little bit of family business."

Swinging a leg over his horse's skull, he slid down from the saddle, slapping the beast on its bony rump. It trotted obediently back to the Lancers' ranks.

He tossed his longsword to a subordinate and strolled casually across to where Mordan was waiting.

"Let's do this properly," he said, stretching his wiry arms and balling his fists. He adopted a boxing stance and raised one eyebrow.

"Not a chance," said Mordan. "I know what you are. You keep your magic, and I'll keep my sword."

"If that's how you want it," sighed Gali. "Either way, you're going to be my slave once this is over—and I think the first thing I'll do is watch you kill your friends."

Barking a complex syllable, he raised his hand again. Mordan dropped and rolled as a ray of multicolored light shot past his head; he thought he saw his brother's tattoos flash briefly as the ray sprang from his hand.

Gali lunged, knocking the rapier's blade aside with a bony forearm. His fist crashed into Mordan's face like a hammer, knocking him onto his back. Blood poured out of his nose; a wave of burning cold filled him with nausea and turned his muscles to water. He tried to ignore it, keeping the point of the rapier between him and his brother.

Gali looked down at him, and then backed off a couple of paces. "Come," he taunted, "at least try to put up a fight!" He waited for Mordan to get to his feet, and attacked again.

This time Mordan was ready. Running to meet his brother, he somersaulted into the air at the last moment, flying over the incoming blow and leaving a deep gash in Gali's forehead. Landing in a crouch, he turned to face his brother again.

"That's better!" Gali grinned. "But it won't do you any good." He wiped the thick, black blood from his forehead with the back of his hand—and as Mordan watched, the cut sealed itself without leaving a scar.

"You see?" he crowed. "Of course, you won't be able to do this after I've killed you. Or cast any spells. No, you'll be much weaker. Just as you always have been. But don't worry—I'll keep you intact as long as you continue to amuse me."

He walked forward slowly, arms spread as if daring Mordan to attack him. A worried murmur spread through the defenders. Mordan felt a brief pang of despair, but then he noticed that blood was still oozing from his brother's side, and dripping onto the sand of the courtyard. He had done some damage with that first thrust.

Still wearing a mocking smile, Gali was just within reach of his rapier. Mordan feinted to the left and then cut back right, burying the blade almost hilt-deep in his brother's chest. Again, he saw shock and pain contort the fleshless face, and the blue-white eyes burned with hatred.

The back of Gali's fist crashed into Mordan's chest, throwing him back a couple of paces. The deadly chill washed over him again, but this time he did not feel any weaker. Instead, he felt a sudden warmth from the charm-bag that the old halfling shaman had given him, spreading through his body and driving the chill out. But his breathing became labored and painful—he guessed that Gali's blow had broken one or more ribs. He couldn't take much more of this punishment—and Gali knew it.

Through the pain and fatigue, a sudden realization came to him. Gali wasn't just toying with him for pleasure—he was giving his magical healing time to work between attacks. Like Brey, Gali was undead, which made him tireless. He was gradually wearing his brother down, and time was on his side. The only way to win this fight was to take it to Gali, wounding him faster than he could heal and overpowering him before Mordan became too exhausted to keep on fighting.

Summoning all his reserves of strength and willpower, Mordan launched a flurry of attacks. The tip of the rapier seemed to be everywhere, weaving and probing, keeping Gali at arm's length. For the first time, Mordan realized that despite all his unnatural powers, Gali was a hair slower than he was. Just as when he was fighting the Valenar, Mordan had to put his faith in speed and skill, in striking and not being struck.

His darting attacks were beginning to have an effect. Gali was oozing dark blood from a dozen small nicks and a couple of more serious wounds. He tried to move inside his brother's reach and use his life-draining fists again, but Mordan skipped backward, cutting a welt across Gali's forearm as he did so.

Gali snarled in frustration and lunged, ignoring a thrust to the abdomen and striking a heavy blow to the side of Mordan's head. He followed this up with a savage kick that sent his brother sprawling, and threw himself forward in an attempt to pin him to the ground. Mordan rolled aside and was halfway to his feet when Gali hit the ground; a lightning thrust through the ribs brought a yell of pain and rage.

Gali leaped to his feet and tried to back off, but Mordan advanced on him, cutting and thrusting with the speed of a striking cobra. Gali dodged and wove, but couldn't avoid all of the attacks. He seemed to stumble, and Mordan aimed a thrust straight at his heart.

But the feinted stumble turned into a roll, taking Gali under the thrust. He clawed at his brother's feet, knocking him down again. Mordan's head hit the ground with sickening force; he was stunned, and the rapier fell from his grasp. In that moment, Gali was on him.

Kaz Mordan gritted his teeth and fought with all his strength. His brother's face blotted out most of the sky, laughing with savage glee as he pinned Mordan down, kneeling on his chest and holding his right wrist against the ground. Mordan lashed out with his left arm, trying to block the punches that rained down on his head and face.

"Why don't you use that filthy mark on me now, worm?" snarled Gali, using the childhood nickname he had invented for his despised younger brother. "Why don't you? It can't hurt me now—in fact, it'll make me stronger!" His fist crashed down in time with his words. Mordan's head was swimming with the force of the blows; he held onto consciousness with all his strength.

At last, the stump of his left arm blocked Gali's fist. They wrestled, Gali trying to reach past the protective arm and Mordan fending him off. With a growl of frustration, Gali let go of his brother's right wrist and struck him hard across the face. From the corner of his eye, Mordan could see where his rapier had fallen, and ignoring the blow, he lunged with his right hand, grabbing the hilt. Before Gali knew what had happened, the rapier transfixed his neck, piercing right through.

Gali's cry of pain hissed through his punctured throat, bubbling the dark blood that poured from the wound. He rolled backward, clawing at the rapier, but Mordan kept a firm grip on the hilt, pulling the sword out of his brother's neck and plunging it into his heart. Gali fell backward, gripping the blade with bloody hands as he struggled to pull it out of his chest. Using the momentum of his brother's fall to supplement his own fading strength, Mordan rolled to his feet, forcing the blade deeper and twisting it in the wound. Gali clawed feebly at his legs, and then his limbs went slack.

"No . . ." he rasped, blood bubbling from his throat. "You . . . worm . . ." Then his head fell back, and his white eyes rolled up sightlessly.

Mordan leaned on the rapier for a moment and then pulled it from his brother's chest. He looked down at the body, as if trying to think of something to say. Then he turned, took half a step away, and fell down on his face.

❋ ❋ ❋ ◉ ❋ ❋ ❋

As if uncertain what to do, attackers and defenders stared at the prone figures that lay in the space between them.

Then a blazing point of red light shot from the ranks of the defenders, blossoming into flame in the midst of the undead lancers. A shout went up, and the surviving defenders surged forward. At their head was a red-haired vampire woman who tore into the opposing ranks with unstoppable ferocity.

The counterattack flowed over and around Mordan's fallen body, and Haldin ran forward to kneel over him. Reaching into a belt-pouch, he sprinkled a bright, glittering dust over the young Karrn, muttering a prayer as he did so. The dust gleamed briefly with a blue-green light, then disappeared; Mordan's eyes flickered briefly, but he did not move. Placing the blue dragon statuette on Mordan's chest, Haldin bowed his head and began a low chant, which he repeated over and over with urgent intensity. A pale luminescence grew in the heart of the dragon, flaring briefly before going out. At the same time, Mordan struggled to sit up.

"What happened?" he asked, a little dazed. "Did I . . . ?"

Haldin nodded. "Come on," he said, shouting above the din of battle, handing the young Karrn his rapier. "Let's finish this!"

He gestured to the fighting. The defenders of Fort Zombie were locked in combat with the remaining wights. In addition to the surviving Vedykar Lancers, they now included several defenders who had been killed and risen as wight spawn.

Mordan put a hand on the gnome's shoulder.

"That thing with the light," he yelled, "can you do it again?"

"No," yelled Haldin, "but I can do something almost as good!" He trotted to within a few paces of the fighting and raised the blue dragon statuette over his head again, howling an incantation. The carving glowed briefly, and a half-dozen of the wights simply crumbled to dust, leaving their mortal opponents staring in disbelief. He grinned at Mordan and unslung his crossbow from his back.

Mordan vaulted into the saddle of a riderless undead horse, wrapping the reins around his left arm and kicking the beast in the ribs. It lurched forward through a gap in the defenders' line, riding down one wight as he plunged his rapier into the chest of another, lifting it off the ground and hurling it back. Seeing him recovered from his duel, the defenders nearest him cheered and redoubled their efforts. From the corner of his eye he saw Brey cutting a swath of destruction through the attackers, breaking backs and tearing off heads in a frenzy. An undead steed reared, as if to trample her—but like a zombie in northern Cyre three years ago, she caught its hooves in her hands and twisted, throwing it aside with inhuman strength. Its rider tried to leap clear, but she slammed into the wight in mid-air, landing with its chest between her feet and the hard ground of the courtyard. There was a crunch, and it stopped moving.

❂ ❂ ❂ ◉ ❂ ❂ ❂

Tarrel made his way to the parapet, to give him a better view of the battle and enable him to place the fireballs from his wand without harming any of his allies. Intent on the struggle below, he didn't hear stealthy feet behind him. A searing cold stabbed through his chest; turning in pain and surprise, he saw a robed elf standing just a few paces away. Without thinking, the half-elf raised his wand and loosed a fireball at his attacker, lighting up the whole parapet in a welter of flame.

A crossbow bolt slammed into the elf's chest, interrupting the casting of his next spell. The half-elf raised his wand for another fireball. Pulling the bolt from his ribs, the necromancer launched himself backward over the parapet; the fireball missed him, exploding harmlessly more than a hundred yards away.

Tarrel saw the elf pull a feather from his belt as he fell, howling a magical phrase; an invisible force buoyed him up before he hit the ground, and he sped off through the air, back to the dark wood.

● ● ● ◉ ● ● ●

In the courtyard, the few remaining bone knights had formed up; led by Brey and Mordan, they were beating the wights back. Some had been turned and were fleeing through the open gates, while others fought on with unrelenting savagery. Running to join the fray, Haldin added his power to the turning, and another half-dozen of the creatures turned and fled. The rest of them wavered for a moment, and then followed their escaping comrades. With a great cheer, the defenders of Fort Zombie went on the attack.

Mordan was first through the gates, his undead steed flying like a Valenar purebred. Whatever else these monsters had done, he thought, they had certainly improved the horses. Close behind him was a small wedge of bone knights, some on skeletal steeds that they too had commandeered from the attackers, and some lagging behind on the fort's own mounts. Beside them, a huge red-brown wolf loped in pursuit of the fleeing wights, its eyes burning with an unnatural red glow.

Dawn was beginning to break on the horizon when they reached a dark wood about a half-mile away from the fort. They had overtaken the wights who had escaped on foot, leaving them to the other defenders as they tried to catch the remaining lancers. They were almost at the wood when a huge black shape lifted into the air, surrounded by a crackling ring of dark energy. It pointed its nose northward, and climbed rapidly as it sped away.

The riders pulled up short, unable to do anything except watch it go. Mordan gestured at the wolf, indicating the light on the eastern horizon.

"Brey," he shouted, "get under cover!" The animal glanced at the sky and headed back to the fort at a run.

"The rest of you," Mordan shouted, holding up his rapier, "follow me!" Wheeling his horse round, he led them back to where the few stragglers from the attacking force were struggling to stay ahead of their pursuers.

Their attack was on a smaller scale than the last charge of the Vedykar Lancers, but its effect was similar. Attacked from all sides, abandoned by their master, the wights had nowhere to go, and nothing to do but die.

One of them, wearing the tattered remnants of a Lancers uniform, managed to fight his way free and run. Riding out of the melee, Mordan chased the fugitive down, felling him with a pommel-stroke. Before the wight could do more than get to his knees, the tip of Mordan's enchanted rapier was tickling the pit of his throat.

"You're not going anywhere," grated the Karrn, "until you've answered a few questions."

CHAPTER 19

Olarune 25, 999 YK

The commander of Fort Zombie was not happy. Mordan, Tarrel, and Haldin sat in the office while the Captain of Corpses paced back and forth behind his desk.

"You know why the fort was attacked," he said as he paced, "and you did *nothing* to warn me?"

Haldin cleared his throat diplomatically. "My dear Captain," he said, "I assure you that if we had known in advance, we would certainly have brought the danger to your attention. But the fact is, we were taken as much by surprise as you were. It is simply that, once the attack was under way, we recognized some of the attackers, and we believe we understand their motive."

"Motive?" echoed the Captain. "Well, I must admit to a certain curiosity regarding why I just lost more than half the fort's fighting strength!" He paused to catch his breath, towering over the seated gnome.

Haldin looked up at him with a polite but neutral expression.

"Well," the Captain said, a little calmer, "let's have it. I'll have to put *something* in my report."

"As you will no doubt recall," said Haldin, "I was sent here to follow up on certain information that has come to the Ministry's attention. It seems that a ring of smugglers has been—shall we say, diverting—zombies that pass through the fort on their way to demobilization, and selling them as laborers on the black market."

The Captain looked puzzled.

"So what's the connection," he asked, "between a gang of zombie smugglers and an undead army descending on my fort?"

"A very fair question," observed Haldin. "We believe they were intent on putting the smugglers out of business, just as we were. It seems that one of the gang's key members had information about them, and they wanted that information suppressed. Like us, they were not sure exactly who was involved; unlike us, they apparently decided on the simple expedient of wiping out the fort's entire population."

"The cavalry were once members of the Vedykar Lancers," Mordan put in. "The smuggler's main agent at Karrlakton was a former Vedykar Lancer named Berend Hintram. Our guess is that he deserted before the Lancers turned undead."

"We have information that associates the Vedykar Lancers with a secret undead development project," Haldin continued. "Initially their mission was to provide security, but it seems that they became subjects in some of the experiments. Regrettably, the project cut off communications with the Ministry shortly before the end of the War, despite our best efforts to locate them."

"We also have a witness," Tarrel interjected, "who saw

necromantic experiments this renegade unit carried out on live prisoners from Thrane, in direct violation of the Articles of War."

"So as you can see, Captain," Haldin said, "it is of the utmost importance that we trace last night's attackers and bring those responsible to justice—and on behalf of the Ministry, I can assure you of our full cooperation. I shall make it clear in my own report that the attack could not possibly have been foreseen, and that the fort's garrison acted with great heroism in the face of enormous danger."

The Captain of Corpses stopped pacing for a moment and cast a critical eye over Mordan and Tarrel.

"And these two?" he asked.

"They are independent consultants," the gnome replied, "assisting the Ministry with the investigation. There is one other—a young lady, formerly of the army of Thrane—who is *resting* at the moment. Your troops may have mentioned her in their reports."

"Ripping off heads and throwing horses to the ground?" said the Captain. "Yes, they mentioned her. They said she's a vampire."

"Quite so," said Haldin. "A most unfortunate victim of illegal experimentation, as my associate from Breland pointed out. As you can appreciate, it is absolutely vital that these miscreants are found and brought to account—not only for their deeds here, but also in the interests of maintaining the peace between Karrnath and Thrane. This matter must be handled with great care or it could result in a serious international incident."

The Captain thought about this for a while.

"I can't spare any troops," he said, "if that's what you're driving at."

"Not at all, my dear Captain," replied Haldin. "The Ministry would not dream of further draining your resources at this most unfortunate time. All we ask is to impose upon your hospitality for another day or two—perhaps less. With the help of your troops, my associates managed to capture one of last night's attackers, and we wish to question him. We shall, of course, be happy to share all relevant information with you."

* * * * * * *

"Are you sure you're really a gnome?" Tarrel asked later. "I thought sharing information for nothing was against your principles."

"Quite sure, my dear Tarrel," Haldin chuckled. "Although I begin to wonder whether you are really a Medani inquisitive. Surely you noticed how I limited the offer to *relevant* information?"

"Without defining what is and isn't relevant," Tarrel said. "You'll have to excuse me; I had a long night."

They made their way across the courtyard, where burial details were taking away the bodies of the slain. Carts piled with the dead—attacker and defender alike—were being loaded onto carts drawn by skeletal horses. From the fort they went to the lightning rail station, where they were stacked like cordwood in covered, windowless carts painted black and bearing the insignia of the fort. Normally used for moving active zombies rather than corpses, they would convey the dead to Atur, along with a request for replacement zombies and bone knights.

Mordan saw two troopers picking up the body of his brother, and he wandered over to watch. Gali's eyes were closed, and he looked almost peaceful. One arm hung over the edge of the cart, and Mordan folded it across his chest.

"Have you decided what you'll tell your family yet?"

Mordan jumped. He hadn't heard Tarrel approaching.

He shrugged. "I don't know," he said. "Have you decided what you'll tell your client?"

"Why?" asked the Brelander. "So we can tell the same story? Don't worry. My guess is, your government will want to keep this very quiet. It might be easiest to let the family go on thinking that he died in Cyre."

Still looking at Gali's body, Mordan made no reply.

Haldin came over to them. "I'd like to examine this one," he said to the soldiers. They hesitated for a moment, and then unloaded Gali's body from the cart. Following the gnome, they laid him on a bunk in the barracks. Dismissing the soldiers with a gesture, Haldin began to examine the body.

"Interesting," he said. "Have you seen tattoos like these before?"

Mordan didn't answer, but Tarrel pulled out the diagram he had taken from the workroom beneath the ruined fort. Haldin took it eagerly.

"Fascinating," he said. "You found this in the Mournland, I take it?"

"That's right," said Tarrel. "There were a few works in progress, too. Brey said the spell-casting zombies that captured her were tattooed as well."

"Ah," said Haldin, "of course!"

Tarrel looked at him quizzically.

"It's a process known as spellstitching," Haldin explained. "The tattoos are patterns of magical energy. I've never seen an actual example before."

"So that's how he was able to kill all those troops when they tried to help me?" asked Mordan.

Haldin shook his head. "No," he replied. "Spellstitching is limited in its effects. That spell was far too powerful. He must have had some other source of magic."

"He must have had another source of strength, too," observed Tarrel. "He was a lot harder to kill than the other wights."

"I have a theory about that," said Haldin, "although it doesn't explain everything."

"Care to share it?" asked Tarrel with a wry smile.

Haldin grinned broadly. "What are you offering in return?" he asked.

"Stop it," said Mordan. "This isn't a game. That's my brother there, and I want to know what happened to him. Haldin, you offered me an exchange of information—let's exchange. Maybe you can make some sense of what we found in the Mournland. Tarrel, what do you say?"

"Brey should be in on this too," said the Brelander. "She actually saw them in action."

"Agreed," said Mordan. "We'll ask her when she gets up tonight."

"I shall look forward to it," said Haldin. "Meanwhile, let's see what our captive can tell us."

"You go ahead," said Mordan. "I'm going to stay here for a while."

Tarrel and Haldin left him to his musings.

❂ ❂ ❂ ⦿ ❂ ❂ ❂

They found the captured wight in the same cell they had occupied only a few hours before. Tarrel's half-elf guards stood on either side of the door, out of reach of the creature's hands. Both wore field dressings over a number of minor wounds.

As the gnome and the Brelander approached the cell, the wight hurled itself at the door, reaching out through the bars with a bony arm, its eyes blazing with hate. Tarrel backed away, but Haldin stood just a couple of inches outside its reach. A few minutes went by, with the wight frantically trying to reach the gnome, and the gnome holding his ground with an imperturbable smile. Eventually, the wight gave up.

"That's better," said Haldin, as if congratulating a small child on its manners. "Now, I have some questions I'd like you to answer. Truthfully, if you please."

"Why?" snarled the wight. "You'll destroy me whatever I say!"

Haldin held up an admonitory finger. "Perhaps," he said, "or perhaps I'll recommend that you be sent to the Ministry for further study and evaluation. There might yet be a place for you in the army of Karrnath."

The wight considered this. Seeing its indecision, Haldin reached into a belt pouch, bringing out something that looked like a severed finger. The wight looked at it curiously, and Haldin moved it in a complex pattern, muttering under his breath.

"Now," he said amicably, "I'm sure we can come to a suitable arrangement. I am willing to believe that you were not a willing participant in the things that were done to you, and neither, perhaps, were any of the Vedykar Lancers. You did your duty and were betrayed by those you were assigned to protect. Am I right?"

There was a pause. The wight searched his face, meeting nothing but a sympathetic smile.

"What do you want to know?" it rasped.

"There," Haldin beamed. "You see, this doesn't have to

be difficult or unpleasant. First, let us introduce ourselves. My name is Garro Haldin—what is yours?"

"Rochus Gaebler."

"Very good," said Haldin. "I am pleased to meet you. Now, why don't you tell me everything that happened to you after you were assigned to Unit 61?"

❋ ❋ ❋ ❋ ❋ ❋ ❋

"Well," said Haldin, after night had fallen and Brey had joined them, "it seems that Dravuliel is a very gifted necromancer indeed. I'm not surprised that he decided to leave the employment of the Ministry and set out on his own account. The accident involving the gateway to Mabar, ironically enough, provided him with an ideal pretext."

"What do you mean?" demanded Brey.

"The laboratory complex was deserted and heavily damaged when you found it," Haldin replied. "If anyone had come from the Ministry to find out why communication had stopped, they would probably have concluded that Unit 61 and the Vedykar Lancers were destroyed."

"But he didn't know that you'd already lost track of them," said Mordan.

"Quite so," Haldin continued, "which is why I became interested when each of you began making enquiries about them."

"So," said Tarrel, "we've told you everything we know, and so has Gaebler. What do you make of it all—beside the fact that Dravuliel is good at his job?"

"Well," replied the gnome, "I can tell you that, from the books you recovered, he has unearthed a number of very potent necromantic techniques, some of which were thought to be lost forever. He also seems to have invented some of his own. I've already mentioned spellstitching, which he seems to have mastered completely."

"Your brother," he said, turning to Mordan, "was another thing entirely. As Tarrel correctly observed, he was much more powerful than a normal wight. More powerful individuals are known to occur from time to time, especially where a person has been unusually violent in life. The records I have seen refer to them by several names, of which the most common is 'slaughter wight.' They are extremely rare."

"Is that what gave him the stronger magic?" asked Mordan.

Haldin shook his head. "No," he said, "and that is what bothered me at first. But in a few of the books that Tarrel so thoughtfully recovered, I found mentions of a process that, so far as I know, is entirely new to necromancy. It emulates a natural process—if 'natural' is the right word in this context—whereby undead creatures sometimes become more powerful as they continue to exist over the centuries. They develop a number of abilities: rapid healing, enhanced strength and force of will, and sometimes the ability to cast one or more spells, even if they knew no magic in their breathing days. Ordinarily, this process takes centuries or millennia, and even then it is far from certain. Dravuliel seems to have found a way to invest a comparatively young undead creature with these abilities. Ancient books refer to this process as 'evolution,' and the documents you recovered include descriptions of experiments to bring this about artificially. It is my opinion that your unfortunate brother was chosen to receive these gifts."

Mordan snorted. "I wouldn't be surprised if he volunteered," he said.

"Could he have made more of them?" asked Brey.

Haldin shrugged.

"That's hard to say," he replied. "The notes you retrieved are incomplete, and there is every chance that Dravuliel and his team have refined the processes since they vacated that laboratory."

"What about that ritual with the dead elf on the post?" asked Brey.

"That is another example of lost knowledge that Dravuliel has apparently uncovered," answered the gnome. "Various ancient manuscripts mention a process called the ritual of crucimigration, and I believe that this is what you discovered. The ritual brings a living subject—who must be willing, the sources claim—to the point of death, where-upon he or she becomes an undead creature—necropolitan is the most common name for such beings—while retaining almost all knowledge and abilities from life. Some see it as a route to eternal life, and others as a means of overcoming the weaknesses of living flesh. In either case, it would allow a scholar to develop knowledge and abilities for decades and centuries, without the need for food or rest, the infirmities of age or the interruption of death."

"That explains the corpse-elves," said Brey.

"What about Dravuliel himself?" asked Tarrel. "I only got a glimpse of him on top of the wall, but he didn't look dead—just very old."

"He may have some other plan for himself," replied Haldin. "Perhaps he intends to become a lich, or it could be that he has some reason for wishing to remain alive."

"I'll be sure to ask him," said Brey. "But what you're saying is, he can still die?"

"What about that airship?" asked Mordan. "Does he have some kind of renegade Lyrandar heir working for him?"

"I think it is unlikely," replied Haldin, "although I did

come across something in one of the books that might explain it. Gaebler was able to provide me with some confirmation, though of course he does not understand the details."

"What?" asked Brey. "Does he have some kind of flying undead bound to the thing?"

"In a way," Haldin said. "Have you ever heard of a creature called a necromental?"

They all shook their heads.

"Necromental?" mused Tarrel. "What's that, some kind of essence-of-death creature?"

"Not exactly," answered the gnome. "It is a kind of elemental, which has been bound to negative energy instead of the elemental energy of its native plane. Just as natives of this plane can become undead, so can elementals."

"An undead elemental?" asked Mordan.

"Precisely," Haldin replied. "It seems that Dravuliel has bound an air or fire necromental to power his airship—and because it is undead, he and his assistants can control it just as easily as a Lyrandar heir might control a living elemental."

"That reminds me of something," said Tarrel. "When the hill caved in, the thing that came out looked like an earth elemental . . ."

"Quite possibly it was an earth necromental," said Haldin. "It might have been an early experiment on Dravuliel's part, bound beneath the laboratory complex until Captain ir'Mallon destroyed the altar, or it might have been created spontaneously from years of necromantic energy leaching into the surrounding soil and rock, together with the unpredictable magical effects of the Mournland. It's hard to say without further investigation."

"You were right," said Tarrel, after a pause. "That Dravuliel is a pretty good necromancer."

"An abomination," said Brey, "that's what he is. That's bad enough, but if he's outside the control of the Karrnathi government . . ."

"He is a danger to the nation, if not the whole continent," Haldin finished her thought.

"Did Gaebler tell you where he's based now?" asked Mordan.

"Yes," the gnome replied, "and that is perhaps the most surprising thing. He is in the heart of the Nightwood—away from prying eyes, yet only a few hours' flight from Korth, Karrlakton, and Atur."

"Dol Arrah," breathed Mordan. "He could do anything from there."

"No doubt he has plans," said Haldin, "and no doubt he already suspects that we have questioned Gaebler and discovered his location. We must act quickly before he has a chance to move elsewhere."

CHAPTER 20

Olarune 26, 999 YK

Mordan leaned against the rail of the airship and watched Karrnath pass beneath him. The southern flatlands around Fort Zombie gave way to lines of low hills fringing the floodplain of the Cyre River. From the air, the mist of the Mournland seemed almost like a cloud, rising from the banks of the river to around a hundred feet, covering the blighted land like a shroud. His heart skipped a beat as the airship altered course to fly over the mist, but the skies above it were clear and peaceful, giving no hint of what lay below.

The hop across the Mournland took only a couple of hours, cutting across a bend in the river. Away to the port side, Mordan could see Karrlakton in the distance, a smudge of brown among the green farmland and the dark blue-gray of the river. Even in Decker's mechanical boat, it had taken them days to cover that distance.

The airship was nearly a hundred feet long, built of Aerenal soarwood. She looked very much like a sea vessel, except for the observation dome in the underside of the hull and the four great struts that held the blazing ring of elemental fire around the ship's waist. Mordan had seen airships before, both in war and peace, and this one seemed built for the former purpose. Her construction was plain and functional, lacking the lavish ornamentation and luxurious furnishings of the private sky-yachts and the Lyrandar liners. At each end, on a raised platform, a heavy ballista stood ready beneath a canvas tarpaulin, and each of the side-rails was fitted with swivel mounts for heavy repeating crossbows. While the ship wasn't equipped for dealing death from above, she was well able to take care of herself.

Haldin lorded it over the ship's crew, providing more evidence of his high status within the Ministry. Mordan wondered if he had met the Minister personally—the gregarious gnome certainly had the charm to move in such exalted circles—and what he was like. Stories were told of the reclusive Count Vedim ir'Omrik and his grisly work. It was said that he had been the first to discover the means of creating the enhanced skeletons and zombies used by the Karrnathi military, and had personally overseen the training of the first bone knights. He had fallen from prominence since the end of the War, as Karrnath tried to downplay its necromantic prowess for diplomatic reasons, and it was rumored that the King had instructed him not to appear at court. Some said that he had a secret laboratory hidden somewhere in the kingdom, where—according to who was doing the telling—he worked tirelessly to create ever more powerful undead protectors for Karrnath, or he engaged in ever more vile and insane experiments.

Rumor was vague about the location of his lair. Some accounts placed it in a secret labyrinth beneath the huge Crimson Monastery in the dread city of Atur, while others maintained that the Count had moved into the Mournland to study the new and strange necromantic phenomena that took place there. At least one account claimed the Count's secret laboratory was hidden deep within the Nightwood, and Mordan wondered if that was true. He also wondered if that was where they were going.

As Karrlakton receded on the southern horizon, the edge of the Nightwood loomed to the north. Somehow, it looked bigger from the air; it stretched out of sight in every direction, a dark green carpet covering the land. The small farming villages that nestled on its southern flank belied the dark tales told of the interior. The outer fringes of the great forest were safe enough for hunters and woodsmen—safe enough, in fact, for much of their extent to be declared a royal hunting-park—but terrible stories were told of the dark depths of the forest, and of those who had ventured into them and never returned.

It was late afternoon when Tarrel joined Mordan at the ship's rail.

"So that's the famous Nightwood," he said. "How big is it?"

"About three hundred miles from east to west, and one to two hundred from north to south," he replied.

Tarrel grinned. "Oh, the King's Forest is twice that size," he said. "It goes all the way from Sharn to Wroat."

Mordan punched him playfully on the shoulder. "Typical Brelander," he said, "everything's bigger and better at home. I'm surprised you people ever travel anywhere."

"Oh, we like to," answered Tarrel jokingly, "so we can tell everyone else how great our country is." He gestured at the Nightwood again. "Is it true there's a chasm in the middle that reaches right down to Khyber?"

"Why do you ask?" said Mordan. "So you can tell me there's one in Breland that reaches through Khyber, out the other side, and down to the bottom of the universe?"

Tarrel became serious. "How are we going to find one necromancer in the middle of all those trees?"

"I expect Haldin's got a plan," Mordan replied. "He seems to be good at that sort of thing."

"What do you make of him?" asked Tarrel.

Mordan spread his arms, indicating the airship and her crew. "If he can get the use of this, he's not just a Ministry filing clerk," he said.

Tarrel nodded. "True," he said. "I was watching him during the attack on the fort, and he's got some powerful magic. Is he Blood of Vol, do you think?"

Mordan shook his head.

"No," he said. "The only Blood clerics I ever met were completely humorless. I'm not sure they even recruit gnomes. And that dragon statue of his—I've seen it somewhere, but I can't place it. He could follow a gnome god, I suppose, or some power the Ministry has a deal with."

"Well," said Tarrel, "after watching him in action, I'm glad he's on our side—small as he is."

"Size can be deceptive," replied Mordan. "I learned that on the Talenta Plains. Some of those halfling hunters are tougher than a dwarf's boots."

Their conversation was interrupted by a howl of pain from Haldin's cabin. Crew members scurried to see what had happened, but the gnome came out rubbing his eyes and waved them away.

"A very clever fellow, our friend Dravuliel," he said, beckoning Mordan and Tarrel inside. The cabin was low and dark, dominated by a large wooden desk. A long-legged chair was upset beside the desk, and upon the tabletop stood a crystal ball on a bronze tripod.

"I got a good enough look at him at the fort, so I thought I would try to scry his location," he continued, "but it seems he was prepared for that eventuality. Not only did he block my vision, but he also managed to send back some kind of magical attack through the crystal ball." Righting the chair, he sat down, holding the bridge of his nose between finger and thumb like a man with a headache.

"Does that mean he knows we're coming?" asked Tarrel.

The gnome nodded. "That was never in doubt," he said. "After the way he showed his hand at the fort, he would be foolish not to expect pursuit, and whatever else he may be, this elf is no fool."

Haldin opened a fitted cupboard behind his desk, taking out three goblets and a glass decanter. "Would you care to join me?" he asked. "I'm afraid all I have is Zil brandy. The Cyran is so hard to come by these days." He poured three glasses. "Now," he said when they had drunk, "based on the rough directions given by our captive, I estimate that we are very close to our destination. I was hoping to establish a more precise location using the crystal ball, but I don't think I shall try that again."

"Why didn't you bring him along?" asked Tarrel. "Maybe he could have guided us there."

"Two reasons," answered Haldin. "I felt it was important that he should go to the Ministry for study, along with the remains of his less mobile comrades. They will also find those improved skeletal horses very interesting, I think. Second, I did not want to bring him too close to his former master, in case his loyalty should return—either by itself or through magical persuasion."

"Anyway," he said, getting up from the desk, "we should consider our course of action upon arrival. Would you be so kind as to follow me?"

He led them along a companionway and down a flight of steps into the heart of the ship. Opening a polished wooden door, he waved them inside with a bow, and they found themselves in some kind of equipment locker.

Racks of weapons and armor lined the walls, and crates of ropes, bottles, and other objects were secured to the floor. The two stood silently for a moment, looking about them.

"Please feel free to take anything you think will be useful," said Haldin. "I have left orders that the same courtesy is to be extended to Captain ir'Mallon when she wakes."

Before they could reply, the ship lurched suddenly, and there were cries of alarm from on deck. The three hurried out to see what was the matter.

Some of the crew were leaning over the rail, pointing in alarm. The ballista crews were hurriedly clearing their weapons of their tarpaulins. Others, including the two half-elves who had accompanied Haldin to Fort Zombie, were securing heavy repeating crossbows to their mounts on the rails and slapping in magazines of bolts.

When they reached the stern-rail, they could see what the alarm was about. Rising from the forest below was a huge winged creature, almost the size of a dragon. At first, Mordan thought it might be a wyvern—there were reports that they laired in the depths of the Nightwood—but soon he realized that there were no membranes on its outstretched, beating wings. It was flying by magic.

The thing gained height quickly—unnaturally fast—until it was about a thousand feet above and behind the ship.

Then, partially folding its nonexistent wings, it went into a shallow dive, like a falcon after a dove.

The aft ballista crew loosed a bolt, but it fell short. The creature was not yet in range. As it closed, Mordan could see that it was made of bone, fused into the rough shape of a flying reptile and partially covered with some kind of wrappings. Haldin brought his crossbow up, and Tarrel his wand. All Mordan could do was watch as the thing streaked toward them.

A fireball exploded on the after deck, where the ballista crew was reloading. Bodies were scattered right and left, and flames started to lick around the ballista and its wooden platform. Crewmen rushed to help their comrades and put out the flames, but scant seconds later they were felled by bolts of dark force that shot from the creature's talons. The heavy crossbows fired, with Haldin and Tarrel adding their own attacks, but the creature didn't even slow down. It overtook the ship, missing the top retaining strut and the elemental ring by inches, and more magic missiles shot down onto the foredeck as it went by.

Fighting the instinct to duck, Mordan looked at the thing as it went overhead. It could have been the partially wrapped skeleton of a wyvern or a large glidewing, but for its skull, which was more like that of an immense bull than a dragon. But his eye was drawn to the writhing designs that had been stained into the exposed bone.

"It's spellstitched!" he yelled. This had to be more than coincidence.

There was a dull *twang* from the forward ballista, and the crew cheered as the bolt—heavy as a knight's lance—struck the thing dead center, passing right through it from spine to ribcage. Apart from a slight shudder, though, it seemed to ignore the impact. Pulling up into a steep climb, it performed a wing-over and prepared to make a second attack.

Working with feverish intensity, the forward ballista crew cranked back the string of their weapon and prepared to load a second bolt. Haldin and Tarrel had run to the front of the vessel, determined to get off as many shots as they could while the horror was closing.

Tarrel attacked first, sending a fireball streaking toward the thing. It flew through the explosion without wavering. Some of its bandages were on fire, but it seemed to be unharmed. The ballista sent a bolt through one of the creature's eye-sockets but failed to slow its approach. This time, nobody cheered: they were all waiting for the attack they knew would come.

Green streaks shot from its claws, hitting the foredeck with a savage hiss. Puddles of acid began to eat away at the decking; by some miracle, they had missed the ballista and its crew. Seconds later, though, they did not escape another rain of magic missiles; other crewmen raced to help them and to replace those who were badly wounded.

A volley of crossbow bolts slammed into the creature as it swept over the top of the ship for a second time, lodging in its wrappings. Crossing the line of the elemental ring, it dipped down to skim the afterdeck almost at head height. Mordan thought for a moment that it might try to snatch up a crew member in its claws, but instead a sheet of flame roared down onto the deck. It washed over the unfortunate crew of the rear ballista, who had replaced the string ruined by the creature's initial fireball and were struggling to wind it back.

Dol Arrah, thought Mordan, how many spells has this thing got? The zombies that captured Brey had had only limited magical abilities, but this creature was much more powerful. His only consolation was that its wrappings continued to burn from Tarrel's fireball, and some of the nearby bones were smoke-blackened.

More bolts thudded into the creature from the rear crossbows. The crew worked the repeating levers with furious speed, sending bolt after bolt into the thing.

Tarrel had run the entire length of the deck as the creature streaked overhead, and took careful aim with his wand as it pulled up for another turn. Anticipating its motion, he sent a fireball to the exact spot where it would hang in the air, weightless between climbing and diving. The explosion engulfed the creature, blotting it from view as the crossbow crews slapped new magazines into their weapons and waited for the next pass.

It never came. When the fire dissipated, the winged monstrosity was diving steeply away, trailing flame and smoke. Tarrel punched the air in victory, and a cheer went up as the creature flew off, hugging the treetops.

"Quick!" Haldin shouted to the helmsman. "Follow it!" He swung the wheel, and the ship dropped. Mordan and Tarrel hung onto the rail to avoid falling.

The creature dropped into a wooded ravine, and the ship followed. The sides became steeper, turning into rocky cliffs, and the creature suddenly slewed sideways, disappearing beneath a large overhang. As the ship flew past, they could see a low, wide cave entrance, shadowed too deeply to tell how far back it went. The winged creature had just landed, and small figures were running to beat out the flames from its wrappings. By the light of the small fire, they could just make out the dark shape of another airship. Fire arrows started to come up from archers at the lip of the cave, and Haldin ordered the helmsman to stand off and hover out of bowshot.

"This is it!" he yelled, dancing with glee. "Come on!" He led Mordan and Tarrel back to the equipment hold, and they set about preparing for their mission.

Mordan slung a leather bandolier over his shoulder, holding several flasks of holy water. He had seen what it could do to undead, and after being so helpless against the flying creature, he wanted to have at least some means of fighting from a distance.

Tarrel rummaged through a collection of scrolls, pausing occasionally to feed one into his wooden scrollcase. The case wound the scroll inside itself like a capstan coiling rope, and waited for the next one.

Haldin already had his repeating crossbow slung on his back. He picked up a backpack filled with loaded magazines, and another bandolier of holy water. Crosswise with this, he slung a second bandolier with many small pouches.

The deck was a bustle of activity when they emerged. All the fires had been put out, and the flying creature's acid had been sluiced with water, leaving only minor scarring on the deck. The wounded had been taken below, and the rear ballista restrung. Wooden crates were stacked on deck beside each of the ballistae; they contained ceramic globes packed in straw. Both the heavy weapons had been swung around to fire from the port side of the ship, and the repeating heavy crossbows from the starboard side had been remounted to port.

"Here's my plan," explained Haldin. "The airship will attack the cave entrance, providing us with a diversion. Meanwhile, we will make our way to the ground and find another entrance."

Tarrel looked skeptical.

"Are we going to wait for Brey?" asked Mordan.

"She can join us when she is able," replied the gnome. "We can use the remaining daylight to scout for way in that is less heavily guarded."

"Just the four of us?" asked Tarrel. "Couldn't we take a few reinforcements from your crew?"

"It would be more difficult to avoid raising the alarm," Haldin replied, "and having seen what the four of us were able to do at Fort Zombie, I am confident we shall be enough. Besides, the ship's crew are not trained for this kind of mission; I fear that we would only be leading them to their deaths."

"So how do we get down there?" asked Mordan. "I'm not sure I could climb down a rope one-handed."

Haldin smiled. "That will not be necessary," he said. In response to his gesture, one of the crew stepped forward, holding a wooden hoop about three feet across and as thick as a man's arm. It was equipped with four hand-holds, and a thin string ran across the center.

"One hand should be sufficient to hold onto a life ring," he said. "Are we ready?"

"Not quite," said Tarrel. Reaching into his coat, he brought out a wand of transparent glassy crystal. "Better if they don't see us coming," he said.

❀ ❀ ❀ ❀ ❀ ❀ ❀

Something unseen disturbed the branches of the trees on the valley side. There was the sound of three bodies landing softly on the ground, and after a few seconds Tarrel dropped the magical invisibility that had covered the three of them.

They made their way along the valley side to within a few hundred yards of the cave mouth. Looking up through the trees, they could see the airship moving to attack; fire arrows flew up from the cave while missiles rained down on from the side of the ship.

Haldin pulled a small piece of bone from a pouch on his bandolier. Holding it up, he muttered an incantation, and as his two companions watched in surprise, a milky glaze formed over his eyes. He looked around for a moment and then trotted off between the trees. After a few minutes, he seemed to have found what he was looking for. Keeping his milk-white eyes fixed on the ground, he motioned the others to follow him.

"Something undead has come this way," he said softly. "Hopefully, we can follow its trail and find a way into this place."

His intuition proved to be correct. Within a few minutes, they found themselves standing at the edge of a steep slope that was littered with dead flesh. Bones stuck out of the debris, and here and there a limb or head was visible. The rest was like a pile of slaughterhouse waste. Flies circled lazily above the rotting detritus, and here and there other creatures rustled and skittered among the carnage. The stink of corruption floated over the scene, stronger even than the smell of Fort Zombie. At the top of the slope, a small cave-mouth was visible in the cliff side.

"This is what I was looking for," whispered Haldin. "They dispose of their waste this way." Tarrel grimaced.

"Messy business, this necromancy," he said.

Carefully, they picked their way around the edge of the refuse. The daylight was fading fast, and Mordan lost his footing more than once in the growing gloom. As he dragged himself to his feet for the third time, Tarrel put a hand on his shoulder.

"You can't see a thing, can you?" he asked.

"Not much," Mordan answered, "but they'll see us coming if I light a torch."

"Hold still," said the half-elf. He pulled a scroll from his case and read from it in a soft voice, keeping his hand on the Karrn's shoulder. Mordan blinked in surprise as the scene leaped into clear vision. There was no color, but apart from that he could see as well as in full daylight.

"That should help," said Tarrel, putting the scroll away. "Let me know if it wears off."

Haldin had gone ahead to investigate the cave mouth they had found. He came back just as Tarrel completed the spell.

"It's guarded," he whispered, "but we should be able to get in without raising the alarm."

"Then what are we waiting for?" The sound of Brey's voice made them all jump. She was standing behind them, with a shortbow in her hand, three quivers of arrows slung over one shoulder, and a backpack on the other. Beneath her cloak, she wore a breastplate of blackened steel, and on her head was a helmet of the same material.

"Welcome, Captain," said Haldin, with a gallant bow. "Your company was the only thing we were lacking. Tarrel, I trust that you have a silence spell among your collection of scrolls?"

CHAPTER 21

Olarune 26, 999 YK

Something struck Mordan on the back, wrapping its arms and legs around his body and pinning his arms to his sides. Despite its light weight, it squeezed him with incredible force, driving the breath from his body. As he struggled, he saw more pale, shapeless blurs flying at his companions.

Brey wrestled with the thing on her back, grasping one of its boneless wrists in each hand and pulling its arms off her. As she stretched the thing out, it looked like the flayed skin of a human being; its arms were like the sleeves of a garment, and its chest was slack and empty. Its head flapped like a deflated balloon, with nothing inside its empty mouth and eye sockets. She tore the thing to pieces.

Haldin had been less fortunate. He was much smaller than the thing that attacked him, and it was able to envelop him completely. Nothing could be seen of the gnome himself, just a thrashing mass covered by dead flesh, struggling like a man in a collapsed tent.

Tarrel was farthest from the things when they attacked, and had some warning from the others' cries of surprise and pain; turning swiftly, he launched a fireball from his wand, throwing his attacker backward and setting it ablaze.

Mordan was able to free his right arm from the skin-creature's grasp and draw his rapier. Carefully, he eased the enchanted blade between the thing's arms and his own chest, and began sawing at the empty limbs to try to free himself. The thing shrank from the blade but kept its hold on him, as though it knew it would be vulnerable if it let go.

Having shredded her own assailant, Brey leaped to Haldin's side and tore the thing off him. He gasped for air as his head reappeared but was unable to help himself. Tarrel launched a second fireball, reducing his attacker to a flaming mass that flopped on the ground amid the stench of burning meat. By the time Mordan had freed himself, the gnome was sitting on the ground coughing painfully and Brey was tossing the pieces of the other horrors into the fire started by Tarrel's wand.

"What were those things? More of Dravuliel's experiments?"

Haldin shook his head, his breathing still labored. "I'm not sure," he replied, wheezing a little more than usual. "Perhaps they somehow arose spontaneously in that heap of offal, or maybe they came to feed on it. They would seem to be independent, since no alarm has been raised."

"None that we heard," observed Tarrel. He looked quickly at Brey, who listened for a moment and then shook her head.

Mordan kept his back to the others, watching for any further signs of life—or unlife—among the bloody refuse.

"As I was saying," Haldin continued, having recovered his breath, "there is a small cave entrance close to the top of this accumulation of refuse. It would seem that waste materials from Dravuliel's necromantic work are thrown out of it periodically, and have built up over time into what we see here. We require a silence spell for our next step, because stationed inside the entrance is a creature that can make a very loud and unpleasant noise indeed." He looked at the half-elf, who brought out his scroll-case and pressed a wooden button on the side.

"Silence," he said softly, and within a few moments a scroll wound itself out of a long slit down the side of the case.

Brey unslung the bow on her back and checked the arrows in her quiver, pulling each one out to inspect it. Directly behind the head of each arrow was a small vial of clear liquid, molded around the shaft. None seemed to have been broken by the skin-creatures.

"I didn't know you could use a bow," said Mordan.

"I commanded a troop of rangers behind enemy lines for almost a year," she replied. "Of course I can use a bow."

With Tarrel in the lead, the four scrambled up the edge of the charnel slope, keeping their eyes fixed on the entrance. As they got closer, they could see that just inside the cave mouth stood something that looked like a huge mushroom, almost as tall as a man. Haldin tapped Tarrel's shoulder and pointed to the thing. With a nod, he raised his scroll and began to read.

Before he could complete the spell, however, a small, dark shape shot out of the cave. Apparently disturbed by the motion, the mushroom-creature started to vibrate, emitting an ear-splitting scream that echoed off the valley sides. It was abruptly cut off when Tarrel finished his incantation, and the four looked at each other uncertainly, and then back at the cave-mouth. Something was moving in the shadows behind the now-silent fungus. They flattened themselves against the rock, out of sight from the entrance.

The thing that had flown out of the cave-mouth circled for a while, and then came to a hover not far from the companions. It looked like a mixture of a hawk, a cat, and a monkey; Mordan raised his rapier, and saw from the corner of his eye that Brey had nocked an arrow and Tarrel was taking aim with his wand.

The creature's mouth was moving, but it was silenced by the spell Tarrel had cast on the fungus. Holding its empty hands up in a gesture of peace, it flew rapidly until it was out of the spell's effect.

"Wait!" the thing said. "I'm not a danger to you!" Its voice sounded human and female, with a Karrnathi accent. The three did not drop their guard, but Haldin spoke to the creature.

"This is a homunculus, is it not?" he asked. "May I assume that I am speaking to its owner?"

"Yes," the creature said. "My name is Dria d'Cannith. I am a prisoner here. They didn't capture my messenger, and I've been using it to scout for a way out."

"D'Cannith?" asked Mordan. "Don't tell me Dravuliel has warforged in there as well!"

The creature dipped briefly in a gesture that might be interpreted as a nod.

"I was sent here to rescue a member of the family who was kidnapped. Since being captured myself, I've found out that my cousin has been forced to work on a project which aims to create undead constructs, with the advantages of both types and the weaknesses of neither. At first he refused, but since they captured me he has been co-operating to save both our lives!"

Haldin spoke up. "Dear lady," he said, "may I therefore suppose that, by the use of your homunculus here, you have been able to gain some knowledge of this facility's layout?"

"Some," the construct replied. "I can guide you from where you are to where they're keeping me, and I know a few other places."

"I see that you have done business with gnomes before," said Haldin with a disarming smile, "since you are so careful to point out the advantages of rescuing you before doing anything else. But do not worry, we shall endeavor to help you, even though we came here for purposes of our own."

"He's all heart, isn't he?" muttered Tarrel.

"What's in the entrance?" asked Mordan. "Your little pet set the shrieker off, and it looks like something's moving back there."

"There are four violet fungi," said the homunculus, "and behind them some zombies. I think the zombies are supposed to raise the alarm if anyone tries to get in that way. One of them is standing by a big gong."

"This could be a trap, you know," said Brey, glaring at the small creature.

Haldin turned to her with a reassuring smile. "Please don't worry, Captain," he said. "I have been examining the homunculus while we were speaking, and I am satisfied that it is a pure construct, with no hint of necromancy in its nature. While he is a necromancer of exceptional ability, I have seen nothing to suggest that Dravuliel has any skill as an artificer. But of course, we should always be on our guard."

Tarrel pulled out his wand of fireballs. "Anyone for roast mushroom?" he said, and grinned.

Aiming his wand carefully, he placed a fireball directly in the cave mouth. Silent flame shot out of the narrow entrance, and the four companions finished the climb, with the homunculus flapping behind them.

Charred fragments of fungus littered the inside of the cave. They advanced cautiously as the cave turned into a narrow passage, their footfalls making no sound. Just before a bend in the passage, Haldin stopped and held up a hand, and gestured his companions to each side of the cave. Then he held up two fingers.

The two zombies never stood a chance; the intruders were upon them before they had time to react. Brey cut one almost in half with two swings of her longsword, while Mordan's rapier gutted the other like a fish. It was strange, almost dreamlike, to be fighting in complete silence, to feel the impact of one's blows but hear no sound.

Tarrel motioned the others to stop and mimed that he was going to look ahead. Holding the crystal wand to his chest, he vanished. A few seconds later, his companions heard the first sound in some time—a slight shuffle, followed by a dull thump. Looking round the corner, they saw Tarrel standing beside a large gong and sheathing his shortsword. At his feet was an armored corpse, its exposed flesh blistering from the holy water that puddled around it. Near the gong was a narrow opening, with a large, dimly lit chamber beyond. Tarrel scanned the area with his mirror.

"Looks like a storage area," he said. "A lot of sacks and crates, but not much else."

They went cautiously through the opening, using the boxes and sacks for cover. To their right, a broad passage led to the landing stage on the cliff side; they could see frantic movement beyond and hear the sounds of battle. Occasional bursts of flame lit the area. It seemed that the Ministry airship was providing them with a good diversion.

Tarrel hissed a warning, and they ducked behind cover as a group of zombies hurried to join the battle. They carried crossbows, and moved faster than any zombies Mordan had seen in the Karrnathi military.

For several nerve-wracking minutes, they made their way across the chamber, following the fluttering homunculus. The few containers that were open held a bewildering array of cargo: black gemstones of various shapes and sizes, an assortment of herbs and powders, kegs of ink, and what appeared to be several barrels of dirt. One group of crates gave off a strong smell of rotting fish, and two barrels, placed side by side, contained miniature skulls—one load cast in iron, and the other carved from a flecked gray stone.

They reached the other side of the chamber, where a rock-hewn passage led away into darkness, broken by the flickering of distant torches. The homunculus hovered in the entrance for a moment, then darted down it.

Following the flying construct, they found themselves in a guard room of sorts. The square central chamber was lined with cells, walled off by iron bars. Nearly all of them contained prisoners. On the left, a young human woman stood gripping the bars of her cell; the homunculus squeezed through them and settled on her shoulder with a trill of happiness, wrapping its tail lightly around her neck.

"Lady d'Cannith, I presume?" asked Haldin, with a courtly bow. She smiled wearily and nodded. Tarrel fished a set of slim, hooked tools from inside his coat and knelt down to examine the lock.

"Captain?"

Brey turned at the sound of a familiar voice. Her eyes widened in shock as she recognized the filthy, ragged creature that looked at her through matted hair.

"Egen?" she breathed. "It can't be!"

Several other figures, barely recognizable as human, shuffled to the front of the cells.

"The Captain!" they muttered to each other, "she's come back for us!" Brey turned away for a moment, wiping a bloody tear from her cheek.

"I don't believe it!" she exclaimed, turning back to her lieutenant. "They kept you alive all this time?"

Egen pushed the hair out of his face with a ghastly parody of a smile.

"Yes, Captain," he replied, "all you see here, at any rate. I can't vouch for the others."

"What did they do to you?" she asked, her voice softer.

"They said it was some kind of research that needed living subjects," said Egen. "I don't know what it was. Mainly they just moved us from place to place and one of the undead elf wizards would look us over now and again. I thought at first it might be some kind of disease, but we're all in pretty good shape, considering." He caught sight of Mordan, and stopped abruptly, his eyes wide with sudden fear.

"A Karrn?" he asked.

Brey smiled. "The War's been over for two years now," she said. "We were captured by an experimental unit that officially never existed, then went renegade and disappeared. That's why it's taken me so long to find you."

"So . . ." the ranger said, "did we win?"

Brey shook her head. "Everybody won, or everybody lost, depending on how you look at it. Cyre was destroyed by some kind of magical disaster, and the remaining nations made peace."

Egen looked confused.

"Destroyed?" he echoed. "So where are we now?"

"In Karrnath," she answered. "The renegades were hiding close to home, yet nobody found them."

A murmur rippled through the surviving rangers, who were at the bars of their cells, hanging on every word.

"I'll tell you more later," Brey said. "But now, we've got to get you out of here." Grasping the door of one cell in both hands, she pulled it off its hinges and tossed it aside. The rangers gasped, their eyes wide.

"Oh, yes," said Brey, "I was one of their experiments. I'll explain it all later, but for now let's just say I'm no longer a paladin. Or alive, as the Church defines it." She went to the next cell and pulled off the door, repeating the process until all the rangers were free. They crowded together in the guard room, looking at her with frightened eyes.

"Don't be afraid," she said. "I'm not quite a monster yet—not most of the time, anyway. But I won't be able to come home with you."

"Oh, Captain!" said Egen, almost in tears. "Surely—you weren't willing—couldn't someone in the Church help?" He seemed quite overcome by Brey's fate, and slumped over, wracked by sobs.

Tarrel opened the door of Dria d'Cannith's cell, and she stepped out to join her rescuers. A slightly built woman with thin features and fine, fair hair, she looked as though she belonged at an embassy ball rather than on a dangerous mission in hostile territory.

She opened her mouth to speak but was interrupted by a sudden gurgle from Egen. He dropped to the floor, writhing in agony, and Brey stood helplessly over him.

"Can't you heal him?" she demanded, turning frantically to Haldin.

The gnome looked at the thrashing ranger sharply.

"Perhaps," he said, "if I knew what was wrong." He took half a step toward Egen, and the ranger's body exploded.

Blood, bone shards, and scraps of flesh flew across the room. The offal burned whatever it landed on, sizzling like an acid. Everyone turned away and covered their faces, but no one could avoid being sprayed with the vile rain.

The other rangers fell to the floor, screaming and trying to brush the stuff off them. Some were apparently close to madness from the strain of their long confinement, and this fresh horror seemed to push them over the edge of hysteria. Brey stood watching helplessly as their screams turned from revulsion to pain, and their thrashings became wilder.

"Get down!" yelled Tarrel, pressing on her shoulder. The others were already diving to the floor. As if in a dream, the vampire woman knelt and covered herself with her cloak, and the lives of the remaining Inmistil Rangers were snuffed out in the same grisly fashion as Egen's.

The explosions were as deadly as they were disturbing. Brey's cloak was shredded by flying debris, and only her armor saved her from further injury. The others were all bleeding from numerous small cuts, although it was impossible to tell which blood was their own and which came from the unfortunate rangers. But worse was to come.

The wreckage of the rangers' corpses began to move. Intestines snaked forward, ribs crawled like multiple legs— and behind them they dragged sightless, staring heads, their faces frozen in the unspeakable horror of their death-agonies. In the midst of each ruined body pulsed a sac of fluid, almost the size of a head. Before the blood-spattered companions could recover from their shock, they found themselves under attack.

Brey found limbs, guts, and tendons snaking around

her legs as the bodies converged on her. Already wracked by emotion from finding her troops and losing them in such a fashion, she found the blood and flesh that clung to her was too much for her vampiric nature to bear. Her eyes blazed red, her face distorted, and her fangs bared themselves as she struggled, ripping and tearing the animated flesh and forcing chunks of bloody offal into her mouth.

Dria d'Cannith flattened herself against the back wall, her eyes wide with horror and her homunculus uttering sharp cries of distress as it clung to her neck. Mordan stabbed at one of the loathsome things with his rapier, puncturing the great cyst at its center. A vile-smelling pus oozed from the wound; the creature writhed and shook on the floor for a moment, and then was still. Tarrel had pulled out his wand but couldn't loose a fireball because of the close quarters.

Haldin held up his blue dragon statuette and began to chant, but a pale, translucent object flew into the room like an arrow, striking him on the chest. As it stopped, the companions saw it was a bony hand, glowing with an eerie green light. Haldin's face slackened, and he stumbled to one side, almost dropping the holy symbol. He seemed to have forgotten what he was about to do.

"Holy water!" yelled Mordan, slashing at the spectral hand. It dissolved in a burst of light as his enchanted blade struck it. Tarrel pulled a flask from his bandolier, uncorked it, and poured it over the nearest of the abominations. It sizzled like acid where it struck the creature, blistering and blackening its horrid flesh.

Mordan peered out of the room to try to see where the spectral hand had come from, and was not surprised to see one of Dravuliel's undead elves facing the doorway. Between him and the spellcaster were a dozen armored zombies, with their longswords drawn. Shoulder to shoulder, they advanced with shields raised. The Karrn stood in the doorway to guard his flanks, and raised his rapier to the ready position.

"More coming this way!" he yelled.

THE MASTER

CHAPTER 22

Olarune 26, 999 YK

Take them alive!" boomed a voice, seemingly from nowhere. With a smooth, mechanical action, the zombies sheathed their swords and dropped their shields, walking over them without breaking their stride. A strong hand seized Mordan from behind, pulling him back into the room and throwing him to the ground. Brey launched herself over him, tearing into the zombies' front rank with her sword.

One of the zombies tried to grapple her, but she struck its outstretched arm with devastating force. Her blow should have severed the limb, but instead her sword struck bone with a dull ringing sound and stopped. When Brey drew her weapon back for another blow, the blade was notched and the glint of metal could be seen in the wound it had made. The thing's bones were made of iron. She struck again, with the same result, then threw down her sword in frustration and wrestled the zombie, holding it in the doorway and blocking the others from entering.

Haldin looked on in apparent confusion, as if he didn't understand what he was seeing. Tarrel grabbed the gnome by the shoulders and shook him, and his eyes cleared a little.

"Do something!" yelled the Brelander. Haldin blinked a couple of times, and then pulled out his blue dragon statuette. Holding it up, he recited a prayer—haltingly, but with determination—and looked expectantly at the doorway.

Nothing happened. Brey and the zombie were still deadlocked, and the others were trying to push them back out of the doorway. Haldin tried a different incantation, with the same lack of result. He turned to Tarrel and shrugged.

Mordan stood beside the doorway, waiting for a chance to strike. The weight of the zombies pushing from behind eventually told, and Brey was forced back inch by inch, still locked in a grapple. Mordan struck the creature from the side, sliding his blade between its ribs. It faltered, and he struck again, dropping it to the ground. Brey looked at him with a nod, understanding in her blazing eyes, and pulled another zombie through the doorway, pinning its arms to present the Karrn with a helpless victim. Two more thrusts of his rapier, and the zombie fell on top of the body of its comrade.

Tarrel was reading from another scroll. As he completed the spell, Haldin blinked and shook his head as if to clear it. Holding up his sapphire dragon once more, he repeated the incantation that had failed earlier—and this time, half of the zombies turned and fled. There was momentary confusion as they hampered their comrades that were still trying to reach the doorway, and Mordan took advantage of the deadlock to fell two more of the creatures.

"Get out of the way!" yelled Tarrel, raising his wand. Brey and Mordan sprang back to each side of the doorway, just as a bead of red light from the wand shot through it. The fireball exploded in the midst of the zombies, destroying several and setting the rest on fire.

For a moment the doorway was clear, and Mordan hurled himself through it. His rapier felled a burning zombie as he rolled to his feet, and he looked around for the undead spell-caster. The elf had already started to retreat, but Mordan was faster; two lightning-fast thrusts and he fell to the ground, still.

Brey was next through the doorway, followed by Tarrel and Haldin. Dria d'Cannith brought up the rear, unarmed and looking around nervously. The remaining zombies were quickly dispatched, and the gnome bent briefly over one of them, slicing the flesh of its arm with a dagger to expose the bones beneath.

"Fascinating," he mused. "They actually look like iron." As he watched, the dull gray color faded, leaving natural-looking bone. "At least it's a fairly short-lived spell," he said.

"Look out!" Tarrel's shout of warning came too late. A beam of crackling black energy struck the gnome, and he fell to the ground, pale and shaking. The half-elf launched a fireball at a robed figure standing in a doorway, but the figure flew into the air, dodging the blast easily and landing at the other side of the chamber. Its mocking laughter filled the air.

"It's him!" yelled Tarrel, running across to where Haldin was slowly picking himself up from the floor. Mordan hurled a flask of holy water at Dravuliel, but the elf stepped aside almost lazily, ignoring the splash as the vessel shattered at his feet.

Brey flew at the necromancer with an incoherent cry of hatred. Holding up a hand, he spat a phrase in the ancient elven tongue of Aerenal. The vampire woman seemed to fold up in midair and came crashing to the ground before him. She struggled to regain her feet, but he made an imperious gesture and she cowered as if in fear.

The others could do nothing but watch. Tarrel raised his wand but could not risk a fireball without harming Brey as well as the elf. Mordan judged the distance between himself and Dravuliel, and realized that he couldn't reach her in time to intervene. Haldin was fumbling shakily with his crossbow but still seemed to be in distress from the dark energy that had struck him. Dria cowered behind a crate of black stones, her homunculus silently hugging her neck.

Brey's face contorted with effort as she tried to regain her feet. The elf looked down at her with an expression of amused contempt.

"My," he said, "haven't you grown stronger! I expected to master your will, as I did with your maker Wultram."

"You . . ." Brey struggled to form words, but only disjointed, strangled sounds came from her mouth.

"I see you found your rangers," Dravuliel said. "I suspected you'd come back for them one day, so I saved them for you. Quite a successful test, don't you think?" Brey's eyes blazed a deeper red, but she could not rise to her feet.

Mordan felt a nudge in his ribs and looked down to see Tarrel crouched at his feet, a crate hiding him from the necromancer's view. He gestured to the Karrn's enchanted rapier, then to himself, then the elf, and finally drew a finger across his throat. He seemed to have a plan. Moving slowly to avoid attracting attention, Mordan handed the sword over. Tarrel touched the crystal wand to his chest, and disappeared.

Haldin raised his crossbow and took aim, but Dravuliel saw him and gestured with one hand, softly pronouncing a complex syllable. The bolt rattled off empty air without touching him. Reaching down, he dragged Brey to her feet, holding her body in front of his. Her eyes were frantic, but she couldn't even struggle.

"Naughty," he admonished the gnome. He raised a hand in Haldin's direction. "*Saighydh*," he said, and five bolts of energy darted from his fingers, striking the gnome in the chest. Mordan moved to help him but stopped when the elf pointed at him.

"Oh, no." said Dravuliel. "You stay where you are." He swept the chamber with a glance, apparently looking for the rest of the companions. In that instant, Tarrel appeared behind him, driving Mordan's enchanted rapier deep into his back.

With a cry of surprise and anger, Dravuliel threw Brey to the ground and turned to strike Tarrel a back-handed blow across the face. Dark energy blazed around his fist, and the half-elf crumpled to the ground.

Mordan threw himself into the cover of a stack of crates. He drew his dagger and edged carefully toward the elf. He saw from the corner of his eye that Dria d'Cannith was still crouching behind a crate, but was fiddling with one of the shields dropped by the zombies. Her homunculus was nowhere to be seen. He hoped she had a better plan than Tarrel.

Bleeding heavily from five holes in his chest, Haldin flattened himself behind the corpse of the zombie he had been examining when the necromancer first struck. He had one hand on his dragon statuette, and his lips moved in silent prayer. He was still pale, and his hands trembled.

Employing the same trick he had used in Falko's warehouse—in another life, it seemed—Mordan scooped up a handful of cast-iron miniature skulls from a crate and flung them as hard as he could. They landed far away with a rattle, and while the necromancer's attention was distracted Mordan rolled from the cover of one pile of boxes to another.

Dravuliel began to speak, but no sooner was his mouth open than an ear-splitting shriek rent the air behind him. As he turned, the flying homunculus streaked away. Dria stood from her hiding-place, holding an iron rib from the discarded shield. She had engraved it with arcane symbols, and a blazing bolt of energy shot from the end of the make-shift rod, striking the necromancer square in the chest. He rocked back on his heels, and Mordan was on him before he could recover, stabbing the dagger at his eyes. When the elf raised an arm to shield his face, Mordan struck him hard in the ribs with the stump of his left arm, releasing wounding negative energy of his dragonmark. Holy water had not affected the necromancer; he only hoped that meant that he was not undead.

Dravuliel shrieked as the negative energy burned into his body—a high, thin shriek of rage. Dark fire blazed around his fist again, but before he could strike Mordan, the Karrn found himself seized by one shoulder and flung backward across the room. He struck the ground hard, rolling to dissipate the energy of the fall, and when he looked up he saw that Brey had recovered from whatever influence the necromancer had wielded over her. The slim and fragile elf bent in her arms, no match for her unnatural strength and bestial rage. Picking him up like a rag doll, she threw him to the ground with bone-crushing force, leaping after him with her fangs bared.

"*Teych!*" he croaked, and an instant before the vampire landed on him, he vanished.

Brey rolled to her feet with a cry of rage, looking around for any sign of her quarry. For a moment, the others stood and stared, unable to believe that their adversary had disappeared.

Mordan hurried over to Tarrel and discovered that he was still breathing. Haldin limped up to them, laid his hands on the half-elf, and began to pray. Tarrel's eyes flickered open.

"Did we get him?" he asked weakly. Mordan shook his head.

"We won the first round," said Haldin, "but he will certainly be back. I expect that he is currently healing himself and preparing for another confrontation. It would be wise for us to do the same."

They found a storeroom off one side of the chamber, with only one entrance. Brey stood by the doorway, watching for fresh enemies.

Tarrel rubbed his face, which was bruised where Dravuliel had struck it. Then he fished a vial of healing potion from inside his coat and took a long drink. The color slowly returned to his skin.

"What did you do to him?" Mordan asked Dria, who had joined the group.

"I built up energy in the rod until it could do some damage," she replied. "It's an artificer trick. What did *you* do? That was more than just a punch."

"Aberrant dragonmark."

Brey was cursing under her breath. Haldin readied his crossbow and joined her in the doorway.

"Captain ir'Mallon," he said, gently, "are you hurt?"

"I was helpless," she growled. "He just—there was nothing I could do."

Haldin smiled reassuringly.

"Please do not blame yourself," he began. "It is in the nature . . ."

"Damn the nature!" Brey exploded. She swiped at a nearby crate with one fist, sending it shattering against a wall. It seemed to have been full of dirt.

"If I may suggest," said Haldin, "engaging him from a distance will prevent him from using that power on you again."

Emotions chased themselves across Brey's face. "I know you're making sense," she said, "but there's a part of me that just wants to tear him limb from limb—drink his blood and feel his life draining away in my hands. You have no idea what I—what he—oh, what's the use?"

"I understand," said the gnome, "even though I cannot imagine what you have suffered. He understands too, and I expect he will try to goad you into close combat again. It is the easiest way for him to destroy you."

Brey began to pace, but Haldin laid a restraining hand upon her arm. She turned in surprise—it had been a long time since a living being had touched her willingly.

"He knows vampires," the gnome said, looking earnestly into her eyes, "and if he can make you fight him like a vampire, he will win. He has made sure that you can no longer fight him as a paladin—but you still have the ranger. You still have your bow. That is where you can win."

Brey's eyes softened as Haldin spoke, and she placed a hand lightly on his shoulder. "You're right," she said softly. "Thank you."

Brey unslung her bow, testing the draw on the string. She pulled out an arrow, looking at the bulb of holy water nestled behind the head.

"This won't help if he's not undead," she observed.

"Perhaps not," answered the gnome, "but an arrow is still an arrow."

"So," asked Tarrel from behind them, "what now?"

The half-elf looked fully recovered from Dravuliel's spell, with just a few tears in his coat. Mordan had retrieved his rapier, and Dria had picked up a discarded sword and shield. Her homunculus perched on her shoulder, its tail coiled lightly around her neck.

"An excellent question," Haldin replied, looking around him. The sounds of battle still came from the landing area; the opposite wall of the storage chamber bore three archways, each leading off into darkness. "Since Dravuliel escaped magically," he observed, "we have no obvious path to follow. However, I doubt he went far."

Mordan looked at Dria and then at her homunculus.

"How much of the place did you scout from your cell?" he asked.

"Not there," she replied. "I was interested in finding ways out, not going in farther."

"So you did not locate your unfortunate relative?" asked Haldin. Dria shook her head.

"Well," said Mordan, "it looks like we could use a scout." He cast another glance at the homunculus, which glared back at him and edged itself around behind its mistress' head.

"I've got a better idea," said Tarrel, pulling out his crystal wand.

Haldin held up a hand. "I doubt that our adversary has forgotten your invisibility of a few minutes ago, since it cost him so dearly," he said. "No doubt he will be prepared for a similar attack." He turned to Dria.

"My lady," he said, "I do not wish to expose your homunculus to danger any more than you do. However, it will be invaluable—even potentially life-saving—to know what lies ahead of us. A brief glimpse through a doorway would be sufficient, if you would be so kind."

Dria sighed. "Which one do you want me to look at first?"

"Your choice, my lady," answered Haldin with a smile.

Dria murmured to her homunculus, and it flitted off toward the central archway. Brey covered the left-hand arch with her bow, while Tarrel covered the one on the right with his wand of fireballs. Mordan glanced nervously from one arch to another as Haldin stood beside Dria. The Cannith heir's eyes had a faraway look.

"A large room," she said, "it looks empty. No visible exits."

The homunculus flapped out, and went through the left-hand arch. Dria gasped.

"What is it, my lady?" asked Haldin.

"Some kind of workshop," she replied. "It's not a creation forge, but the components look like—"

"Like your kinsman may have been at work there?" asked the gnome.

She nodded.

"Is it empty?" asked Mordan.

"I didn't see anyone," Dria replied. Her eyes cleared as the homunculus flew back into the chamber, and she started for the archway.

"Wait," said Brey, "what about the third one?"

"I have to look for my cousin," Dria replied. "The third one's all yours." She took another step, but Brey was in front of her, blocking her way.

"Now listen," she said with a snarl, "we're not going anywhere till you check out that other arch."

"I have my duty," Dria said coldly. "I wouldn't expect you to understand."

"Oh, really?" snapped Brey, "and do you expect us to drop everything and watch your overbred, dragonmarked rear while you carry out your *duty*? It would still be sitting in that cell if we hadn't let you out!"

"And *you*," Dria retorted, leaning into Brey's face, "would still be cowering in front of that robed scarecrow if I hadn't blasted him—so I think that makes us even!"

Brey's face began to distort in anger, and Mordan hurriedly interposed himself between the two.

"We don't have time for this!" he said. "That elf could be back at any moment! Now, if you don't want to check out the third arch, I will. Brey, Tarrel—cover me!" He strode purposefully toward the arch.

"Wait," said Brey. "I'll do it."

He stopped and turned. The vampire woman shifted to the form of a bat—smaller than the one that had flown the chasm in the Mournland—and flew through the arch. Within a minute, she returned and resumed her natural form.

"It's a temple," she said. "Seems empty, looks like there are some rooms beyond it."

"Thank you, Captain," said Haldin smoothly.

Dria's gaze dropped to the ground.

"So," the gnome continued, "our choice appears to be simple. If we investigate the workshop, perhaps we will rescue Lady Dria's kinsman, and possibly gain some mechanical allies into the bargain. If we go to the temple first, we will do so with only our current strength, which we already know is sufficient only to stalemate our foe." He looked expectantly from face to face.

"Well," said Brey, "if you put it that way. . . ."

"Whatever we do," said Mordan, "let's *do* it. I don't want to be still standing here when Dravuliel comes back with reinforcements."

"You've got my vote," said Tarrel. "Nice logic, by the way."

Haldin smiled. "When you are small of stature," he said modestly, "you learn to calculate the odds with great care. Shall we proceed?"

With Brey in the lead, the five headed into the workshops.

ANOTHER REUNION
CHAPTER 23

Olarune 26, 999 YK

A short passage led to the area that Dria's homunculus had scouted. As she had said, it looked like a workshop—it was filled with tables and workbenches, like the workshop Mordan, Brey, and Tarrel had discovered in the Mournland, but the tools were far different.

Here and there, a corpse lay on a table. Laid out on other surfaces were jointed metal limbs and plates, looking like pieces of armor. A few of the corpses had metal limbs attached, while others had apparently been subjected to amputations. The stout leather straps securing them to the tables, and the expressions of agony frozen on their dead faces, suggested that the operations had been carried out on living subjects.

Dria examined them as the other four scoured the room for threats.

"Let me guess," said Tarrel. "He's trying to make undead warforged."

"I fear his plan is more subtle than that," said Haldin,

looking at a vat full of a dull brown liquid. "Theoretically, undead warforged would be little different from armored zombies, and as we have seen, Dravuliel's research has moved far beyond that level. I suspect that his aim is to produce a creature that blends the undead with the construct, combining the strengths of each."

"You are correct!"

They looked around for the source of the voice but saw no one. Tarrel gestured at a closed door, and both Brey and Mordan moved toward it.

"Who is there?" asked Haldin, in a conversational tone. "Would you be so kind as to show yourself?"

"As long as you don't try to kill me," the voice replied. Haldin waved the others back from the door, and they joined him reluctantly.

"Am I correct in supposing," continued the gnome, "that I am addressing . . ." He looked at Dria.

"Adalrik d'Cannith," she finished the question for him.

The door opened slowly, and a tall man stepped out. At least, he was mostly a man; his right hand and arm were sheathed in metal, and a steel mask covered half his face. Dria let out a gasp.

"No!' she breathed. "They didn't tell me . . ."

" . . . that I was a renegade?" Adalrik d'Cannith smiled with the uncovered half of his face. Brey nocked an arrow, and Tarrel raised his wand, though neither moved to attack the newcomer.

"Don't worry," said Adalrik, stepping forward and displaying his empty hands. "I have no intention of attacking you." He turned to Dria and bowed. "I assume you were sent to rescue me?" Dria, nodded silently, unable to take her eyes from the metal sheathing her cousin's body.

"We met once," she said quietly, "more than ten years ago. At Morcar and Alina's wedding. I don't expect you'd remember me. My name is Dria." Adalrik's one mobile eyebrow shot up in surprise.

"Dria?" he said. "Fintar's daughter?" He took half a step back, and looked her up and down. "You've grown."

"As touching as this is," said Brey, "let's not forget that there's a very unfriendly necromancer somewhere around here, who's liable to come back with reinforcements at any minute."

"If I bring you back," said Dria, in a small voice, "do you know what they'll do to you?"

"I can imagine," her cousin replied, "but your archer is right."

"I'm not *her* archer," said Brey.

"My apologies," said Adalrik. "Still, I agree that we should deal with the immediate threat first, and worry about the future—once we know we have one." He looked back at Dria.

"I put a few things together," he said, "when I realized the place was under attack. I managed to make some real breakthroughs recently." Turning to the door, he whistled softly, and was answered by the sound of heavy metallic footsteps.

The others tensed as a squat, bulky shape edged itself through the doorway, but Adalrik held up a hand to still them. It stumped over to Adalrik's side, looking like nothing so much as a metal barrel with legs and arms.

"This isn't a combat model," he said, "just a menial. I have some papers and materials stored in its body." The construct stood a couple of yards behind its master.

"These, on the other hand"—he whistled again, twice, and three more figures sprang lithely into the room—"are intended for combat. I hope they will help us get out of here alive."

The companions stood and stared at the creatures for a long moment. They were humanoid, and patches of dead-white flesh could be seen here and there between the steel plates that covered their bodies like a lobster's carapace. The arms of each one terminated in a pair of bright, curved blades.

Tarrel groaned. "Undead warforged."

Adalrik half-smiled. "Not quite," he said. "As you correctly deduced, my purpose here was to combine the most desirable qualities of the undead and the construct in a single creature. These are but a step in that direction. They are half-golems—partially flesh, but entirely constructs."

"So," he said, with an expectant look on the visible half of his face, "what's the plan?"

"The plan is this," said Brey, standing behind Dria, "while it's heartwarming to help out with your family reunion, we came here to kill Dravuliel and destroy all his undead friends. There's a temple nearby, and my guess is he's beyond it somewhere, getting ready to wipe us out."

"Or take us alive," put in Mordan. "At least, that's what he told his iron zombies. I'm guessing that would be worse." Brey nodded.

"Then let's go," said Adalrik. He gestured, and his three half-golems loped out down the passage.

* * * ● * * ●

The temple was larger than they had expected. It also bore no signs of the Blood of Vol cult. Among the unfamiliar symbols carved into the pale stone altar and painted on the walls were a scythe and many skulls. Prominently placed on the wall behind the altar was the skull of a dragon.

"I don't recognize these," said Brey.

Haldin examined the dragon skull. "I do," he said. "I take it you have heard of the Dark Six?" Brey nodded.

"Unless I am very much mistaken," Haldin continued, "this temple is dedicated to one of them—a stealer of souls known as The Keeper."

"So he changed sides?" asked Tarrel. "The temple we found in the Mournland was definitely Blood of Vol."

"It would seem so," replied the gnome, reaching into one of his equipment pouches.

Mordan saw Brey examining the altar. "Don't touch that," he said. "Remember last time?" Before she could respond, Haldin backed into her. He was sprinkling silver dust in a circle around the temple, humming to himself as he did so. Then he opened a flask of holy water, sprinkling it on top of the silver filings. Brey gasped suddenly, and put a hand to her head.

"My apologies, Captain," said the gnome. "I am just ensuring that our opponent has no advantage here. The positive energies I am raising may be inconvenient for you, but they should not be harmful." Brey grimaced.

The two Cannith heirs had taken the half-golems forward to explore the area beyond the temple. A sudden sound of clashing steel made the others look around just as Adalrik and Dria hurried back into the room.

"Wights," said Dria, "about a dozen of them."

The half-golems retreated back into the temple, their arm-blades weaving a web of steel in front of them. They blocked many of the wights' attacks, but their armor was battered here and there, and blood oozed from cuts in their exposed flesh. At a command from Adalrik, one of the constructs fell back as its two fellows blocked the doorway.

Brey was the first to act, sending an arrow between the half-golems and into the lead wight. It hissed in pain as the arrow penetrated its shrunken flesh, cracking the vial bound to the shaft and sending holy water deep into the wound. Tarrel and Mordan both flung flasks of holy water over the constructs' heads, shattering them against the ceiling of the passage and showering the undead beneath.

Haldin sent a crossbow bolt after Brey's arrow. It struck the wight directly between the eyes, exploding in a ripple of silver-white light; when their vision cleared, the companions saw that the creature had fallen to the floor, its head split almost in half. Another leaped forward to take its place.

Tarrel moved around behind the half-golems, aiming his wand carefully. A bead of red light shot from the wand, streaking toward the back of the pack of wights—until a wight fighting in the front rank inadvertently moved into its way. The bead exploded, shooting fire back into the temple and scorching the two-half-golems as well as Tarrel himself. Beating out several small fires on his clothes, the Brelander stood back with an apologetic shrug.

Slowly, the wights forced the half-golems back through the doorway. Mordan stood ready, running one of the things through the body as it came into the temple; he noticed that it wore the armor and insignia of the Vedykar Lancers, like its comrades. With grim determination, he redoubled his strokes, placing lightning-fast thrusts wherever an opening appeared in the half-golems' weaving defense.

The wights fought their way clear of the doorway and started to spread out in the room, and Brey unlimbered her bow again. Adalrik sent the third of the half-golems into the fray. Haldin prayed, holding up his blue dragon symbol, but the wights did not waver in their assault.

When the last of the wights had cleared the doorway, Dravuliel appeared behind them. A crackling aura of black energy surrounded him. In one hand he held a massive scythe with a jagged blade of black iron; in the other, a leather-bound tome, from which he read aloud. In response to his words, the wights redoubled their attacks, as if infused with hellish fury.

Brey loosed an arrow at him, but it glanced off his robe as though the garment was made of adamantine. With a cruel smile, he put down the book and uncorked a flask of filthy-looking water. Throwing it in the air, he intoned another spell—and a driving rain of foul, fetid water began to fall inside the temple, almost hiding him from sight. Haldin yelped as the unclean rain struck him, bringing up red welts on his exposed skin as if it were boiling water. Brey loosed another arrow, but the lashing rain spoiled her aim and it flew wide of the mark.

As the gnome struggled to protect himself, Dravuliel held up a hand, and the floor of the room began to shake. Like something from a nightmare, a section of the rocky floor shot into the air, folding itself around the gnome and sealing him inside. It looked like nothing so much as a sarcophagus.

One of the half-golems fell before the slicing blades of the armored wights. Adalrik and Dria dragged it back out of the battle and knelt over it, their lips moving and their hands working frantically. Mordan and Tarrel battled on, though the Brelander was barely holding his own against the creatures. He fought hard with his short sword, but could not back off far enough to use his wand.

One of the wights struck Tarrel a vicious blow to the head, knocking him back like a felled tree. Mordan, who was fighting two of the creatures at once, could do nothing to help as the wight straddled Tarrel's body and prepared to deliver a killing blow. With a cry, Brey dropped her bow and rushed forward, tackling the creature before it could strike. The momentum of her charge drove the wight backward, and they sprawled at the necromancer's feet.

The elf smiled a smile of pure malice and reached down as if to touch her lightly on the back. From inside his sleeve appeared a wooden stake, shod in silver, and her head snapped back in a scream as he drove it through her body. Then, the great scythe swept down, severing her head from her body and cutting the wight beneath her in two. The head rolled a couple of feet, red hair plastered to the scalp and the stone floor by the vile rain, red blood oozing from the neck. Wide with shock, Brey's eyes turned glassy, and then her head and body began to crumble like sand washed away by the tide. In a matter of moments, only her clothing and armor were left.

"No!" Mordan flung himself aside as the seed of the fireball shot past his shoulder. Tarrel was standing, his feet braced and the wand in both hands, his mouth open and his face a snarling mask of hate. The explosion toppled three of the remaining wights and one of the half-golems, but the necromancer stood his ground.

Adalrik ripped at the magical sarcophagus with his iron hand. After a few blows, cracks started to appear in the stone box; when they widened enough, he thrust his metal fingers into the widest crack and pulled with all his strength. The lid came free with a jolt and fell to the ground. Haldin's eyes took in the scene quickly, and he held his sapphire dragon aloft.

A silver light sparked in the depths of the faceted stone, and as it had in the courtyard of Fort Zombie, a burst of light swept out in all directions. The wights fell like corn before the scythe, leaving Dravuliel to face his intended victims alone. The filthy rain stopped.

Dria barked a command, and the repaired half-golem leaped at the elf, its arm-blades weaving a pattern of death. Mordan leaped forward as well, his eyes blazing and his rapier seeking the necromancer's heart. With a strength that belied his thin frame, Dravuliel swung the great scythe in a figure eight, deflecting the rapier with its iron-shod butt and slicing an arm off the construct as he stepped back into the passage.

Holding the weapon in front of him, he screamed a string of syllables, and the air in the temple thrummed with power. Then a wall of liquid darkness filled the passage, and he was lost to sight.

The wall rippled like the surface of a lake, and a low moaning came from it. In its dark substance, faces came and went, like those of the drowned trying to regain the surface. Adalrik tried to push through it with his metal hand, but shrank back with a yelp of pain.

"Quickly!" Haldin was running toward the exit of the temple, gesturing for the others to follow. Tarrel was staring down at Brey's empty clothes, and Mordan dragged him out by one arm. The two artificers followed, with their constructs bringing up the rear. Before they could reach the exit, however, something appeared, hanging in the air between them and the archway. It was so horrific that they stopped in their tracks and stared.

It was somewhat reminiscent of a newborn baby, but it was as tall as a half-orc, with a distended belly and shriveled, distorted limbs. Half its head appeared to be missing, and it gazed at the mortals with one unblinking, fathomless eye. Blood vessels were visible beneath its sickly-pale skin, pulsing grayly as it turned slowly in the air.

The temple had become cold—not the normal cold of a deep winter, but the bone-chilling, strength-draining cold of death.

"Dol Arrah!" yelled Mordan, "what *is* that?" Its eye lighted on him, apparently drawn by the sound of his voice, and the coldness intensified a hundredfold. As it had at Fort Zombie, the halfling charm-bag around his neck began to flood his body with warmth—but then it crumbled, falling to the floor.

"Don't let it look at you!" yelled Haldin, ducking behind the remains of his sarcophagus. A blast of frigid air struck the stone a split-second later, riming it in ice and widening the cracks that Adalrik's fist had made.

"Get out of here!" barked the artificer, and the half-golems sprang forward between the living and the floating abomination. It regarded them emotionlessly for a moment and then reached down with one of its shriveled arms, striking the nearest construct a casual, almost playful blow. The half-golem rocked back on its heels, responding with two fast slashes that would have severed the limb of a natural creature. Instead, the thing's skin was barely scratched, and the cut sealed itself as the companions watched.

Dria edged around the constructs and reached the passage that led to the rest of the complex, her face a mask of horror. Pushing Tarrel in front of him, Mordan followed her. The Brelander shuffled along numbly, his eyes still seeing the death of the woman he had been sent to recover. Haldin shot a questioning glance at Adalrik, who nodded and motioned him to go. The horror was completely focused on the constructs, as if curious about them; it struck one experimentally with a ray from its single eye, and watched as nothing happened. Adalrik stayed with the half-golems till the gnome was out of the temple, and then left them to their fate.

The storage area was deserted as the companions emerged from the passage, although there seemed to be great activity in the landing-cave. As they ran toward it, they could see that the skeletal flying creature had launched itself into the air again, apparently recovered from the damage it had suffered in their previous battle. Heedless of its own safety, it was grappling the side of the Ministry airship, chewing at one of the elemental binding struts and sweeping crew members off their feet with great buffets of its bony wings.

Haldin, however, pointed with a shout to the dark airship that was still moored in the cavern. An ant-like line of figures was running toward it, carrying books, chests, barrels, and other items, as robed figures on the deck exhorted them to greater speed. Standing on the foredeck, still holding his great scythe, was Marbulin Dravuliel.

CHAPTER 24

Olarune 26, 999 YK

Tarrel launched fireball after fireball at the ship. Flames erupted from the stern, and Dravuliel turned sharply, gesturing to his crew. Ropes were cut, and a ring of black energy flared from the binding struts as the ship lifted into the air.

Haldin took aim with his repeating crossbow and sent bolt after bolt into the winged undead. Struggling to keep their feet on the lurching deck, the crew of the forward ballista reloaded their weapon with one of the ceramic globes, and sent it flying into the creature's head. A cloud of vapor erupted from the creature as it shattered. Mordan skidded to a halt at the edge of the landing-platform; pulling a flask of holy water from his bandolier, he hurled it with all his strength, but it fell short.

The necromantic airship was almost clear of the cave mouth. Tarrel's fireballs kept striking her, and the stern of the craft was blazing fiercely. As it turned to escape along the valley, a couple of her undead crew fell from the afterdeck, blazing like shooting stars as they plummeted to the valley floor.

Dria yelled a command, and her homunculus launched itself from her shoulder, following the escaping airship. It finished its turn and set off along the valley, lost to the sight of those inside the cave. Tarrel stood still, his wand still aimed at the place where the ship had been, emotions chasing each other across his face.

Haldin pulled a new magazine from his bag, slapped it onto his crossbow, and continued to sent bolts at the flying creature. Another globe from the ship's ballista struck it square in the face, and its skull began to dissolve like icing in the rain. Slowly its grip weakened, and it fell off the Ministry ship, pinwheeling to the valley floor below. A cheer went up from the crew, and the companions in the landing bay joined in.

The airship dropped to the cave mouth and hovered partway inside as the crew let down a climbing net from the side. Dria was first on board, and Mordan climbed awkwardly after her. Haldin and Adalrik helped Tarrel to the net, and Adalrik's construct climbed aboard with surprising ease. At Haldin's command, the helmsman swung the wheel round and the airship moved out of the cave, rising into the air.

Dria's eyes had a faraway look as she monitored the enemy ship through her homunculus. Rising above the network of canyons, the airship sped away as crewmen pulled in the boarding net.

Tarrel sat on the deck with his back against the rail, his head bowed. The wand was still held loosely in his hand, as if forgotten. Mordan looked at him, thought about saying something, but decided against it. Having lost the person he had been sent to find, the inquisitive was probably wondering what he would tell his client. For the first time he could remember, Mordan felt lucky; his family already thought Gali was dead, so he wouldn't have to tell them anything. He wouldn't even have to face them again unless he chose to do so. Tarrel would have to go back to Thrane and give an account of his activities.

Hanging from his iron hand, Adalrik was inspecting the damage to the ship's elemental binding strut, keeping up a shouted conversation with the ship's engineer. Mordan couldn't make out what they were saying, but from the amount of nodding he inferred that the damage was not sufficient to cause concern. As the artificer swung himself back aboard, a cry went up from the lookout on the prow; the enemy had been sighted.

Rushing to the forward rail, Mordan saw the dark shape speeding through the canyons below them. Evidently Dravuliel had hoped to lose his pursuers in the twisting canyons, but thanks to Dria's homunculus they were able to follow his vessel, cutting across the top of the forest in a more direct route. The fire at the stern of the ship had been extinguished, but it had clearly caused extensive damage.

Something bright shot up from the fleeing vessel, landing square in the middle of the pursuers' deck. As it struck, it exploded into a small flare of light, showering the whole midsection of the airship with shards of bright energy. The crew of the forward ballista ducked behind the shelter of the raised weapon platform, and the other crew members ran away from the light as fast as they could, toward the areas at the bow and stern of the craft where the shards did not reach.

His reverie broken, Tarrel scrambled to his feet and ran for the forward rail. He launched two more fireballs at the enemy ship, sending bodies flying off the ruined afterdeck and re-igniting a number of small fires. Beside him, several crew members were dropping the ceramic globes from the ballistae onto the enemy. Some were filled with alchemist's fire, adding to the flames; others contained holy water, burning the undead crew like acid. Mordan threw the last few flasks from his bandolier before discarding it and helping to drop the ballista globes.

The bright shards of energy were still ripping through the midships area, and showed no sign of abating. The helmsman was out of their reach, but the magical maelstrom completely blocked his forward vision, and left him relying on Dria, who stood beside him. She had launched her homunculus again, and sent it to the observation dome on the ship's underside where it gave her a view of the enemy ship. Following her directions, he kept his airship stationed above and behind Dravuliel's necromantic vessel, preventing her from rising out of the canyon and escaping.

Adalrik opened a compartment in the chest of his barrel-like construct and rummaged through its insides as if looking for something. Only Haldin was still; he crouched in the cover of the ship's rail, looking down at the enemy through a gap in the wooden balustrade, his lips moving silently. The narrow canyon walls forced Dravuliel's pilot to keep making small course corrections, which slowed the vessel; slowly but surely, the Ministry ship was gaining. Soon, they were completely above their quarry, and then they began to pull ahead.

Haldin rolled a bundled climbing net over the side of the ship. With a shout to his companions, he began to climb down; arrows and spells flew all around him, but none struck him.

Mordan looked at the gnome in disbelief for a moment, and then ran to the net. Larger than Haldin, and slower as he climbed down one-handed, he would be an easy target. He paused for a moment, judging the distance and relative speed of the two craft, and then dove over the side.

Somersaulting in midair, he hit the deck at the same time as Haldin, in a fighting crouch with his rapier drawn. As the gnome dug in an equipment pouch, Mordan wove a defensive web around him with his rapier, dropping five zombies in as many heartbeats.

Haldin held up his sapphire dragon statuette with a loud cry, and the area in front of them cleared. Some of the zombies simply crumbled to dust, while others turned and headed aft as fast as they could go. Mordan destroyed a couple more with quick thrusts through the back as they retreated. His instructors at Rekkenmark would have been appalled, but this was not an enemy that understood chivalry.

A fireball blossomed on the deck, finishing off some of the fleeing zombies and interrupting one of the undead elf wizards who was starting to cast a spell. Mordan looked up and saw Tarrel jump from the rail of the airship above. His feather fall pin slowed him a little too much; instead of landing beside the other two, he drifted down until one of the elemental binding struts slammed into him.

Mordan dashed back along the deck, reaching the level of the binding strut just as the half-elf landed softly on the deck. The side of his face was already beginning to swell from the impact, but he seemed unhurt otherwise.

Haldin trotted up to join them, looking around to make sure that there were no more of Dravuliel's minions behind them. More of the Ministry crew had started to scramble down the boarding net, following their leader's example. Among them, Haldin saw Adalrik d'Cannith, climbing one-handed and holding a rod of some kind under his mechanical arm.

They fought their way to a hatch with a ladder leading below. Haldin glanced down and gestured that there was no threat from that direction. Apparently all hands were already on deck, trying to keep the airship going and fighting off the boarders. Haldin pointed aft, to where the helmsman stood on the raised afterdeck, and the other two nodded. As they crossed the middle of the ship, Mordan glanced up at the underside of their own ship and saw Dria's homunculus gazing down from the observation dome.

Dravuliel was on the afterdeck, standing behind the helmsman and gesturing to his followers with his great scythe. Despite the weapon's size, he seemed to wield it effort-lessly, sweeping and pointing as easily as he might have done with a wand. As they approached, they could see a thin skin of reddish energy surrounding the blade.

Adalrik caught up with them and pointed his rod at the necromancer. Energy flared, and Dravuliel stepped aside— but the bolt struck the wheel, throwing the undead helmsman back like a rag doll. With the wheel unmanned, the ship began to slew from side to side; she struck a tree that stuck out from the canyon side, slowing slightly and slewing to one side. The necromancer held the wheel with one hand; his mouth was moving but they could not hear his words over the rush of air and the noise of battle. Then he let go, and the wheel remained steady, turning now and again as if controlled by an unseen hand.

Mordan winced as something sharp thudded into his side, and turned to see a spellstitched zombie standing a little way off with one scabrous arm raised. Tumbling like an acrobat, Mordan reached the thing before it could loose another spell or draw a weapon, spitting it through the ribs.

They had reached the back of the main deck. In front of

them, wooden doors led into the cabin area, and some narrow steps ascended to the afterdeck. Haldin fired his repeating crossbow, putting three bolts into one of the undead wizards that guarded the stairway, and Mordan half-climbed, half-leaped his way to the top. Quickly dispatching three zombies, he found himself once more face to face with Dravuliel. Despite the rents in his clothing and the minor cuts on his face and hands, the necromancer showed no signs of serious injury or fatigue.

He made as if to block Mordan's rapier with his scythe, but then let it go. It hovered in front of him for an instant, and then sliced down towards the Karrn's head. Twisting to the side at the last moment, Mordan dropped back and watched the animated weapon, judging the time it would take to ready itself for another attack.

As the scythe swung back, Dravuliel made a series of complex gestures, mouthing words that only he could hear. Dipping a finger into a belt-pouch, he traced the image of a skull on his forehead, and black flames leaped from his body, completely enveloping him. Tarrel appeared behind the necromancer, delivering a stab with his short sword. Unable to check his blow, he winced in pain as his arm entered the sheath of black flames.

Dravuliel winced too, with the unexpected pain of the attack. Turning, he spat a single word at the Brelander, slapping him across the face with a hand wreathed in black fire. Tarrel stumbled and fell to his knees, his face twisted in agony while many of Dravuliel's minor wounds magically healed.

Momentarily distracted by the sight, Mordan found the scythe-blade whistling down at him again. At the last second, he twisted aside, aiming a lunge at the necromancer's heart—and everything went dark. His first thought was that the darkvision spell Tarrel cast on him before they entered Dravuliel's lair had worn off; instinctively, he stepped back a few paces, and found that his sight returned—still in mono-chrome. Working his way around the edge of the blackness, he saw Dravuliel fleeing toward the rail of the ship, with a large feather clutched in one hand.

Mordan ran after him like a panther, bringing him down mere feet from the edge with a flying tackle. The black flames burned Morden with a cold fire, but he gritted his teeth and held on despite the pain. A dagger stabbed into his side, and at the same time a knee crashed into his groin as the necro-mancer struggled. Dravuliel sensed the loosening of his grip and kicked him off, springing to his feet. His hands wove a pattern of darkness in the air, and his body turned pale. With a shock, Mordan realized that he could see the timbers of the ship through the necromancer's body.

With an arrogant smile, Dravuliel began to sink through the deck, just as he had walked through the walls of Fort Zombie. He was using magic to escape for a third time, and Mordan's heart plummeted at the thought. He lashed out with his rapier, and was surprised to see it draw a bloody line across the necromancer's spectral forehead. Dravuliel looked equally surprised—his eyes widened and his mouth dropped open, and he began to sink faster.

Only his torso and head remained above the deck when Mordan struck again—a savage, twisting thrust downward through the pit of the throat. He felt the blade glance off the elf's collar-bone and penetrate lungs and organs before it was stopped by the solid timbers of the deck. The necromancer stopped sinking through the deck; his ethereal body hung on the enchanted blade that transfixed it, as helpless as though he had been solid. Dravuliel's mouth worked noiselessly, blood trickling from the corners—and then his eyes rolled back in their sockets and his head slumped.

Mordan stood over the spectral figure, his hand still on the rapier-hilt, hardly able to believe that the necromancer was dead. For several heartbeats, he watched and waited for any sign of a new trick, a new evasion, but the elf remained unmoving. Then, little by little, Dravuliel began to solidify again. His spell had ended with his death, and now his corpse was returning to a solid, material state. Timbers creaked and bones cracked as the necromancer's body tried to occupy the same space as the deck planking; blood pooled around the corpse, but it remained caught as Mordan withdrew his blade.

Tarrel limped over and looked down at the dead elf; Mordan answered his questioning glance with a curt nod. The Brelander relaxed a little, closing his eyes for a moment.

It was only then that Mordan noticed that the airship was flying above the forest now, beside and a little behind the Ministry craft. Haldin stood at the helm. He was steering with one hand while the other held his sapphire dragon over the wheel, and he seemed to be talking continuously. It seemed that he had come to some arrangement with the undead elemental that powered the craft. Meanwhile, Adalrik crouched beside the control column, inspecting the workings of the mechanism with great interest. Bodies littered the main deck, but to Mordan's relief most of them seemed to be long dead; casualties among the boarders seemed to be few and light.

A sudden ray of light made Mordan look around; behind them, the sun was rising. With one last look at Dravuliel's corpse, he sheathed his rapier and leaned on the rail, watching the color slowly return to the world as the darkvision spell wore off.

"So have you decided what you're going to tell your folks?" Tarrel joined him at the rail, taking a long pull from a flask of a healing potion. He offered it to Mordan, who drank gratefully.

"Not yet," he said. "It's going to be a little while before I'm sure what happened myself."

He paused and looked at the Brelander.

"What about you?" he asked. He didn't envy Tarrel the task of reporting back to Brey's father.

"I don't know," he said, scratching his head. "I might just leave out the unpleasant details and tell him she died fighting evil, like a good paladin. That is, if your government ever lets me go. I have a feeling they're not going to want word of this to get out."

"It is going to be a little complicated, I must admit," said a wheezing voice from beside them. They glanced down at Haldin, and then at the helm; a half-elf crewman was manning the wheel.

"Don't worry," said the gnome, "he's a good helmsman. And the necromental keeping us aloft is surprisingly reasonable for an undead creature. We should arrive in Korth in a matter of hours."

CHAPTER 25

Korth
Therendor 2, 999 YK

Mordan sat in his room, staring idly out of the window at the rooftops of Korth. It was comfortable enough, but that didn't make it any less of a prison.

In the days since the party had returned from the Nightwood, he had been kept strictly separated, and submitted to polite but determined questioning by various Ministry officials. He guessed that the others were going through the same process. Still, he thought to himself, free room and board. It wasn't as though he had any pressing business anywhere. For the first time since he returned from the Talenta Plains, he wondered what to do next.

He also thought about what—if anything—he would tell the family. The official report of Gali's death on the Day of Mourning had taken a terrible toll on both his parents, and telling them the truth could only make things worse. The news that their beloved elder son had been corrupted by an evil necromancer and turned into a murderous wight would be bad enough, without adding the fact that the disgraced

Kasmir had added fratricide to the list of his crimes. He decided to wait until he knew what the official report of the whole affair would say, and decide then.

He also debated whether it would be better to remain Kaz Mordan, the veteran from the Company of the Skull, and let the disgraced—and still wanted—cadet Kasmir ir'Dramon fade from memory. That was harder to decide. He knew the charges against him were false, but he also knew that proving his innocence would be almost impossible. He had known that all along, which is why he had deserted in the first place. Why should he even try? He had no rose-tinted expectations of being forgiven and welcomed back by his parents if he could clear his name. He would never replace Gali in their affections, no matter what the truth might be.

But he knew, too, that there was more at stake than the reputation of one former cadet. He still knew the things he knew—the things that had nearly resulted in his death—and that would never change. He could bury his head in the dust of the Talenta Plains for a hundred years and it would make no difference. Kasmir ir'Dramon had been raised in the Karrnathi tradition of service and loyalty, for all the self-centered cynicism of Kaz Mordan.

The idealistic cadet and the world-weary veteran argued back and forth inside his head as he waited for whatever the Ministry of the Dead would decide. There was a cancer festering at the heart of the Rekkenmark Academy—the place that, above all others, stood as a shrine to Karrnathi ideals—and the thought that he could do nothing about it was becoming intolerable. It was his duty to both king and country, the cadet maintained, to bring this evil to light. The veteran cautioned that one man stood little chance of success against such a well-entrenched conspiracy. The traitors had tried to kill him once and would almost certainly do so again—and again, until they succeeded. His only protection was anonymity.

He found himself wondering what Brey would advise him to do. She had certainly altered his opinion of Thranes. During the War, he had accepted the propaganda view that they were all dangerous fanatics bent on subjecting the whole of Khorvaire to their theocratic tyranny. She didn't come across as a brainwashed fanatic, though. There was something more than unthinking fanaticism in her constant struggle against the darkness of her vampiric condition, and even though she knew her church and her country would never accept her back—even though she could no longer so much as speak the name of her deity—she never let the darkness win. It was more than simple revenge against those who had destroyed her life: she fought to remain herself, to stay true to her ideals despite everything. That took real strength. He knew what she would say. Never give up, always fight for what is right, no matter what it costs you. But he was no paladin.

He thought of Tarrel, the Medani inquisitive. The dogged half-elf had tracked Brey across half a continent and found her even though she didn't want to be found. Then, rather than simply dragging her back to her father and collecting his payment, he joined her to help redress the wrongs done to her. In the end, she had died saving his life. What would he say? Perhaps Mordan owed him an explanation, since he had rebuffed him so rudely on the boat that night. He made a mental note to try to talk to him, if he saw him again.

Then he thought of Dria d'Cannith. Like him, she had been searching for a missing relative. Although captured and imprisoned, she had never given up, using her flying homunculus to look for a way out and, in the end, to bring them to her aid. Like him, she had been shocked by what she saw when she finally found her cousin. Unlike him, her family would want to know, and he wondered what she was going to tell them. Would she lie to protect Adalrik, or would her duty outweigh her personal feelings?

And what of Adalrik himself? Had he been coerced into helping Dravuliel with his plans to create undead warforged, or was he willing? Was that what he meant by calling himself a renegade, or had he violated the laws of House Cannith in some other way? It seemed that he would not be welcomed back with open arms by the House of the Mark of Making, any more than Kasmir would be welcomed back by the house of ir'Dramon— but judging by the shock and grief in Dria's eyes when she first saw him, his fate would be worse than simple banishment.

Thinking of all this, his own problems came into clearer perspective. They were still not trivial by any means, but they did not seem so completely insurmountable.

Haldin was the one he couldn't figure out, though. From what he had seen at Fort Zombie and in the Nightwood complex, Mordan knew that he must be a powerful cleric, and yet he had never spoken of religion. Mordan wasn't even sure what god or group of gods he followed. The sapphire dragon statuette was some kind of holy symbol, from the way the gnome had used it against their undead foes, but Mordan had no idea what it signified.

Then there was the question of his status within the Ministry. Quite apart from his divine powers, the fact that Haldin could secure the services of an armed airship and her crew for his mission spoke volumes. So did the amount he knew about undead—although, Mordan admitted to himself with a wry smile, gnomes were notorious for the way they hoarded knowledge. But out of all of his erstwhile companions, Haldin was the only one he felt he didn't know. He had no idea what the gnome would do in his position, although he suspected that he would have found some way of avoiding getting into it in the first place. Would he ask a gnome for advice? That was usually an expensive proposition.

Hearing footsteps in the passage outside his door, Mordan stood and waited for the guards who would escort him to another interview with another official. When the door opened, though, he was surprised to see Haldin there, alone. The gnome smiled.

"I do hope the Ministry's—ah, rather insistent—hospitality has not inconvenienced you unduly," he said. "I made it clear to my superiors that you and our other friends should be afforded every comfort that the circumstances permitted."

Mordan spread his arms and turned to indicate the room.

"I've stayed in worse places," he said laconically.

"Excellent," said the gnome. "Now, if you would be so kind as to come with me, I have something to say to all of our company." He held the door open wider, indicating the passage outside with a courtly sweep of his hand. Mordan saw that there were no guards with him.

Mordan followed Haldin through a labyrinth of wood-paneled corridors and down several flights of stairs. Finally, they entered a large, carpeted room furnished with several overstuffed armchairs and entirely walled with bookshelves, except for a large and impressively carved marble fireplace. The others were already waiting, and they got up to welcome him. Haldin waited for the greetings to be over, and discreetly cleared his throat.

"My friends," he said, "if I may call you that, I have been instructed to tell you certain things on behalf of the Ministry, and I also have some things I would like to say on my own behalf. First, and most important, you are all free to go. There was to have been a condition of secrecy—indeed, those of you who are not Karrnathi citizens were originally to have had the memories of recent events magically removed—but I was able to prevail upon my superiors not to do this. I suspect, Tarrel, that when you inevitably encountered the gap in your memory you would be very much concerned with filling it, and I know that you are well equipped to do so."

The others smiled, and Tarrel bowed modestly.

"Besides," the gnome continued, "the Ministry has been able to arrange things so that there is no longer any evidence of what you encountered, and would of course do everything in its power to discredit you if you should ever try and pass on what you know. This all falls into the realm of state secrets, as I'm sure you will understand."

"So the Vedykar Lancers," said Mordan, "they still died on the Day of Mourning?"

Haldin nodded.

"As esteemed, loyal, and greatly lamented members of the Army of Karrnath," he said. "Their treachery never took place, for they could not possibly have been assigned to provide military support for an experimental facility that never existed. In fact, some independent explorers chanced to discover their remains quite recently; the banners and other insignia are on their way to Vedykar, where I am told a memorial is to be constructed. Meanwhile, the bodies of the lancers themselves are being returned to their families for burial. In closed caskets, sadly, as the peculiar nature of the Mournland has rendered the sight of their remains somewhat disturbing."

"Will the regiment be re-formed?" asked Mordan. The gnome shrugged.

"That is a matter for the army's commanders to decide," he said, "although it would seem regrettable for such a long and glorious tradition to come to an end with the Day of Mourning."

"And the Inmistil Rangers?" asked Tarrel.

"They were never in Cyre," replied Haldin. "The government of Thrane assures us that this is so, and it we would never dream of doubting their word. Accordingly, neither the Ministry of the Dead nor any other branch of the government of Karrnath has any knowledge of them. But permit me to anticipate your next question—that of the remarkable Captain ir'Mallon. It is known that she was in Karrlakton, from the spell that her esteemed father, the general, purchased to locate her remains when she was presumed dead in the Mournland. Such spells are powerful and expensive, and their results are not often wrong."

He paused for a moment, and then continued.

"Officially, the government of Karrnath has no knowledge of her activities or even her existence," he said. "However, it will become known through certain unofficial channels that she played a prominent role in tracking down and bringing to justice a desperate war criminal whom Karrnath had been seeking for some time—and whose existence, of course, the government of Karrnath will also deny. Unfortunately, she lost her life in the process, but—still unofficially—her death was entirely befitting a paladin of the Silver Flame. Tarrel, I assume that you will be able to locate those unofficial channels without further assistance?" Tarrel nodded.

"Her ashes have been recovered," Haldin went on, "and have already been presented to the Church of the Silver Flame here in Korth. I understand they will be returned to Thrane with full honors. The Karrnathi ambassador in Flamekeep has been instructed to convey to her father the unofficial condolences of King Kaius himself."

The gnome paused again and coughed softly. Picking up a small bell from a table beside his chair, he rang it.

"I must apologize," he said. "All this talking makes my throat quite dry. I trust that some brandy would not go amiss?" A uniformed servant brought in a tray bearing a decanter and five glasses, serving them all. Haldin sipped at his glass and grimaced.

"It is only Zil, I'm afraid," he said. "The Cyran is almost impossible to acquire these days."

"Try the Black Dragon in Karrlakton," suggested Mordan. "They seem to have no trouble getting hold of it. Tell them I sent you." Haldin's face brightened like a summer sunrise.

"I shall indeed," he said, beaming.

"Now," he said, after they had drunk, "as I said earlier, you are all free to go. Tarrel and Lady d'Cannith, I understand that both your houses have been enquiring after you with some concern. I trust that you will be able to set their minds at ease."

"And myself?" asked Adalrik d'Cannith, with an ironic smile. Haldin smiled back.

"Yes, my lord, your house is most eager to effect your return," he said, "and that matter has necessitated some delicate negotiations. You will not be surprised that House Cannith has made clear its displeasure at your recent activities—I believe the word *excoriate* was mentioned?" He raised his eyebrows questioningly, but neither Dria nor Adalrik spoke.

"However," Haldin went on, "the—involuntary—nature of your captivity is regarded as a mitigating factor. As is the fact that—no doubt deliberately—you made sure that your work did not progress beyond the most elementary stages, giving nothing useful to your captor." Adalrik's face was inscrutable.

"Given the circumstances, the Ministry of the Dead has requested House Cannith to permit you to remain with us as an expert informant, so that the extent and ramifications of your research can be assessed. I cannot say yet what their answer will be, as the dragonmarked houses have always maintained neutral stance in international affairs, which might be jeopardized by their allowing one of their members to work with the government of a single nation. The Ministry has, of course, stressed that your work will only be used for peaceful purposes, such as ensuring that no similar research is under way or can be completed at any Karrnathi facility. This is in line with the government's stated policy of removing undead from front-line service where practicable, and ceasing all further research into the creation of undead troops."

"And until they decide, I am free to go?" asked Adalrik.

"That is correct," said Haldin. "Although your personal assistance would be valuable, we already have your notes and the materials from your workshop. House Cannith has not requested that you be detained—no doubt because they do not know that you, or your charming cousin, are currently our guests. If such a request were to be received, it would be quite problematic, I suspect. Since the dragonmarked houses are carefully neutral in their dealings with national governments, it follows that the governments must observe the same neutrality in their dealings with the houses. I am sure that House Cannith would think carefully about any demand from the Karrnathi government to hand over one of our citizens who had sought sanctuary with them."

Dria looked at Adalrik with concern.

"I'll have to tell them something," she said. Adalrik smiled with the half of his face that was still human.

"I know," he replied. "Tell them the truth. I wouldn't want you getting into trouble on my account. And if they send you after me again, I'll try to be harder to find."

Haldin raised his glass.

"That is all I have to say," he concluded. "Except to give you my personal thanks, and to toast our successful completion of a very difficult operation. To all of us!"

The four returned the toast, and Haldin rang the bell again. After a few moments, a procession of servants brought in everyone's weapons, and the other belongings that had been taken from them when they arrived at the Ministry.

Slipping the baldric of his rapier over his head, Mordan wandered over to Tarrel. The Brelander was busy filling a number of small pockets and pouches that were sewn into the lining of his coat.

"So will you be heading back to Thrane now?" he asked.

Tarrel looked up. "Not right away," he said. "I'll send a report back by Sivis requesting further instructions, and while I'm waiting I'll tap into those unofficial channels Haldin mentioned."

"Well, if you're not busy any evening, I can show you the best Talenta Cuisine off the Plains. I'll even make sure you get enough headroom."

Tarrel smiled.

"It's my treat," he said. "I'm still on expenses!" He paused, looking over Mordan's shoulder. "I think someone else wants a word with you," he said.

Mordan turned to find Dria and Adalrik standing behind him. Adalrik was holding a package wrapped in sackcloth.

"I don't know how you feel about things like this," he said, offering it to the Karrn, "but I had to do something while they kept us waiting. Luckily they let me have my tools."

Mordan went to take the package but decided it would be easier to unwrap it if it stayed in Adalrik's hands. It was a mechanical left hand, made of brass with a silver inlay. Unlike Adalrik's own metal hand, it was as fine and delicate as a natural one.

"I had to guess the size," said the artificer, "but it shouldn't take more than an hour or so to fit it properly. I'll warn you right now, they hurt like the Fury's teeth when you first put them on, but after that you'll forget it's artificial."

Mordan began to thank him but was interrupted as Haldin bustled over, standing on tiptoe to inspect the hand.

"Most impressive," he said with a nod of the head to Adalrik. "I must say, it is almost equal to gnome craftsmanship." Adalrik half-smiled, inclining his head to acknowledge the complement.

"I'm afraid," the gnome went on, "that my own poor gift will pale by comparison." He gave the d'Canniths a significant glance, and they wandered off to talk to Tarrel.

"I suppose it is possible," said the gnome, "that one day you might bump into the cadet I mentioned in our first conversation—Kasmir ir'Dramon. If you should do so, perhaps you would be so kind as to relay a message to him. It is this: There are those at Rekkenmark who believe in his innocence and stand ready to help him clear his name. The message comes from an instructor-sergeant named Rangoth, and was forwarded to me in strictest confidence by a distant cousin in House Sivis. I hope you will respect that confidence." Mordan looked at him sharply, but the gnome's face was expressionless. He remembered Sergeant Rangoth.

"If I ever run across him, I'll be sure to tell him that," he said. "And as far as gifts are concerned, I'll settle for one small piece of knowledge."

"Ask," said Haldin. "I'll answer if I can, though I may ask you something in return. I am a gnome, after all."

"Understood," replied Mordan. "The sapphire dragon—what god is that? I was never much good at theology, but it's been bothering me."

Haldin smiled broadly.

"Ah," he said, "so you appreciate the agony of not knowing something! It is easily answered. I have heard you swear by Dol Arrah of the Sovereign Host; the blue dragon represents her colleague Aureon."

"Of course," Mordan said, "the god of law and knowledge. Isn't he normally depicted as a wizard?"

"You humans draw him as one of your own," Haldin replied, "and I'll admit that the blue dragon is one of his less common symbols. However, as every gnome knows, he is one of our ancestors. What else could he be?"

They laughed for a moment, and then Haldin's face became more serious.

"Knowledge has a price," he said sternly, "and now it's my turn to ask you something."

Mordan suddenly wondered what he had let himself in for. The gnomes were notorious bargainers, especially when it came to giving away information. Catching his expression, Haldin tried to keep a straight face but couldn't suppress a chuckle.

"Don't worry," he said, "it's not that bad! If it were, I wouldn't have given you anything first!" Mordan relaxed a little.

"It's just this," the gnome continued. "Having seen you in action, I know your capabilities as an undead fighter. I can't promise, of course, that every assignment will be as interesting as this one, but you'll find the Ministry pays a little better than the Company of the Skull. What do you say?"

Mordan raised his eyebrows. "You're offering me a job?" he asked.

"Quite so," replied the gnome. Mordan searched his face for any sign of humor, but he seemed to be quite serious. "I would have made the same offer to our friend from Thrane, if she had survived."

Mordan thought for a moment, then shook his head. "Thanks for the offer," he said, "but I actually have a couple of things I need to take care of right now."

With a small sigh of disappointment, Haldin nodded.

"I believe I understand," he said, "but if you should ever need employment, please go to the nearest Ministry office and ask to be put in touch with me."

"I will," said the Karrn, tucking the mechanical hand under his left arm and extending his right to the gnome. When Haldin shook it, he had something in his own hand; an opal ring, signifying membership in the Order of Rekkenmark.

"It belonged to the brother of the cadet I mentioned," said the gnome softly. "I thought he might find it useful."

"Now," he said brightly, as Mordan pocketed the ring, "I suggest you go with our friends from House Cannith and see how well their gift suits you."

THE LOST MARK TRILOGY

Matt Forbeck

Twelve Dragonmarks.

Sigils of immense magical power.

Borne by scions of mighty Houses,
used through the centuries to wield authority
and shape wonders throughout Eberron.
But there are only twelve marks.

Until now.

MARKED FOR DEATH
Volume One

THE ROAD TO DEATH
Volume Two

THE QUEEN OF DEATH
Volume Three
OCTOBER 2006

For more information visit **www.wizards.com**

ENTER THE NEW WORLD OF

THE DREAMING DARK TRILOGY

By Keith Baker

A hundred years of war...

Kingdoms lie shattered, armies are broken, and an entire
country has been laid to waste. Now an uneasy
peace settles on the land.

Into Sharn come four battle-hardened soldiers. Tired of
blood, weary of killing, they only want a place to call home.

The shadowed City of Towers has other plans...

THE CITY OF TOWERS
Volume One

THE SHATTERED LAND
Volume Two

THE GATES OF NIGHT
Volume Three
NOVEMBER 2006

For more information visit **www.wizards.com**

THE DRAGON BELOW TRILOGY

Don Bassingthwaite

In Eberron, there are terrors older than the nations of men. In the dark places of the world, the secrets of the Dragon Below are better left undisturbed....

THE BINDING STONE
Book 1

A chance rescue brings bitter rivals together. With a mysterious ally, the two warriors embark on a mission of vengeance, but the enemy waiting for them in the depths of the Shadow Marches is far more sinister than any they've faced before.

THE GRIEVING TREE
Book 2

The heroes, now in possession of the magical Dhakaan sword, head into the monster kingdom of Droaam. New enemies vie to control them or kill them, and their nemesis Dah'mir returns to wreak havoc upon them.

THE KILLING SONG
Book 3
DECEMBER 2006

For more information visit **www.wizards.com**

ENTER THE NEW WORLD OF

THE WAR-TORN

After a hundred years of fighting the war is now over, and the people of Eberron pray it will be the Last War. An uneasy peace settles over the continent of Khorvaire.

But what of the soldiers, warriors, nobles, spies, healers, clerics, and wizards whose lives were forever changed by the decades of war? What does a world without war hold for those who have known nothing but violence? What fate lies for these, the war-torn?

THE CRIMSON TALISMAN

BOOK 1

Adrian Cole

Erethindel, the fabled Crimson Talisman. Long sought by the forces of darkness. Long guarded in secret by one family. Now the secret has been revealed, and only one young man can keep it safe.

THE ORB OF XORIAT

BOOK 2

Edward Bolme

The last time Xoriat, the Realm of Madness, touched the world, years of warfare and death erupted. A new portal to the Realm of Madness has been found – a fabled orb, long thought lost. Now it has been stolen.

IN THE CLAWS OF THE TIGER

BOOK 3

James Wyatt

BLOOD AND HONOR

BOOK 4

Graeme Davis

For more information visit **www.wizards.com**